ACTING LIKE W[...]

Play My Part

MIRIAM ROSENTVAIG

Copyright © 2022 Miriam Rosentvaig

All rights reserved.

No portion of this book may be reproduced in any form without written permission from the publisher or author, except as permitted by U.S. copyright law.

This is a work of fiction. Names, characters, places, and incidents either are the product of the author's imagination or are used fictitiously. Any resemblance to actual persons, living or dead, events, or locales is entirely coincidental.

Author's Note

I wrote this story for all the people out there who are fighting battles that nobody else knows about. And I want you all to know that you are not alone, nor you will ever be. You are loved, cherished, and appreciated, even when you feel you're not or that you don't deserve to be.

Throughout the book there are multiple songs mentioned. I would like to encourage you to grab your headphones and listen to them since, from my perspective, they will only heighten the experience. You can check out [Play My Part's playlist](.).

Writing this novel was an absolute pleasure, and I love all the characters living in this universe fiercely. You might disagree with some of their choices or feel confused about their reactions, but all I can promise you is that each one of them have their reasons for choosing the path they did.

Finally, I hope you will enjoy your read, and that it will bring at least a small smile on your beautiful face.

Disclaimer:

All the characters and events inside this book are fictional. Any resemblance to real persons, living or dead, is purely coincidental!

This book isn't recommended to people under the age of 18. It contains multiple explicit sexual situations, as well as mentions or depictions of the following triggers,

- abortion
- abusive relationships
- alcohol consumption
- mental illnesses
- emotional abuse
- physical abuse
- pregnancy
- rape
- sexual abuse
- sexual assault
- sexually explicit scenes
- violence

Prologue
Lucas

It was the first of May when I learned what disappointment feels like. How sadness can and will rip your heart to pieces. How happiness isn't just the absence of sadness, but the feeling that rises from the ashes of what sorrow burned. Happiness is a phoenix. And the person who feels it is supposed to teach it how to fly.

As a child, I was the silent type. The one who liked to observe rather than to interfere. I liked to watch people like a spectator in a crowded theater. Unnoticeable and easy to forget. I was always clapping for the people on the stage even if I was just another face in the crowd. My father once told me that every person experiences life through their own set of lenses and we shouldn't force anybody to wear our glasses. Such a wise man my father was! He always had a metaphor ready to make the life lessons he taught my sister and I a bit clearer. Not because he thought we didn't understand what he was saying, but because we loved getting lost in his stories. We admired that man with all we had. And when I gathered up the courage to tell him that I love him, it was already too late.

I never knew how to express my feelings when I was younger. I loved so many people, but I never told them those words. I was afraid they wouldn't say it back, and I knew that would wreck my small heart. I know now that's called a defense mechanism. And I find it rather odd that a seven-year-old had to build one to hold himself together.

Miriam Rosentvaig

I loved my dad, John. I loved my mom, Amber. I loved my sister, Sandra, and I loved her best friend, Melody. Mom and Dad left this world when I was just fourteen and my sister was twenty-four. They loved each other, their children, and watching the sunrise. My mother once told me that I'm the incarnation of a smile because she could never stop smiling from the second she saw me. She taught me that feelings don't need words, just facial expressions, and that I should always be kind. She came to tuck me in every single night, and told me that I should never expect something in return for being a good person. My parents loved each other, and went on dates every Wednesday evening.

For as long as I could remember, I bragged about how my family was the greatest family in the whole wide world. Not because I wanted to impress my friends, but because I actually believed that. At the age of fourteen and a day, my family stopped being the greatest family in the world, turning into a pair of siblings who thought the sun would never rise again because their parents weren't there to watch it.

It was the first of May when the part of my heart my parents gifted me stopped beating. It flatlined, and nothing and nobody in the world could've resuscitated it. I knew something was wrong the moment I sat in that classroom, listening to what my math teacher was saying. I was happy and interested until, all of a sudden, I became sad and had a lump in my throat. I tried to ignore that uneasiness, but with every second that passed, it only grew and grew until I couldn't take it anymore and let a tear fall on my cheek. Nobody around me noticed it and that was the first time I regretted my decision of being unnoticeable. I needed comfort and the people that loved me weren't there to give it to me.

Right as I wiped that tear, the principal came in and looked at me with pity in her dark eyes. Despite the circumstances, I felt a burst of happiness because my sudden sadness became justified. The thought of being sad without a particular reason scared me. I don't remember much of what happened between that moment and the one when I got to my house and saw Sandra

Play My Part

being held by Melody. My sister was breaking apart in front of me and I couldn't do anything for her. I couldn't do anything for myself, either.

Melody looked at me with her dark, hazel eyes and reached out, silently telling me she would take care of the both of us. I didn't hesitate for a second before hugging her and let her put her arm around me. I didn't know why I was crying, but I knew something terrible happened. I knew I wasn't ready to find out the reason for all of us having tear-stained cheeks.

"It's all right! I've got you, okay? I've got you!" Melody said, kissing Sandra's hair and hugging me tighter to her chest.

I let go of Melody, and went to hug my sister from behind, kissing her shoulder.

"Hey, Luc." The sadness in her voice hit me right in the chest and made my knees weaken.

"What happened, Sand?" I asked in a terrified voice.

She looked at Melody and cried harder, burying her face in her hands. My sister was shaking her head frantically and stayed silent for what felt like hours. Sandra turned around, and hugged me like she never did before. Not hard, not desperate, but with warmth. I didn't realize I was cold until I felt her warmth.

"They're gone, Luc," she whispered, kissing my blond hair.

"That's all right, Sand. They'll come back, right?" They always came back. And despite knowing what *gone* meant, I forced myself to believe that my sister was referring to a different place, not a different world.

I put my chin on my sister's shoulder and looked at Melody who gave me a tender look.

"This time they won't, Luc-Luc! This time they went to a different place. A better place," she sniffed. "But they'll be with us all the time, right? We'll keep them in our hearts, so they'll always be close."

That was when the realization dawned on me, and an endless set of shivers ran through my body. I was fourteen, and my mother will never remind me to be kind again.

Miriam Rosentvaig

"They didn't even say goodbye before leaving to the cabin," I whispered, "they just said, *We'll see you later tonight*!" I paused and looked at both of the girls who were sitting in our mansion's living room. This gigantic house just became bigger, and any happiness we ever felt since we moved here six years ago vanished into thin air. "They said we'll see each other tonight!" I screamed. "Why didn't they say goodbye? Now I'll never be able to tell them goodbye!"

"You will," Sandra cupped my face and kissed my forehead, but I pushed her away. The gesture reminded me too much of Mom, and I wasn't ready to let anybody else kiss me the way she always did. Sandra didn't budge, and kept holding me like she was trying to protect me from all the torture my soul was going through. She was always the strong one between the two of us. While I was shy, and never managed to form connections with anybody, she was outgoing and befriended everybody she thought worthy of her time. She and Melody clicked from the second we first got here, when we stepped out of the car and met our then twenty-year-old neighbor.

Melody Byers was a gorgeous woman, with long, dark hair and lips that could make angels start a revolution in Heaven. She lived in Austin and came to visit her parents here, in Fredericksburg. We moved here from Los Angeles because my parents both decided to retire early from their acting careers. When I was old enough to realize how Melody made my soul vibrate and my body ache, something inside me knew that every time Melody and I meet, it will always be by accident, and short-lived.

"We'll be fine, Luc! I promise we'll both be fine!" she said, shifting on her knees.

"How can you say we'll be fine, Sand?" I said, kissing the top of her head. "How can you say we'll be fine, when all I feel is an unbearable pain and that from now on I'll only be a wandering soul looking for a missing piece that will never come back?"

All three of us stood there in silence, letting it swallow us whole. The only sounds I could hear until nightfall were the sobs that each of us took turns to let out. I loved my parents, but Melody did too. She always came back to visit from time to time, and every Friday night she came to dinner at our place with her parents. Her family was our extended one and vice versa. We were immensely happy, until that day, when our world crumbled to dust, only to be blown by the wind.

It was the first of May when I lost my parents and thought that I would forever be broken.

The police officers came back the same day, not giving a single fuck if we needed privacy or time to mourn. They kept telling us how sorry they were right before insisting that one of us needed to go to the station and fill out some paperwork.

I didn't care that it was an accident. I didn't care that the hole in the asphalt was covered by dirt and my father couldn't have noticed it even if he tried. I didn't care that it was unfortunate that the storm last night made the dirt slippery. I didn't fucking care about how unfortunate it was, because I needed someone to spit my venom onto. I needed someone to be guilty of my parents' death and I couldn't even fucking have that.

I felt lost. Unnoticeable, and just another face in the crowd, as always. And I started feeling like I didn't want to be that anymore. I wanted to be noticed and loved. I wanted to laugh loudly and love freely. I wanted to experience all the things my mother promised life would bring me at the right time. I wanted friends and a lover. I wanted to kiss someone's lips while feeling my heart stutter. I wanted all those things as a reward from life for forcing me to go through this tragedy with no lifeline to hang on to.

We buried my parents the next day, and I never cried more than I did then. I think that was the moment when I finally understood that my father, John Temple, would never hug me again and my mother, Amber Temple, would never tell me that I was one of her world's greatest wonders. That I would never see or hear them again. And my young heart didn't know what to do other than to whisper a promise that I would follow my mom's advice and be the greatest version of myself when I grow up. I would do it for her. I would do it for both of them. And I would never let anybody tell me I couldn't be great or that I should go back to wanting to sit in a dark corner while everybody else was bathing in the spotlight. I wanted to share that spotlight with them.

It was the third of May when I decided I would become an actor, just like my parents. And that I would not only be their son, but Lucas Temple, the man with Academy Awards on his shelves. Lucas Temple, the man who will never live off his parents' fortune, but do his best to make a name for himself. And Lucas Temple, the man who will take care of the people who took care of him. I would do it for John and for Amber, but also for Sandra, Melody, and Melody's parents.

I would become the man the world needs to make people restore their faith in humanity.

Melody

It was the first of May when I came back to Fredericksburg to visit my parents. To this day, I remember going out on the porch to try and put my thoughts in order after another endless fight with them. I was thirty and tired of hearing the same thing over and over again. *You should settle down, Melody. We're not getting any younger, Melody, and we want a grandchild. Why is it so hard for you to find someone, Melody? You're too picky, Melody!* I wasn't picky, I just hadn't found the right person for so long, that I gave up looking for them altogether.

I decided to focus on my career instead. I had a master's degree in public relations, specializing in the film industry, because while I sucked at acting, I was a sucker for movies. For six years I spent every Friday evening at my best friend's house, hearing her parents talk about that world. And I realized I wanted to live there. I wanted to be behind the scenes, and to laugh with the cast over drinks. But they have been gone

Play My Part

for four years, and the fact that they will never tell me their stories again made me sad every time I thought about it. At the same time, knowing that Lucas's career was shining brighter and brighter was the perfect antidote for that sadness. He always was a good kid. Even as a teenager, he was always polite, kind, and considerate. And beautiful to say the least. I was sure that whoever got to become his wife would be the luckiest woman out there, if she could cope with the crazy lifestyle that all famous actors have. And I was sure that being known all over the globe was the next step for him.

I felt a pang of jealousy when I thought about another woman holding Lucas's hand, but I blamed it on the fact that we were always close. Even though we started seeing each other less, and less, we still called each other every day. We stayed on the phone for hours, talking about our lives with me spilling all my frustrations, joys, and secrets. He always was a good listener and the rock I needed. He knew about my crushes, the night I spent in jail because I got into a bar fight with a woman who offended one of my friends, and he knew how often I masturbated. He was the only person who got the full version of me, who I trusted enough to tell absolutely everything without ever feeling afraid of being judged.

I didn't know when this started. I just remembered he called me because Sandra didn't pick up and he felt lonely. He was sixteen and a half, filming a series far away from home, and needed to hear a familiar voice. So I stayed with him on the phone until he didn't answer my questions anymore, I hung up, smiling to myself for helping him fall asleep. And from that night, we did the same thing over and over again. We were both alone, trying to fit in the world.

To my surprise, as I was sitting on the porch that one night, I realized that the lights in his room were on. I knew he planned to come home to check on the mansion he didn't want to sell, but I didn't know it was so soon. So, I ran inside his house, happy that I would finally get to see him again.

Miriam Rosentvaig

I went inside his room and saw him sleeping on his back, with his right hand on his chest, wearing nothing but boxers. The fact that my mouth started watering, and my brain was pushing me in his direction, took me by surprise. And despite trying to convince myself that this was a bad idea, the part of me that thought it was the best idea won.

So, I lay down next to him and kissed his cheek, threading my fingers in his dusty blond hair. I wanted him. I wanted a man who had just turned eighteen a day before, and I wanted him more than anything at that moment.

He woke up and gave me a smile like he was expecting me to be there. I thought he would've been surprised, but his face was expressing nothing but recognition. Like something deep inside him recognized something deep inside me. We stayed like that, looking into each other eyes, frozen in time, until I felt his lips on mine. I opened my mouth to deepen the kiss, and I regretted doing that the second he ended the kiss. Only to stop regretting it when he grabbed my hair and kissed me back with a passion that made me start taking my clothes off.

We didn't speak much that night, because for the first time we didn't need words. I vaguely remember "Don't Let Go" by En Vogue playing in the background while we let our bodies express everything we felt. The only thing he said was "I've never done this before," and the only words I'd spoken were, "Don't worry, I'm on the pill and clean!" I had sex with my best friend's brother that night, and despite him being a virgin, he made me climax twice. And I sucked his cock, told him to hold back his orgasm, and fucked him until he came inside me.

And after I was sure he was fast asleep, I went back to Austin. Because the part of me that told me this was a bad idea suddenly took over, and I felt like nothing would ever be the same between us.

It was the second of May when I stopped taking Lucas Temple's phone calls.

Chapter 1
Melody

I'm a woman. I make mistakes. I deserve to be told when I'm wrong. What I don't deserve is being punished for every small thing I do wrong. Apparently, my ex-husband didn't get the memo.

It was the third of May when I got married to Bart Trello, the successful doctor every woman in Austin swooned over. A man younger than me, but beautiful in all the ways that mattered. Or, at least that's what I thought. A man who promised to make me happy, only to bring me suffering and pain.

I finally managed to divorce him after several fights, a messy lawsuit, and threats that made me willing to go back to him more than once. The only reason I didn't do that is because I promised myself I deserve a chance at a normal life and that a woman should never be slapped only because she forgot to put sugar in her husband's coffee. And I wanted to let every woman out there know that they shouldn't settle for monsters because they apologize right after punching you. That love doesn't look like this. I did it, not being afraid of the fact that the whole city knew my husband and thought the best of him. He had them eating from his palm simply because his smile was blinding and he did pro bono work.It's been almost a week since my divorce was announced and I would love to feel happy, but I enjoy feeling numb too much to allow myself to step out of this state. My career is the only thing that gets me out of bed each morning and makes me believe that there is hope in the world. That nightmares and dreams can coexist. My job is my fairy tale, and my ex-husband is the horror movie nobody dares to watch.

I feel dead at the same time I feel like I have so much life in me, it's making my skin burn. My worst fear is that if I die now, I'll miss out on a lot of surprises that life has to offer. And I want to experience so many things. I want to have fun and be reckless. I want to laugh, to love honestly, without dark tentacles staining that beautiful feeling. I want to love without being scared of doing it.

I married Bart two years ago and ran from his home a year into our marriage. I don't think I'm incapable of having a healthy, sane relationship, I just think that life didn't offer me the chance to prove myself that I can. But I do have hope. And that's what makes me believe that the warrior I once was is ready to go out there and fight tooth and nail for what she wants and for what her soul craves.

Bart and I met in very unethical circumstances. I was his patient for a short period of time, and right when I thanked him for being an excellent doctor, he asked me if I would be interested to find out if he's an excellent man, too. I was at my lowest point in life then, and I needed somebody who could hug me and promise me that everything would be fine. To hold me and to make me feel like a woman was supposed to feel. He took me out the next evening and his jokes, wit, and confidence made me like him. We kept going out and spending time together, and when he kissed me after our third date, I started believing that he was the man I was supposed to spend the rest of my life with.

His flaring nostrils when the waiter was two minutes late after we told him our order and his eyes void of any emotion when a beggar asked him for some change should've told me that behind that mask there was a monster waiting to come out. I was suffering, and I didn't know better, but I can't stop blaming myself. It was me who chose not to believe the rumors about him abusing his ex-girlfriend. It was me who decided that if he started throwing punches with every man that said something wrong in his direction, it didn't mean he could never touch a

Play My Part

woman the wrong way.

I thought he was my hero, my knight in shining armor, but he was nothing but a villain wrapped in tin foil. I thought he would always be my everything and now I wish I was his nothing. He was the first man who told me I looked great when I wasn't wearing any makeup, and turned out to be the reason for me adding an extra layer of foundation on my face and throat.

Bart first hit me on our wedding night. He said I looked in a certain way at his brother, the same brother who is gay. He slapped me so hard I fell on our bedroom floor, asking myself if it actually happened, or if it was just a bad dream. He proceeded with grabbing my hair, throwing me on the bed and telling me I was now his. That he owned me and that I should be grateful he accepted to play with a broken toy that nobody ever wanted or would ever want. He thrust inside me, making me scream in pain, while he told me that it was my fault, that I was solely responsible for him behaving like that, because I should never look at another man while I was holding his hand. He raped me for the first time that night, all the time while telling me that I was whore that he would tame and turn into a good, obedient wife and forced me to thank him for it. I woke up the next day and packed everything I had there, only to realize he changed the locks at some point. I was my husband's hostage both physically, and spiritually.

When he woke up, he behaved like the previous night never happened. He was the same sweet man I met a year before, who kissed me after taking the first sip of his coffee, making the taste linger on my lips. I asked him if he'd have the decency to at least apologize, and his answer was that he had nothing to apologize for. That I knew he was a jealous man and still married him. That it was my fucking fault for everything he did to me.

I had nowhere to go, even if I could escape from the jail I was locked in. I ended my rental agreement two weeks after I moved in with Bart. My parents sold their house in Fredericksburg two years ago, deciding to finally accept Sandra's offer to come and live with her in the United Kingdom together with her husband and their baby daughter. That awful morning, when Bart was looking at me with madness swimming in his eyes, it was the first time I hated my best friend for taking care of my parents, instead of feeling grateful to her for giving them the life they well deserved.

I was scared of the man I forced myself to fall in love with, and I felt like something flipped in my brain, making me want to do anything to avoid making him angry. I didn't want to make him happy because I loved him, I then realized. I wanted to make him happy like a prisoner would their captor, adjusting my behavior only to avoid punishments.

He pushed himself off the kitchen counter and grabbed my hair, pulling until my scalp burned, and making my eyes tear from the pain. He shoved me on the wall and lifted the skirt I was wearing that day. It was my favorite skirt, and I burned it in our backyard the next day, when he left for work.

"I'm going to fuck you now, Melody!" he said in a serious voice. "I'm going to fuck you and put a baby in you, so you'll have a reminder that you're only mine until you fucking die. You will make me all the babies I want, and I'm going to breed you until I won't have any cum left in my balls!"

I couldn't say anything. I didn't want him to do that. I didn't want to bring a child into this nightmare I was living in. He was a provider, but he could never truly be a father.

He shoved himself inside me and I screamed because of the pain I felt between my legs. I still wasn't healed after what I was forced to endure less than twelve hours before. My heart didn't want him and neither did my body. I never wanted to feel his skin on mine again, but I was horrified by the consequences that my rejection might have caused.

"Don't scream, you whore! We both know you like it!" he said when he started thrusting inside me. "Such a fucking disgusting liar, pretending you don't want your future baby daddy's cock in your pussy!"

Play My Part

I couldn't hold it in me anymore so I started crying, putting my forehead on the wall. Bart was thrusting harder and deeper inside me and I felt like he was tearing my whole body apart. He already did that to my soul, so my body would be just collateral damage.

"How about you stop crying and start moaning, huh? Moan for me, slut!" He put his hand around my throat and squeezed until I couldn't breathe anymore. I panicked and turned my head to look at him, hoping the pleading look I was giving him would be enough to make him stop. His face expressed insanity. He was feeding on my suffering like a lion would feed on an antelope carcass.

"Say *please* and I'll let you breathe. Don't and I'll kill you and fuck you until your body turns cold. I'm sure I'll be able to come inside you at least twice until that happens," he said in a chilling voice.

I tried to push him off, but considering the fact he was twice my size, I didn't stand a chance. Defeated, I let a new set of tears fall from my eyes and mouthed *please*. He let me go and I started coughing and gasping, my lungs filling with the oxygen they were deprived of for so many seconds.

"I love it when you beg me. I'm controlling you, Melody. I'm controlling every single part of you and I just proved to you that your life depends on me and my good mood. Only on me and my good mood. So you'd better behave when you're going to work tomorrow, right?"

I didn't answer. Me going back to work was one of the things I held on to when I needed my brain to produce a small amount of serotonin. And Bart ruined that for me. He ruined everything for me. He hit my head against the wall, increasing his pace and yelling at me to answer him.

"Yes, I will behave," I whispered.

"I'm going to fuck you again in the morning, so that you will go there with my cum leaking from your slutty pussy. That will teach that motherfucker Charlie that you're my property and he shouldn't look at you!"

Charlie was my boss and the walking definition of an imbecile. He was mean, loud, judgmental, and utterly stupid. The only reason for him leading the film PR agency I was working for was because our former manager retired and Charlie's father had enough money and influence to put his spawn in a leading position. Life was terribly unfair on all fronts for me, and there was no light at the end of that tunnel.

When I felt Bart's cock throbbing inside me and his moans getting louder, it was the first time I felt every single part of me cracking into small pieces.

Bart kept his word and raped me again the next morning. I wasn't even awake when he positioned himself between my legs. I screamed again when I felt the same pain. I was having the same nightmare and, as it happened the day before, when he got close to his orgasm, I started crying and begging him to stop. Needless to say, my pleas remained unanswered. If anything, they made him thrust even harder.

But that was then, and now I need to focus on building the person I want to be.

As I'm entering the office building where Charlie waits for me, I realize my life hasn't changed much. Sure, I've started therapy, and talked about all the scars different people or events left on my tired soul. But I sometimes feel like I'm still trapped in Bart's prison. Even though I'm now legally free from that monster, and I do have a temporary restraining order keeping him from coming close to me in the near future, I feel like my brain doesn't understand that fully. I discussed this yesterday with my therapist, and she told me that healing has no timeline, and that my brain isn't able to realize I'm out of danger yet. Hence the moments when my body starts shaking out of nowhere and the feeling that my lungs are constricting even if I'm surrounded by people.

I rented a new apartment, one closer to my job and as far as possible

Play My Part

from Bart's home. I send a prayer each and every night to every entity willing to listen that I won't wake up in the middle of the night with that monster inside my house. That's why I'm so afraid of falling asleep, and that's the reason for waking up screaming during the rare nights my exhausted brain shuts down.

I'm still working for the same imbecile. I'm still hoping that someday me and the other members of his team will finally get him fired. I have nothing to focus on other than my job, and that's exactly what I will do. I will be the best film PR specialist out there and make everybody call me Melody Byers, not *Bart Trello's ex*.

It's nine a.m. and the heat outside is unbearable. Living in Texas and wearing long-sleeved shirts and pants all the time to hide the bruises on my hands and legs only made my life harder. But now I'm wearing a sleeveless sundress that ends right above my knees and sandals. It's my own way of saying *Fuck you, Bart! Look at me blossoming!*

I walk into the building and right when I enter the elevator, my phone rings. I roll my eyes when I see it's Charlie, but instantly regret it, fearing that some of the people around me might see it. But nobody really sees me. Because if they did, they would've helped me when I was silently begging to be dragged out of the darkness and being allowed to shine bright. I'm unnoticeable. I'm just another face in the crowd. The people on the stage can't see me because the light of their happiness is blinding and makes them oblivious to other people's pain. It's not their fault. It's only mine.

"Hi, Charlie!" I say in a much more cheerful voice than I actually feel.

"Melody, love! Where are you?"

"Just came inside the building. Do you need me?" I ask in the same tone.

"More than anything, and you know it. Come to my office, please. We need to talk. I've got great business for you!"

I'm sure he does. He always puts on my plate the most difficult clients. The most pretentious and entitled producers and directors.

Miriam Rosentvaig

I step out of the elevator wishing a great day to everybody on my way to Charlie's office. When I knock on his door, his obnoxiously loud voice tells me to enter. He is sitting at his desk, looking at some papers he's holding between his thick fingers. Everything is thick about him. He's obese because he eats everything he can get his hands on. He lives on fast food and alcohol and he changes his wardrobe on a monthly basis because his old clothes don't fit him anymore. And if he were to be a kind soul, this wouldn't matter. But his appearance is just a confirmation of the uncaring, and self-centered character he has.

"How can I help you, Charlie?" I ask, taking a seat on the chair in front of the coffee table in his office. A coffee table he uses as a shelf for his cheap vodka and his IKEA glasses. For a man with a fortune as big as his, you would've thought he has better taste and a bit of class. He doesn't.

"By accepting my offer, Mel, I'm doing you a favor by bringing this to you, trust me!" Of course he's doing me a favor. Because with Charlie, every project he gives you is a favor, not something he should normally do, considering this is my fucking job.

"I can't wait to hear more." I fake a smile.

"CastleCat Productions is making a movie," he says, leaving the papers aside and looking at me with his brown eyes. He untucks his red tie and wipes the sweat on his forehead and his bald head with a discarded tissue from his desk. I force myself to swallow back the bile that rises up my throat. "And it won't be filmed in the US!" he continues in an excited voice.

This sounds like the perfect opportunity to take a break from all the shit that I went through. Let people here forget about the divorce that was the main topic of the whispers in each and every corner. This might be my chance to start from scratch, go and live somewhere else while doing what I love, and come back to a world where people won't stare at me when I'm grocery shopping.

"I'll take it," I say, faking calmness. I'm anything but calm. I want to leave this place as soon as possible. I would do it now. Leave only with my passport and my credit card, not giving a damn about anything I leave behind.

"We all have to go with them," Charlie says. I nod, because that's exactly what I want. I don't care who they are. They can be the worst crew ever known to mankind and they would still be an army of angels compared to the demon I was married to.

"And where exactly are we supposed to go? For how long? What will we need to bring? Maybe besides a social media expert, they will need the graphic designer on site. Should I tell Chris to start packing, too?" I rush out.

"Whoa, easy there! You know I can't keep up with your enthusiasm." Charlie laughs and I purse my lips. "So, as far as I understood, you'll have to go to Budapest, Romania."

"Don't you mean Hungary?" I ask in a timid voice.

"No, no! I'm sure it's in Romania," he answers, looking through the papers he held earlier.

"Bucharest, then," I correct him.

"Yeah, let's call it Europe, just to be on the safe side." He laughs, and I force myself to smile.

"And what exactly is going to happen in Bucharest, Romania, Europe?"

"They're making a movie." The moron laughs again like he just said the best joke ever heard. I sit there, watching him and waiting for him to be done.

"What kind of movie? Do we have a title? A timeline? Did they set some expectations for their PR representatives?" I immediately go into work mode. I need to prove to Charlie that I am the right choice, although I am not entirely sure that he actually appreciates me for how professional I am.

"It's called *Dysfunctionally Perfect* or some shit like that." That puts a real smile on my lips.

"That's a great title," I say.

Miriam Rosentvaig

"It's a shit title," he says, saliva coming out of his mouth. "And the plot is shit, too. It's about—and I quote—*how broken people can find love and use it to heal their wounds.* Boo-fucking-hoo," he mocks, but I'm already back to being sad. I wish I could be healed. I wish I can be truly loved. I wish somebody could help me heal my wounds and let me heal theirs.

"They signed all the great names," he continues in the same annoyed tone. "Yonathan Friedmann in the role of a manwhore billionaire. Psht! Go figure." He scoffs, rolling his eyes. Yonathan Friedmann is well known for being exactly that in real life, so the role indeed suits him. Honestly? I can't blame the man! He looks like a fucking gift that God sent to Earth, only to make women swoon and sigh every time he comes up on the screen.

"Then we have Tzipporah Angelberg, of course, because one Jew isn't enough on your set if you want to win an Oscar, right?" Charlie laughs again, and I want to stand up and leave this place and this judgmental imbecile behind. But I can't. I need to sit here and listen to his shit only to be able to get this project. A small price to pay for a few of months of freedom.

"So, they are the main characters?" I ask, desperate to change the topic.

"Kind of. Sort of. There are three relationships moving forward throughout the movie. Billionaire meets a law student, grumpy whatever shit he is gets together with a successful journalist, and a sociopath falls in love with the daughter of a priest." He frowns and rolls his eyes right after. "It's a complete shitshow, I'm telling you. This movie has all the controversial shit in it. Because it has to be *politically correct!*" He air quotes the last two words and I have to fight the urge to roll my eyes.

"Got it." I nod, urging him to move on from the cast so I can find out when I am supposed to leave.

"And the weird one is played by a Gypsy. Can you fucking believe that?" Jesus Christ. This is the manager of one of the most prestigious film PR companies in the country. I don't understand how people still hire us and the firm still stands. "Oh, wait! You told me about him at some point. That dude, Manon something!"

Play My Part

"Toussaint. Manon Toussaint. And I think the term you're looking for is *Roma*, not *Gypsy*," I say in a much angrier voice than I would like Charlie to hear coming from me.

"Only you could know a rascal like him." He scoffs, and if I didn't need this project so much, I would quit right this instant. I'm fed up with Charlie and his shitty mentality. "And the grumpy one is played by Lucas Temple. As far as I understood, these three are best friends or some shit. I still don't know how a great guy like Lucas could befriend those two, but I guess this is great for the movie producers. They sure as hell need one of the best actors of our time if they want this shit to bring them some money."

I freeze and look at Charlie, hoping that I heard him wrong. He couldn't have said Lucas Temple.

He couldn't have mentioned that the boy with the hair kissed by the sun and with the eyes enveloped by a forest in the blooming season will be spending the next few months in the same place I will. My best friend's younger brother. Much younger brother. The one who taught me how to be a warrior and how frail feelings could be. I gave him all my love when he was a teenager and he gave it back tenfold. He became my younger brother, only to become everything I ever wanted in a man.

The same man who I last saw five years ago, when everything between us changed. When my downfall began, and his career started. Lucas Temple, the man who wrote me an insane amount of letters, to which I never replied. Because I was scared, crippled by the idea that I might love him in a very wrong way. To this day, I remember the words he wrote in his last letter to me.

> *Wherever life takes you, I hope it will be the best place you'll ever know. I hope you'll be happy, Mel-Mel. And I sincerely wish you all the best. I hope one day you'll meet a man that will turn your life upside down the same way you did mine. I hope he'll make you blush and hang the stars from the sky in*

your bedroom. You deserve nothing less, but so much more.
And for all the love you gave me, even though it didn't come in the shape I wanted it to, please know that I'll forever be grateful. Words can't express how much you mean to me. They really can't. I hope our paths will cross again. If not in this lifetime, maybe in one of our next ones. But until then, please remember me. Please never forget me.
I cherish you, Melody. I will never stop cherishing you.
Kisses from another life,
Your lost boy,
Lucas Temple

He was always my blind spot and the boy I would've fought everybody and everything in this world for. I owed him so much, but I never got to pay my debt. Maybe life decided to give me a break and connect with an old friend. Is he a friend? How can someone you slept with and haven't spoken to since be a friend? How can he be more than somebody I was lucky enough to spend time with?

"So?" Charlie interrupts me.

"Where do I sign?" I answer in a determined voice.

Apparently, my past life decided to invade my current one. And I'd be damned if I don't let it.

Chapter 2
Lucas

"I'm not sure I understand, Yonathan," I tell one of my two best friends, who is currently sitting on my living room couch, reading the script for the movie we'll soon start filming. "They asked you to play Hail first, and then they changed their minds and casted you as Bo?"

"They changed their minds, I changed mine, what difference does it make?"

"Pardon my remark," Manon, the last part of our trio, interrupts, "but are you still keen on answering every question you're asked with another question?"

Yonathan frowns and takes off his black-framed glasses, putting the script next to him.

"And what if I do, Non? Does that annoy you?" He smiles and looks at me with mischief in his eyes. When Yonathan gets like this, it means he's in the mood for teasing either me or Manon about different things we've done in the seven years we've spent together.

I met both of them when I was sixteen. I was still living with Sandra, and it happened a couple of months before she met her husband. A British tourist who got lost on his way to Austin and stopped to ask my sister for directions. According to him, he forgot everything about his plans when she smiled at him. According to her, they fell in love two months later, when he was still in Fredericksburg and asked her if she ever visited the United Kingdom while eating ice cream during one of their endless walks.

She went to visit London six months later, and never came back, trusting Yonathan and Manon for some unknown reason to watch over me until I turned eighteen.

"Call it a gut feeling, Luc," she said, smiling. "I really think these two will take care of you better than I ever did."

She had no idea that nobody could've taken better care of me better than she did. She could never understand how much I appreciated the fact that she chose to stay in Fredericksburg and be the town's therapist instead of moving to a bigger city only to be close to me. Our parents left behind an insane amount of money, and we both spent as little as possible of it. We only bought groceries, cooked together, and paid the bills. There were no expensive clothes, or unnecessary indulgences. We were just two people who looked out for one another while trying to fill the emptiness the death of their parents left behind.

I was getting more and more successful by the time she left. The series all three of us featured in was filmed in multiple cities in the USA, so I told myself that it's better she met Richard and left the country. The thought of her being all alone in that huge mansion and me being away from her could've made me decline the part and lose the chance that drove me right at the top of the *most-wanted actors* list.

I always liked our small group of three. Maybe because it reminded me of myself, Sandra, and Melody, or maybe because I always liked being the mediator. The one with a clear mind who always tries to fix the problems inside our small group. I did it when I promised my father he will always have me, and that he should let Sandra spend more time with her friends since she was a teenager already. I did it when I started listening to Melody's secrets when she considered me a better listener than my sister. A sixteen-year-old boy with nothing but good listening skills, that's what I was for her.

I've always been the mediator and I will never stop doing it. It's my safe place. My comfort zone.

Yonathan is the oldest of us three. He's thirty-three, followed by Manon who just turned twenty-seven, and then there's me, the baby of our chosen family, being twenty-three. Yonathan wears an armor made of indifference, arrogance, and sarcasm that keeps him protected from all the bad the world can throw in his direction. And God knows he needs all the protection he can get after the horrendous childhood he had. I'm incredibly proud of how my chosen brother turned out after everything he went through. Running away from home at the age of sixteen, moving to a different continent, only to make sure your family won't find you until it's too late is definitely something that could damage your sanity.

But that didn't happen to Yonathan. Not then, at least. He not only kept his mind intact, but went to auditions since the first moment he set foot in Austin. And after countless nights of sleeping in abandoned cars, somebody finally gave him a chance. He was the lead actor of one of the most successful TV series in history. And I played his long lost younger brother when they started filming the fifth season in my hometown.

I never thought they'd choose me for the role. There were thousands of kids coming from all the cities around mine to audition for the part. I never knew if my last name had anything to do with the producers offering me that chance. If it did, I don't regret it. I proved my potential. I not only met the expectations, but I raised the bar higher. There wasn't a single bad review of the first episode that featured me. And I still hope that wherever my parents are, they are smiling and proud of me.

I didn't like Yonathan in the beginning. In the first days, he blamed me if a scene wasn't going the way he wanted it to. Then, he switched to completely ignoring me. And, when he wasn't, he was incredibly rude to me. The day he told me that I would never be as good as my father and that I should give up acting was the last straw. He could talk bad about me all he wanted, but mentioning my dad was always off-limits.

I told him to go fuck himself and that he was half the actor he thought he was and turned my back to him. I heard him chuckle on my way out and that only made me angrier. I turned my head to look at him, and when I saw that he was looking at me with pride in his eyes, I crossed my arms and frowned.

"What the fuck is wrong with you?" I asked him.

"Wrong? Why would you say there's something wrong with me?" he challenged.

"Because I just told you to go screw yourself and you're looking like I paid you the best compliment."

"But that's not what you actually said, was it, baby Temple?" he came closer to me. "You said I should go fuck myself. And that's the kind of fire I like seeing in people." He sighed and unbuttoned the jacket of his suit. "The world is such a fucking boring place most of the time. There are so many lost sheep running around like their life actually has a purpose. It might have." He shrugged. "But if you're spending your days with your head down, accepting all the shit your lousy boss throws at you only because you want to have something to eat for dinner and pay the bills, you sure as fuck won't find it."

"So, living like a daredevil is key?" I asked in a high-pitched voice, typical for all teenagers my age.

"Living. Living is key. Most people forget that they were born to live, not to meet the expectations of the people around them. If you live only for pleasing others, can you really say you have a life? Or are you just breathing for the sake of others?"

"That's why you were treating me like shit? Because you thought I'm not living according to your standards?" I scoffed.

"Nah, not because of that." He half laughed and threaded his fingers through his ebony hair that reached the tip of his ears. "I tried to push you. I needed to know if you're willing to fight a bit for what's yours. You want to succeed in this world? Then you better be ready to tell more people to go fuck themselves. I didn't know if you had it in you and I wanted to find out if you're worthy of my help."

"And why would I need your help, Yonathan? What makes you believe that I can't make it on my own?" I asked, moving closer to him and looking directly in his light blue eyes. "I don't need you."

"You do, Lucas, and it's completely fine if you're too proud to acknowledge it now. I'll help you either way. I'll take you from this shitty village and show you the greatness of the world. I'll teach you how to leave the past behind and live the fuck out of your life!"

"I don't want to leave the past behind. I have a wonderful past, thank you very much!" I wasn't about to open my heart in front of the man I was almost sure was a complete sociopath.

He squinted his eyes and looked at me like he could see everything I was hiding. I didn't like it one bit.

"Is that why you refuse to call the people who play the role of our parents *Mom* and *Dad*?" he said in a cold, detached voice.

"I just think Joseph and Lucy sound better. It gives the show a taste of authenticity," I lied.

"Authenticity?" he chuckled. "For an uprising actor, you're completely shit at lying, Lucas. Is this little boy still sad that Mommy and Daddy left him in this cruel world?" he asked in a mocking tone.

"Don't talk about my parents," I said taking another step closer. When I felt my forehead touching his chest, I looked up and fought back tears.

"Oh, I'm sorry." He half laughed. "I just wanted to find out more about Lucas Temple's *authenticity*." He put an emphasis on the last word.

I pushed his chest and yelled at him to shut up. One time. Two times. More times than I could count. I was irrationally angry. He had no right to talk about my parents. Not then and not ever. Although their bodies were no longer on this planet, they still lived inside me and every time somebody mentioned them something inside me flipped. I couldn't stand hearing other people talk about them, not even when they were giving them praise or posthumous awards. They were mine to cherish. Only me, Sandra, and Melody were allowed to mention their names.

Yonathan didn't react to my burst of anger. He stood there and let me push him and punch his chest for several minutes. I don't know what I was screaming at him, but I felt like I finally found a way to let out all the sorrow and the pain I bottled up in the past two years. I lost my mother and father. I was losing Melody, who was constantly pushing me back, most probably because she realized that a boy twelve years her junior was desperately in love with her. Not because she was there for me when nobody except Sandra was, but because she was fucking stunning, kind, and smart. All that hurt. It fucking hurt.

Suddenly, Yonathan wrapped his hands around me. I fought him in the beginning, but when I realized he wouldn't let me go, I just surrendered and started crying, burying my face in his chest.

"I know, kiddo. Trust me, I know," he said in a low voice. "I know how losing the people you love the most in this world feels. But you're a big boy and you're strong, aren't you?"

"Why did they leave me?" I asked between sobs. "Why does everybody I fucking care about leaves me behind, Yonathan? Why can't they just stick around and love me the same way I love them?"

He sighed and hugged me harder, like he wanted to tell me more about his own story, but changed his mind at the last second.

"Because sometimes you need to leave people so you can grow. And other times you need to leave them behind so you can watch them growing from a distance," he said in a choked voice. "You don't need anybody to be great, Luc. You'll do phenomenal things if you surround yourself with the right people. A person like you should never pay attention to the ones

Play My Part

below you. You're a fantastic kid and you'll be the best fucking actor in the world, you hear me?"

I nodded and took a step back, trying to figure out what happened in the past half an hour. We walked into this room as enemies and now he was telling me that I was a great person and that he wanted to help me despite me never asking for his help.

"What do you actually want from me, Yonathan?" I asked in a suspicious voice.

"To go and tell your sister that you're leaving for Philadelphia after we wrap up here," he said in a determined voice, cocking an eyebrow.

"The producers didn't say if they still want me on the show."

"They will." The indifference in his voice told me that convincing them was just mundane work for him. "Do you want them to tell you now or should they wait until Sandra comes to pick you up from the set?"

"You know my sister's name?" I asked, feeling my eyebrows reaching my hairline.

"I know everything I need to know to make your dream come true, baby Temple. Now, answer my question. I need to let the crew know." He took out his phone from his pocket and looked at me impatiently.

"I think they should wait," I answered.

He gave me a single nod and typed something. When he put his phone back, he put his hand on my shoulder and looked at me with amusement in his eyes.

"Do you want me to introduce you to somebody you could fuck like she's a bitch in heat? If you prefer boys, I have some contacts, too. Just say the word, Lucas!"

"I don't, Yonathan. I just want to live my life and be the greatest version of myself."

"And the greatest version you will be," he said in a reassuring voice. "So, just making sure I understood correctly. You're not in the mood to fuck, but you did fuck somebody at least once in your life, right?"

"Can we please stop talking about my sexual life?" I pleaded, feeling my cheeks turning redder by the second.

"At least tell me you know what cum tastes like."

"Yonathan, I'm begging you!"

"Oh, the amount of times I heard that coming from a woman's mouth," he laughed. "I could never grow tired of hearing it, you know?"

I knew he wasn't lying, because besides crude, Yonathan was ruggedly handsome in a way that had women throwing panties at him. He was tall and charming, and no woman could resist him once he decided to seduce her."Can you please stop, Yonathan?" I said through gritted teeth.

"I was joking, Luc," he said, raising his hands at his chest level in surrender. "Well, not really, but anyway, let's talk about the details. I never had a minor on my watch, so I need to know how to convince you that heroin isn't the right choice."

"That's not in your job description, so don't worry about that. I have some great people in my life that have guided me in the right direction. I have an older sister, so I'm not sure I need an older brother, too."

"Let's just wait and see, shall we?" he asked like he already knew how strong our connection would become through the years.

Now, I'm looking at Yonathan and shaking my head, silently asking him to drop it and not pick up a playful word fight with Manon. We should start packing for our departure to Romania that will happen tomorrow. Instead, we all gathered in my five-bedroom apartment to exchange impressions on the script. Not that we didn't already do it several times since we accepted the roles, but this is something we will never get tired of. We always give each other tips and tricks on how to put more or less emotion in a certain scene. That's when Yonathan actually reads the script before the filming starts.

"It doesn't irritate me, Yon," Manon answers in an indifferent voice. "I just consider it childish."

"Oh, do you?"

"Yes, I do. So how about you answer Luc's earlier questions instead of trying to irk me. I'm already tired and not in the mood for your banter."

Yonathan rolls his eyes and looks first at me and then at his perfectly clipped nails.

"I told them you're more suitable for Hail's part!" he shrugs. "After all, Hail is Bo's younger chosen brother, not the other way around. Also, I think I'm more suitable to play Bo rather than that poor lost soul who would beg any average woman to give him an ounce of attention. I'm a billionaire and I like to fuck. This role fits me like an XXL condom fits my cock." He laughs.

Manon gives me an amused look and I can't help myself and start laughing.

"Did you read the full script, Yon?" my brown-skinned friend asks.

"Of course," he scoffs before continuing. "Of course I didn't, I mean. That's why I have an agent. If she said she finds that part more suitable for me, who am I to say that it doesn't?"

"Oh," Manon sarcastically says, "did you take in consideration that said agent is desperately in love with you and hopes that one day you'll be hers forever?"

"She's not *desperately* in love with me. She may like me more than any agent would like her boss, but it's not my fault that I'm terribly attractive." Yon laughs again.

"Surely not. But I think that Ashley might've said that only because she hopes you will end up falling in love with her the way Bo fell in love with Arrow. Maybe in her fantasies she's the one who makes you realize you are just a lost soul looking for his one true love."

"Who the fuck is Arrow? And what the fuck are you even talking about, Non?" Yonathan asks and picks up the script, flipping through the pages until he gets to the last ones.

Both Manon and I bite our lips trying to keep ourselves from laughing until our friend finishes reading the ending of the story. I can't look at Non because I know a single look would make both of us burst out laughing, so I keep my eyes on the floor, focusing on the pain my poor bottom lip feels.

"No," Yonathan says letting out a huge exhale and standing up. "This is fucking impossible. It's a mistake! It has to be! Ashley never read it or they sent a different version of the script. No, no, no! I need to fire her! This isn't right!"

I can't hold it in anymore and start laughing, and Non follows right after. The fact that Yonathan starts pacing the room calling everybody who had access to this script and yelling at them that they're morons doesn't help us stop, on the contrary. We laugh harder, falling to the floor when our knees become too weak to keep up with us.

"Well, I'm happy I'm amusing you. No feeling is better than seeing your friends laughing because you're experiencing a tragedy," Yonathan says after firing Ashley's secretary over the phone.

"Come on, Yon! This is everything but a tragedy," I say. "And I can't believe that you didn't know how Bo's story ends! How could you make such a rookie mistake?"

"I hired an agent especially for this kind of thing, Lucas! This is her fucking job!" he yells, and that only makes me laugh harder.

"Well, maybe you won't fuck your next agent. That should do the trick!", Non says, wiping the tears from his cheeks. "But how could you not know? We were together when the pitch came in. Didn't *billionaire meets law student* give you a hint on what was going to happen?"

"Meets!" Yonathan screams again in frustration. "*Meets* is the key word here! They meet, they fuck, they fuck again, they grow tired of each other, they move on!"

"It's a romance, Yon!" I say. "How could you expect one of the main characters not to have a happy ending?"

Play My Part

"My definition of a happy ending is completely different from society's one, I guess," he says in an exasperated voice. "Falling in love with the most boring woman known to humanity is a worse ending than *Sweet November*'s!"

Manon takes the script from him and starts writing down things on it. He's a fast reader, so this is easy for him to do. Despite us being so different from each other, we are always there when one of us needs help, even though sometimes it comes really hard for all of us to verbalize it. We just jump to help whenever it's needed. No questions asked and no rewards expected in return. My chosen brothers and I know each other. We know when one of us needs our help and we never hesitate in giving it. Not a single time.

"See if this helps," Non says. "I underlined some scenes that you could rewrite. Make them less romantic while sticking to the main idea."

Yonathan groans and throws the papers on the table. He stands up and pinches the bridge of his nose, squinting his eyes like he is in pain. I frown, because I can see how much this upsets him. His frustration is no longer funny, because I can see how he feels trapped and stuck in a helpless situation.

"Are you okay?" I ask, putting my hand on his shoulder and squeezing, the same gesture he did to me all those years ago.

"No, baby Temple! I'm anything but okay!" he shouts. "I'm in pain! Physical pain!"

"I can completely understand that this can give you a headache, but you're a fucking great actor, Yonathan. It's not like this is the first time you'll play this type of character," I say, trying to make him feel better.

"It's not my head that hurts," he says as loud as earlier. "My whole existence and the fucking depths of my heart hurt. This?" he points to the script he threw on the blue leather couch in the center of my living room, "This is bullshit. I can't connect to that moron! Not now, when I found out that he's just a troubled mommy's boy who tries to fight his anxiety first by fucking every woman with a pulse only to end up being obsessed with that… girl," he spits.

"And you don't see any resemblance between you and Bo?" Non interrupts.

"None." Yonathan shakes his head and rubs his five o'clock shadow.

Manon picks up the discarded script again and starts reading.

"*Bo pinches his nose and rubs his stubble. He stands up and looks at Hail.*

She doesn't want to fuck me, Hail! Me, the most-wanted bachelor in the United States of America, according to thousands of women and various tabloids."

He carefully puts the scripts on the table, frowning when he doesn't manage to make the papers form a ninety-degree angle on the table's corner.

I leave Yonathan's side and go to stand next to my other best friend.

"Let me help you," I say in a gentle voice, giving him a kind smile.

"No!" he screams, slapping my hand that went to the pages. He immediately gives me an apologetic look. I know he didn't mean to harm me and that his illness sometimes gets the best of him, so I keep a smile on my face and nod. "I'm the one who has to do it, Lucas. If you help me, something bad will happen to you and I don't want that. I can't let fate rip my heart out of my chest that way. Let me do it."

"Sure, Non, whatever you need."

All three of us stay in complete silence, letting Manon position the script in a way that is satisfying his brain. After he's done, he takes a step back and looks at the table again. Nodding to himself, he taps his thigh for five consecutive times with his index finger and picks up the conversation from where he had left off.

"No resemblance whatsoever, Yonathan," he sarcastically says. "Tell me something. Aren't you the one who preposterously fucks his way through life, bathing in debauchery and craving the tabloids' attention?"

Yonathan rolls his eyes, sitting back on the couch, paying extra attention to the coffee table, so he doesn't ruin Manon's work.

"That I am. But the problem is that this imbecile falls in love with this fucking creepy sociopath, and that's where I get stuck. I don't know how to switch gears so fast!"

"First of all," I say, taking a seat next to him, "Arrow is neither creepy, nor a sociopath." I let out a laugh. "She's sweet and caring. And she falls in love with Bo the same way he falls in love with her. It's the perfect example of opposites attract, Yon."

"Like I said, a sociopath with no friends, putting all her eggs in that poor man's basket," he replies in a disgusted voice.

"They don't need anybody else," I say in an exasperated voice. I know that he can be stubborn and pretentious, but this time I have the feeling that he's taking this out of proportion. He won a Golden Globe last year for his role in a drama telling the story about a man who reunited with his high school sweetheart and faces life's challenges next to her. I really don't understand what his problem is.

"Oh, bless your hopeless romantic soul! That is the most insane way to spend your life. Only needing one person to be happy makes you nothing but a lunatic who settles with whatever destiny, fate, or life gives you. But you have to fight, baby Temple. You have to fucking fight for getting the cake, eat it, and fuck the baker, too." He sighs and rubs his temples. "When there are so many options out there, why would one choose to live a boring life?"

He unbuttons his jacket and leans on the sofa bench, covering his eyes with his left arm.

"I don't know how to bring him to life without letting my frustration get the best of me. This man is everything I never wish to become. He's my exact polar opposite. All the dumb jokes, all the kindness he wants to spread is just too much, I swear."

"Should I keep reading the script out loud?" Manon asks. "Or are you maybe ready to admit that the reason for you being so agitated about this situation isn't that Bo is your polar opposite, but the only thing you're afraid you'll become?"

"What the fuck do you mean by that?" Yonathan asks in a revolted tone, opening one of his eyes and looking at our best friend.

"In my humble opinion, you connect with who Bo is in the first half of the movie," Non answers in a calm voice, "but him falling madly in love with Arrow scares you shitless because of how pure the love they share is. It scares you because deep down inside you, you hope that you'll find something similar, but the arrogant bastard that you pretend to be refuses to let that side of you speak up."

I purse my lips, taking into consideration what I've just heard. I don't have time to ruminate it because after only two seconds, Yonathan's irritated voice cuts the silence.

"Okay, Dr. Freud. Thank you *so* much for your input! I will take it with me and throw it in the closest trash can I find. Your imagination is so vivid, it would make Shakespeare jealous if he wasn't fucking dead!"

He sighs and gives Manon a questioning look, pointing at the script. When Non answers with a nod, Yonathan takes the script, puts his glasses back on, and goes back to reading.

"You know that you're supposed to wear those glasses all the time except when you're reading, not the other way around, right?" I ask, getting closer to him so I can see what part of the script he decided to analyze.

"I wear them when I remember I have them and when I want the woman I'm fucking to tell me that she's been a bad student who needs to be punished. I can play various parts, even in bed. The professor taming the brat is definitely one of my favorite ones."

He shifts in his seat, probably lost in one of his fantasies.

"So, maybe you should make a career shift and explore the porn industry. You won't get any Academy Awards, but you won't have to play Bo," Manon jokes, taking a sip of his can of Dr. Pepper.

"Fuck you, Non. Fuck you poorly sans lube," Yonathan replies.

Play My Part

"Does that mean you'll take my advice into consideration? I heard sans lube pays better. God knows you'll need the money since your passion for high maintenance women is greater than your ego," Manon throws back.

Yonathan groans again, and I cut him off before he can continue.

"You know, I think you could ask your co-star to help you connect better with Bo and actually live their story. Maybe the chemistry between you two will make it easier for you to play this part," I suggest.

"I already fucked Joanna. Multiple times. Zero chemistry there, and she doesn't know how to properly suck cock for the life of her. She does have an appetite for anal though, hence the multiple times," Yon replies, not taking his eyes from the page he's reading.

"Well, I'm sorry, but I don't have any other suggestions. That's what helped me connect with Hail when I started practicing."

"Of course it helped you. You're going to be naked next to Tzipporah Angelberg. Not only that, but you'll pretend to fuck her."

"So?" I frown.

"So?" he asks in an incredulous voice. "That woman is a perfect ten. Flawless. If she wasn't Jewish I would've fucked her already." He grins mischievously.

"The fact that you two have the same religion is what's stopping you?" Manon asks in a sarcastic tone.

"The fact that she has a religion is what's stopping me." Yonathan scoffs. "I need to play with her mind first. Make her realize that screaming my name louder than she does God's when she's praying is an improvement she didn't know she needed."

"And then?" I ask.

"Come on, baby Temple, you don't need me to draw you what happens when a woman is screaming your name, do you? I thought you already lost your virginity and you felt at least one warm mouth wrapped around your cock." I did, but that isn't the point. I don't care much for sex or intimacy. Not since five years ago, at least.

"I was referring to what happens after you'll have sex with her, you shallow soul." I laugh.

"Oh, that," he says in an indifferent voice. "I'll send her to oblivion the same way I did with all the other women that worshiped my cock like it's a gift sent from up above. They don't need to know that at the same time they think they've found a new god, they're actually lying in bed with the devil!"

Chapter 3
Melody

I finally arrived at the airport. I thought I'm going to feel the biggest sense of freedom anybody ever felt. Instead, I have the feeling that all the men walking past me are either sent by Bart, or Bart himself. My heart is beating at a fast pace, not only in my chest, but in my throat, and in my ears, I feel it pulsating in every part of my body.

Some people laugh carelessly, wearing sun hats and reminding their children to drink water. I give them a bitter smile, thinking that if my life took a different turn, I would've had a child of my own. A small version of me who would've cried because they lost their favorite toy and who forgot to drink water.

I keep walking toward the lounge when I will patiently wait for my company's private jet to take off, shaking every time I see a man wearing a shirt similar to the ones I used to arrange in Bart's closet. Maybe this was a bad idea. Maybe I should've stayed home, where I knew exactly how to avoid the monster that used to feed on my pain. Maybe this isn't my chance at a new beginning, but a continuation of the nightmare that started so many months ago. Maybe this trip won't be Heaven opening its gates for me, but purgatory welcoming me into its perpetual confusion.

I stop to buy a bottle of water from one of the shops around me, and the young woman who takes my money wishes me safe travels. I wanted to tell her that I don't know how safety feels, but ruining her day because I made some poor choices isn't something I'm comfortable with. I just wish

Miriam Rosentvaig

I could live her life only for a day. I would give everything I have for at least twenty-four hours of not having the past that I do now, or at least, of being able to stop remembering it. I would trade every single penny I have only for a moment of tranquility.

I force my brain to remember the good times, when it was me, Sandra, and Lucas against the world. Three people of different ages, but united by something no human being will ever be able to describe. There was a magnetic pull between all three of us, even though at some point, I started being more and more attracted to Lucas than willing to spend time with his sister, my best friend. For that, and so much more, I feel guilty. I feel guilty for not being there when my best friend needed me, lying about having an important meeting. I hid the fact that I wasn't in the mood to see her when all she wanted to do was share the news about her engagement.

I feel guilty for being thirty and wanting a man who just turned eighteen. I felt like if I would've pursued what my heart was whispering to me, I would've robbed him of all the experiences I already went through. I would've stolen the fun he was supposed to have at that early age, even though I knew he would be anything but an average young adult. His talent was and still is absolutely insane. I would never tell him this, because I'm afraid it would hurt him more than make him feel good, but he's much more talented than his parents were. And his parents had an impressive collection of acting awards. The way he puts everything he has into the roles he's playing is visible to everybody who's watching his movies. And I'm always watching his movies. I'm always watching him, even though I know I shouldn't. The fact that I'm going to spend the next six months so close to him does nothing to calm my already tired heart. If anything, it just makes it beat faster. My brain is either remembering the good times that we had, or building images of both of us laughing and sharing inside jokes like we used to. And images of us kissing and promising each other that we will never make the mistake of staying far from one another ever again. I know I shouldn't be thinking of this, especially since now he, most

Play My Part

probably, barely remembers me. With all this success on his hands, only a fool would take trips down memory lane. He lives for the future while I'm stuck in the past. And, on some level, I feel like I deserve every single thing that ever happened to me. I royally fucked up and was majestically fucked back.

I've missed Lucas since the second I left his house that night. I always missed him, but now I miss him even more. I spent the past two nights thinking about the moment we will see each other again, wondering if he will look at me the same way he did all those years ago. Will he hug me or pretend he doesn't know me? Would he be able to see how nervous I am, how much I've changed and how my hands are shaking? Or would he ignore me?

Either way, I would never hold a grudge if he decides that leaving me in the past is what he needs. He deserves everything he has. He always deserved the world, and the world only gave him pain and suffering in the shape of his parents' deaths and his sister moving to Europe. When John and Amber left this world, Sandra was already an adult, but Lucas was just a teenager whose only care in the world should've been his grades and how to ask his hot classmate to be his girlfriend. He lost so many people, only to lose me again and again throughout his life. I put him through hell and forced him to pretend he was sitting with the angels. One other thing I will never be able to forgive myself for. God, I'm such a fucking wreck!

"Come on, Melody," I whisper to myself. "Put your right foot in front of the left one and move!" I start walking, trying to focus on the shops around me. All I can see is people. Lots and lots of people, some of them laughing, others being engaged in conversations. We're so different, us people. Every single one of us has an interesting story to tell, but only a few of us are ready to share it, and even fewer are willing to listen.

I take a deep breath and put my earbuds in. I need a soundtrack for this moment. My new life deserves a good song, so I push Play on "Young Volcanoes" and let Fall Out Boy sing that anthem in my ears. I smile and

Miriam Rosentvaig

I start imagining what these people's stories might be. The man in the suit running realized he made a mistake letting the love of his life go, and now he's rushing to stop her from leaving. Maybe he'll propose. The old woman next to me is heading to her retirement vacation, planning to visit all the countries and places she added on her bucket list. She hopes she will make friends wherever she goes, promising they will meet again.

And all the children around me are just waiting to write their stories. Maybe one of them will find the cure to a rare autoimmune disease and maybe another one will become an astronaut. I can only hope that they will all have a peaceful, happy life and that they will let their passion lead the way.

Another thing I am realizing just now is that I am completely alone in this world. And I don't know if this world even wants me anymore. I know that we are all just stardust in the bigger picture. Just a small grain of sand in the endless beach of this universe. However, I find myself wanting more. I want to be a bigger grain of sand, or, at least, a rock that will slowly change into dust, when the wind is blowing too hard and the rain is pouring. I want to be eroded, but I want that on my own fucking terms. And there is no time like now to mentally write down those terms and create a set of boundaries that I would force everybody around me to abide by.

I inhale deeply and exhale. Once. Twice. I breathe like I never breathed before. Or maybe I did but it was too long ago for me to remember how it felt. A smile forms on my lips and it easily transforms into laughter. I'm laughing and crying at the same time because I feel so fucking relieved. I feel like I just escaped from prison, and, to some extent, I did exactly that.

I start looking around me, this time actually noticing the space, not only the people. I want to buy perfumes, jewelry, and bags. I want to indulge myself for the first time in such a long time. I deserve this, for fuck's sake. I deserve this and so much more, despite all the mistakes I've made in my past. I'm only human and I'm allowed to make mistakes. God only knows I suffered the consequences more than enough. I need to stop pitying myself and realize that life might have thrown shit my way, but I'm the only one entitled to make the decision to either wipe it off my face and continue walking, or cry because I'm dirty. And I will fucking keep walking.

After a shopping session that cost me more than half of my last month's salary but feels like my soul had multiple orgasms, I start walking toward the bar I like the most in this section of the airport. My job grants me access to multiple perks, flying private included, so why not take advantage of everything? The bar is definitely more expensive than the other ones, so the self-indulgence session couldn't end in any other way. Money is such a fucking small thing in the greater scheme of things that I don't even care if I max out all my cards. And that would be pretty impossible, to be honest, because I make enough money to live a spoiled-rotten life. The reason I'm not doing it is because I'm afraid of the future and of ending up unemployed and having no one to help me. It happened to me once and I'll be damned if I ever let it happen to me again.

If I want to start from scratch and have a new life, then this is what I will do. I will go to Romania, make memories while doing my job, not giving a single fuck if Lucas wants to talk me or not. I was on my own for enough time to be able to breathe even if he is right next to me.

But if he does, then I don't know how I will be able to refrain from telling him all the things I wanted to tell him these past years. To tell him that I want him and that I'm sorry. To remind him how we were there for each other through the good times, but especially through the bad ones. To ask him for one more chance. For one more glance. For one more touch.

I'm scared to death as much as I'm excited. I have no idea where my life is headed, but at least I know that I will keep on walking. I have nothing left to lose since my home could never be my safe space. I feel anything but safe there, and that's how things will be, at least in the near future. However, Austin is known territory. Being so far from it makes me think of how things will be when I'll come back. Will Bart forget about me? Will he finally be in prison for all the shit he put me through? Will I ever be able to gather the courage to find a good lawyer and press charges, to share all the proof I have of what he did to me with somebody else? I have so many fucking questions, so many uncertainties, and so many mixed feelings. One second I feel happy and determined, only to feel scared and powerless the next. I feel like I'm like a genie in a lamp. Free for a short amount of time compared to the eternity I'm forced to spend inside the prison my brain built.

I go inside the bar and I leave all my bags on the floor, smiling when I see how well the new red purse I bought goes with my shoes. Despite all the shit I had to endure in the past years, I still care about my appearance. I still care about matching outfits with accessories. Maybe that's why all the film and entertainment companies trust me with taking care of their movies' social media pages and their events. I love beautiful things, whether it's admiring or creating them.

"Can I bring you something?" the young waiter asks me when I open the lid of my laptop.

"Sure!" I smile. "Can I please have a macchiato with two sugars and an extra shot?"

"Wait, aren't you that doctor's ex-wife?" he asks me in a condescending voice. "The one who went after his money and divorced him when he couldn't offer her everything she was asking for?"

Of course, that's the narrative Bart came up with. Of course he had all the right people endorsing him and basically declaring that I'm nothing but a gold digger who never loved him. But I did love him. Or, at least, I convinced myself that I did. Either way, that's beside the point. I never wanted his fucking money. I only wanted someone to hold me and promise me that I'll be whole again.

"No, actually, I'm that doctor's ex who got beaten to a pulp by him and got raped daily," I spit. "Now, can you bring me my coffee or should I find a bar who doesn't hire judgmental, misogynistic pigs who would

Play My Part

believe anything that a man says?"

He gives me a spiteful look and I give him one back. I'm done with being stepped on and I'm done with avoiding gazes and hiding myself. I didn't do anything wrong except go out with that putrid soul one evening when I lost everything.

"Non, don't you hate it when people shout in public spaces?" a thick, raspy voice coming from behind me says as loud as it takes for me to hear.

"Yon..." another voice warns.

I see red. I'm done with men giving me shit day in, day out for all kinds of reasons. Last week it was Bart, a couple of minutes ago it was the waiter, and now this. I just need them to fucking stop noticing me and criticizing me altogether. I need all the men populating this planet to mind their own fucking business.

I turn around and see the most annoying and difficult Hollywood superstar. Yonathan Friedmann. Sipping from a glass that contains what I assume is whiskey and two ice cubes and wearing his typical attire. An expensive three-piece suit, like he's the fucking president, not an actor who the media never knows how to treat. One day he's unhinged, the other he's smiling like he wants to fight for Greenpeace and human rights at the same time.

Next to him sits Manon Toussaint, the mysterious and broody actor that keeps his private life as hidden as possible from the public eye. His tattooed arms are crossed over his chest, and the scowl on his bearded face tells me that he's unhappy about something. Maybe about what Yonathan said earlier, but that may be just my brain's wishful way of thinking. I would love to have somebody in my corner right now. I feel so fucking drained and the day has barely started. I have a flight leaving in less than two hours, and the jet lag will drain me even more. This may not be my greatest day, but I will sure do my best to force it to make it at least to the top five.

I look at them, noticing that there's a missing part of their trio. However,

I'm too fucking angry to spend time thinking about where Lucas might be before getting closer to their table.

"Good morning, Mr. Friedmann! Don't you fucking hate it when people behave like they were raised by wolves when they pretend to be pretentious and educated as fuck?" I ask in an aggressive voice.

Manon leans back on his chair and uncrosses his arms, letting out an exhale. I look at the symmetrical tattoos on his fingers and arms, and I find myself curious about them. Are they telling a story? And if so, does it continue on his back, or on his chest, under the black T-shirt he's wearing? There's no sexual desire on my side, just simple curiosity. The thought that I might be broken since neither of these two men seem attractive to me crosses my mind, but I push it away. I'm not broken, just bruised. I am still able to feel sexual pleasure since I masturbated last evening imagining all the things I would do to and with Lucas and came harder than I ever did in my life.

"You know what?" Yonathan half laughs. "I actually do. I take it you're speaking from experience? You definitely look like you just came out of the woods and bought all that shit," he points at my bags on the floor, "just to let people believe that you're highly educated and pretentious as fuck."

"Better faking to be pretentious, as you put it, rather than being a fucking asshole like you are."

I thought my comment will affect him in some sort of way, but he gives me a bored look, toying with the golden cufflinks of the white shirt he's wearing under his Armani jacket.

"I beg to differ," he finally says. "Better an asshole than the incarnation of the cloth my maid uses to clean my shoes," he muses in an amused voice. "You people don't care about decency, while I care too much for it. I'm not in the wrong here, by any means."

Yonathan frowns, and raises his index finger to his lips.

"You seem familiar."

"I'm surprised to hear you remember people's faces." I retort.

"Tell me, sweetheart. What was the best part? Fucking your throat, playing with your clit, or forcing your ass to take my whole dick while praising you for crying?"

"Jesus, Yon!" Manon exclaims, and my eyes turn glassy only from hearing how he forces women sexually. I suddenly realize that I despise the man the same way I despise Bart, if not even more.

"Not in my book, Non." Yonathan turns to his best friend. "Jews don't believe in Jesus. At least, the ones that aren't part of a fucking cult, who just want to be interesting and become religion influencers." He exhales. "Can you imagine being so boring that you need to come up with a sub-religion, only to feel like you did something relevant? Pathetic."

He grabs a napkin from the box on the table and places it in front of him before putting his glass on it. "Actually, no. Religion, in general, is pathetic. Placing your fate and your future in somebody else's hands is the worst kind of weakness. And if that somebody is just an invisible force, well," he shrugs, "that makes you the lowest form of life on the planet. Mosquitos have a higher purpose than those people. At least they feed frogs. The religious and pious people not only do not feed anybody superior than them, but they just consume. Money, energy, and other resources from us hard-working people!"

He pauses and looks at me like he forgot for a second I was there. And why wouldn't he? I'm so easy to ignore. To forget.

"You didn't answer my question," he says in a more relaxed voice than the one he had earlier.

"Sorry, I think I fell asleep during your speech about religion. Guess pious people aren't the only boring ones, are they?" I give him a half-smile that is the exact opposite of the hateful look I'm sure I have in my eyes.

"That's all right," he says, giving me the same type of smile. "I love nothing more than repeating what I said, so stupid people can keep up. I was asking which hole of yours I fucked."

"Fuck you," I say, gritting my molars.

"So, all of the above?" he laughs, shaking his head.

"So, none of the above! I'm not a huge fan of pigs," I say clenching my jaw.

"Yet, you're rolling in the mud." He cocks an eyebrow. "Otherwise you wouldn't enjoy this subpar conversation we're having."

"You started it by speaking ill of me," I say, louder than I meant to.

"I speak ill about a lot of people. Most of the people I know, actually." He takes another sip of his whiskey. "Honey, what do you exactly need? Why are you still standing there like a poor deer caught in the headlights?"

"Apologize and I'll let you be," I say, fidgeting with my fingers to keep my hands from shaking.

"Yeah, that's not going to happen!" he indifferently retorts. "So, I hope your plane's pilot is willing to wait for you for a long, long time." He laughs, and I notice Manon rolling his eyes before looking out the window. "You entertained me for a bit, so I'm willing to repay that favor with one of my own."

"You can take that favor and cut your cock with it. Feed that to the wolves that raised you!" I say, hoping that my remark will shake him a bit.

"Predators don't eat other predators, darling. The organ you're craving right now is more than safe in a pack of wolves."

Nothing seems to rattle this man. He's like a block of stone. I envy him from a certain point of view. From the point of view in which he doesn't die in terrible pain.

"If you want to do me a favor, please tell me how you come up with such original pet names," I sarcastically say.

"Unlike your Fendi bag, my terms of endearment are, indeed, original." He crosses his arms at the back of his head, holding my gaze. "Not the ones I'm using on you because you're not worth a single thought process." He takes a deep breath, straightening up and arranging his tie. "Now, shoo! Your presence isn't neither required, nor necessary for the time being. Don't call me and I definitely won't call you. Unless my friend here would like to ride you. I would recommend against it, because weak links are the reason chains break," he says, disgust dripping from his voice.

I feel tears pricking my eyes, because he hit a soft spot. He's not wrong. I am a weak link. I was so fucking weak for more time than I am willing to admit. I am the one who broke multiple chains, by cracking and giving up.

"For fuck's sake, Yonathan!" Manon says, standing up and taking my hand, confusing me. "What's your name, cutesy?" he asks in a sweet voice.

I shake my head. I don't need to do this now. They will find out soon who I am because I'll be forced to follow them for pictures and interviews. I just want to leave this place and forget about this rendezvous for the time being. I need time to wrap my mind around what I just said to the star of the show. To fucking Yonathan Friedmann.

I don't know what got into me. I don't know who the woman who talked to him was. I think I met her at some point. I thought I lost her, but I now realize I just forced her to go into hiding. And now, the Melody who doesn't take shit from anybody just made an appearance. And what an entrance that was.

"I'm sorry," I say to Manon and take my hand from his. "I'll just go."

"No, no. Stay," he says in a soothing voice, giving me an apologetic look. Only it's not him who should apologize. "Let me pay for your coffee."

I don't need him to pay for anything. I just started the journey of taking care of myself and not needing anybody to rely on. I am the only person I need and Manon won't be the one who would make me stop walking on this path I chose.

"You're beautiful." He looks at me with the same kind eyes that fill up with panic all of a sudden. "God, that came out wrong. I'm-I'm not hitting on you. I-I-I…" he stutters, and genuine fear takes over his face.

Yonathan immediately stands up and gently takes him by the arm, forcing him to look outside again.

"What do you see, big boy?" he asks.

"The sun, a plane, the clouds, the track, and a discarded luggage," Manon rushes out, inhaling deeply.

"Good. Now, what can you touch?"

"You, the window, the table behind me, and my can of Dr. Pepper." His breathing slowly decreases, but his muscles are still tense. I watch in awe, trying to understand what is happening.

"Perfect, Non! You're doing great! Now, three things you can hear," Yonathan says in a calming voice. I'm completely sure he's insane. Somebody right in the head could never go from one state of mind to the exact opposite in the blink of an eye.

"Your voice, the clinking of the glasses from behind the bar, and the music from the speakers," Manon answers, and I notice that his legs start shaking.

"Two you can smell."

"Your cologne and mine." He leans his forehead on the window, and my heart cracks a bit. He is clearly fighting something.

"And what can you taste?" Yonathan asks him in a soothing voice that sounds strange coming from his mouth.

"Mint. From my chewing gum," his friend answers.

"Amazing, Manon! Fucking brilliant. And who are your chosen brothers that will forever be next to you?"

"You and Lucas!" he says in a determined voice.

I let out a whimper when I hear his name, and I curse myself internally for reminding these two men that I'm still here and that I witnessed what they just went through.

Yonathan frowns and takes out his wallet from his jacket pocket.

"How much?" He taps his finger on the leather.

"How much what?" I ask incredulously.

"How much money do you want for taking what you saw to the grave?"

"Are you fucking kidding me? What, you think that I would run to the press and tell them that Manon Toussaint struggles with anxiety?"

Play My Part

"Yes!" He sounds so sure that he could convince anybody that I'm that type of person.

"I would never mock or sabotage somebody for fighting their demons and their ghosts. So fuck you, Yonathan Friedmann."

We stare at each other, throwing invisible daggers to each other's faces. He completely misjudged me without me wronging him in any way, shape, or form. I despise him and I don't know how I will be able to stand next to him in the upcoming months. There are only two men who can make my stomach churn, and Yonathan is definitely one of them.

"You still didn't tell me your name," Manon whispers, trying to cut the tension that's pulsating in the air.

"Melody. Melody Byers. Went by Melody Trello for a short period, but apparently, it didn't stick."

But it's not my voice who says that. It's the one belonging to the man who I dreamed about the last two nights and many other ones too.

The voice of Lucas Temple.

Chapter 4
Lucas

"Byers?" Yonathan asks, cocking an eyebrow, his usual gesture when he's suspicious of something. "You can't possibly mean…"

"Yes," I cut him off.

"Well," he chuckles and stands up, "I'll be damned! You took your time, didn't you?"

"What do you mean?" Melody asks. My Melody. The incarnation of a song performed by an angel choir. God, how I missed her. The last time I saw her, her dark hair was much shorter. Five years ago, when we happened to be back home at the same time, she had the brightest sparkle in her eyes. Now, it's so dimmed that it's barely visible to any other person but me.

I remember waking up in my old room that Sunday. We had a break from filming, so I decided to spend the weekend at the mansion in Fredericksburg that I still own. I don't know what led me there. Maybe it was fate, pushing both of us to the same place at the same time.

Her sweet lilac perfume was still haunting the room, reminding me from the second I opened my eyes that she was there, with me. I fell asleep next to her and I woke up alone, knowing she regretted what happened. But I didn't. I could never regret spending the night with the person who was there for me when I needed someone the most.

Play My Part

"He doesn't mean anything," Manon says and I internally thank him for being the kind person he is and trying to make this encounter bearable. Unfortunately, his efforts are futile because Yonathan would never leave something unsettled until he says everything he has on his mind. I love him for being so loyal to me, but sometimes I have the feeling that he forgets that I'm an adult, perfectly capable of taking care of myself.

"Actually," Yonathan continues, taking Manon's hand from his arm, "I mean that you disappeared from Lucas's life when you crawled back to whatever hole hosted you. Selfish, but understandable." He squints his eyes and gives Melody a look that could make Freddy Krueger shit his pants. His almost transparent eyes complementing his dark hair always make him look scarier than he actually is.

"Yon," I say in the calm voice I usually use when I'm trying to ground him. He ignores me and steps closer to Melody.

"Yet, if I remember correctly, and I'm sure I do, you called him five years ago. You spent the night with him in Fredericksburg." Suddenly, the annoyance on his face changes to stupor, and I frown again, not understanding where this is going. "Such a strange coincidence you're here right now."

"Strange, indeed," Melody whispers.

"Right," Yonathan retorts like a lawyer who just presented the proof that will guarantee his victory to the jury. "So what? Did your husband find out that he married a whore and now you thought it's the perfect time to stalk Lucas and rekindle that flame between the two of you?"

Melody slaps his face, making everybody in the bar turn their head in our direction. I mutter a curse under my breath, and Manon is clearly panicking since he starts doing things in sequences of five. Five taps on his soda can. Five steps front and five steps back. I see him walking to a different table farther from ours, where he takes a seat and buries his face in his palms.

He starts shaking his head, probably trying to silence the demons that are eating his reality alive. I'm torn between going to try to calm him down and doing my best to avoid the disaster that Melody and Yonathan are one step away from creating. He looks angry, but she looks angrier. Neither of them speaks, but the look on their faces tells me that they're waiting for the other to blink first.

I have no idea what happened while I was talking on the phone to my agent. I have no idea why Melody is here. I have no idea how I will make Yonathan and her like each other, but I know I have to. Because now that Melody accidentally came back in my life, I will never let her go again. I've been attracted to her like a needle to a magnet for as long as I can remember. And this time I won't back down. Nobody can convince me to back down.

I'm not stupid. I know she was married and that her divorce was pronounced just a few days ago. I know that the whole shitshow was more public than she would've liked. Or, at least, more public than the Melody I know would've liked. I'm not sure the way I remember her is the same as the woman she is today.

I know that she didn't ask for anything from her ex-husband besides never seeing him again. I know she must've loved him. I know she might still love him, but I don't care. If there is something, I learned from Yonathan it's that if you want something you have to go and get it. And I always said to myself that Melody never replied to my letters or contacted me because she was happy. Because she found Bart, and that they were living a happy life, in their white picket fence house.

I made a promise to myself five years ago. I decided that as long as fate doesn't make our paths cross again, it had a reason for doing so. But now she's here. Close to me. So close that I can smell her lilac perfume again and can get drunk from a single inhale. She's so fucking beautiful that I can't breathe. She always was special. Smart, witty, and beautiful. With curves to die for and a smart mouth that could kill.

She was the perfect woman while I was the perfect boy. Time was

Play My Part

against us more times than not, but it isn't anymore. I am more than a stable adult. I am fucking famous. People know me all around the world. Directors and producers fight each other to have me in their movies. I am way past the stage of negotiating contracts. Everybody knows that I won't get out of bed for less than five million dollars per movie. I'm not arrogant, it's just the truth.

And Melody deserves to be at my side. She deserves the same kind of attention I get. She deserves everything on this fucking planet. I'm not only physically attracted to her, it's like my soul can only stay in my body if her own agrees with that. She stole my heart, my soul, and everything that made me feel alive. And I need to feel alive again. I need to have my Melody played by the piano of my existence.

"How fucking dare you?" she says through her slightly crooked teeth. She always refused to wear braces because she thought people would mock her if she did. If I would've been her age, I would've told her that I liked her even more. But I was a kid. A fucking kid who didn't know more than the fact that he missed his parents. I wasn't old enough to offer her the validation she definitely needed.

"How dare I what?" Yonathan says, rubbing his stubbled cheek. "How dare I say you're a whore or how dare I point out the fact that you need money for all those fancy clothes? What can I say, baby Temple? She's a keeper," he sarcastically says, fixing Melody with his gaze.

She tries to go past him, but he grabs her wrist to keep her in place. The second his hand moves, she takes a step back and flinches. That makes me suspicious as fuck. I do a quick mental search, trying to remember if her parents ever hit her, but I come up empty. Melody and her parents had a lot of conflicts throughout the years, but neither of them were violent people. They fought over her visiting more often, or them trying to make her accept their money when she was between jobs. It was never something serious and it was never terrible.

I keep asking myself if maybe I just imagined it. That maybe now that she's here, I'm trying to find out things about her and my brain decided to think the worst. To find another way to blame myself for not fighting harder for her and keep her from abandoning me in a similar way everybody except Yonathan and Manon did.

I try to convince myself that Melody is fierce enough that she would never allow herself to be a victim. She always fought for being independent, screaming to the world that she could and would take care of herself. I'm almost positive that if somebody would ever dare to raise a hand at her, she would unleash hell on them. But that fucking dimmed sparkle says more that any words could tell.

I don't know what skeletons Melody hides in her closet, but one thing's for sure. I will open that closet and kill the skeletons again and again, replacing the bones with blooming roses.

When I see Yonathan frowning, I know that I'm not the only one who noticed it. He gives me a barely visible nod, encouraging me to come closer. When I do, I feel like the oxygen in the room vanished, noticing the small scar on the left side of her neck. It can definitely go unnoticed, but I memorized every single inch of her skin when I saw her naked all those years ago. And that fucking scar wasn't there.

I feel pure rage. I feel a fire burning inside me that can only be extinguished if I find the person responsible for ruining her perfect white skin and burn them to the ground.

"Who did this to you?" I ask in a cold voice, flicking my chin toward her neck.

"Myself," she whispers, pulling her hand from Yon's.

"You're lying," Yonathan says. "You expect us to believe that you stabbed yourself in the neck one sunny day?"

"No," she says, rolling her eyes, but the gesture is forced, not natural. She's trying to fake annoyance, but I'm an actor. And a fucking good one. I know poor theatrics when I see them. "I expect you to believe that I was trying to take a glass from the kitchen cabinet and the door hit me!"

Play My Part

She starts laughing and looks at Yonathan with disdain. "And why do you care, anyway? One moment you're calling me a whore and a weak link and the next you're interested in my well-being? Are you completely insane, Mr. Friedmann?"

"I'm just not a fan of seeing women getting fucked up. Whore or not, you're still a victim."

"Can you stop calling her a whore?" I say, getting closer to them. "You're my brother, Yon, but I swear to God, sometimes you need to put a filter on your thoughts before letting them come out of your mouth."

"Oh, I'm sorry," he mocks. "How dare I disrespect the woman who just happened to be here, looking for her one true love, right?"

"Stop, Yonathan," I say, trying to hide the fact that I would wish nothing more than that being the truth. I would sell my soul to the first buyer only to have Melody in my arms again, telling me that she made a mistake and realized we're meant to be.

I don't care about her previous marriage. If anything, that is more proof that we could never be with somebody else. I need her. I need her so fucking much that it's overwhelming me. In the past years I tried to bury her memory deep down inside me. I tried having sex with multiple women, only to realize that I wanted them to be her. I wanted her thick hair wrapped around my fist. I wanted her hazel eyes looking at me while I'm thrusting into her mouth at her own pace.

"I'm not stopping until I find out what's the real reason for her being in this fucking airport at the crack of dawn. So, better start talking, Melody."

"I'm not stalking him, you fucking moron," Melody says. "But I guess that since every hole you ever fucked only wanted you for money and fame, you think that everybody out there has a hidden agenda. News fucking flash. Not all women are desperate enough to fuck a man like you only for some extra dollars."

"Such a dirty mouth for a mediocre woman."

"Stop, Yonathan," I say. "Just fucking stop, already."

"And where's the fun in that?" He laughs. "Can't you see she's all bark and no bite? I'm just helping you dodge a bullet, baby Temple."

"I don't need your help. Not this time."

"You will always need my help." He looks like he needs to hear this more than I do. "And I will always be there to shove it down your throat even when you don't want to swallow it. You know damn well I'm the type of person who helps even those not asking for it."

"Not. This. Time," I say through gritted teeth, trying to make him understand that he needs to leave. "I'm not a lost teenager anymore, Yonathan. I don't need you to make decisions for me, especially in situations like this. Now, please. Can you let me have a word with Melody?"

"And then what?"

"And then we'll be on our way," I answer immediately. I would fucking ditch the whole movie and take Melody to the other side of the world, where nobody could find us if I could.

Seeing her after all this time makes me feral. Makes me feel like an animal, wanting to defend their cub. The tables have seemed to turn now that we're both adults.

"Have it your way, baby Temple. But when she fucking breaks your heart again, you'd better not look for my shoulder to cry on because I won't be there for you. Not again, Lucas."

"Enough!" I shout.

"Enough, indeed," he says in a disappointed voice. I hate that I make him feel like this after everything he did for me but I hate more the fact that he has never been in love. This man locked his heart in a box and buried it in the deepest waters he could find. He could never understand what seeing Melody does to me.

Unlike Manon, who had his share of disappointments, Yonathan is only able to fuck like an animal. The moans that I heard every night from his room when we were living together while filming the series that launched both our careers are the perfect testimony for his skills in bed.

But love? Love is out of the question for the complex human being that is one of my best friends and my ultimate protector.

Yonathan checks his Rolex before nudging me with his shoulder.

"You have fifteen minutes, baby Temple. If I have to drag you to that plane, I'll do it." He then gives Melody a nod, and throws a final knife at her that makes me roll my eyes. "It wasn't a pleasure. I don't like you. Just let him down gently and go on with your shitty life. You don't belong with him, Melody Byers."

Time stops. Every-fucking-thing stops when Melody looks at me through those long eyelashes that don't need a drop of mascara. Her pale complexion is fucking astounding and the way her eyes turn a bit brighter when she looks at me almost makes my knees buckle.

I take two steps and her face is on my chest. I'm not the short teenager who barely reached her shoulder anymore. I'm a grown man now. A man who just wants to wrap her around me and never let her go.

"Hey, you," she whispers in that sweet, angelic voice of hers.

"Hey, you too," I say in a choked voice, fighting the urge to touch her.

"How have you been?" she asks, sounding like she has something stuck in her throat.

"We only have fifteen minutes, Melody. Let's not waste it on small talk, shall we?"

"I don't know what to say..." she drifts off.

"Tell me who hurt you," I say in a determined voice.

"I already told you—"

"That's bullshit!" I spit and grab her shoulders, looking at the black void that are her eyes. "You never lied to me, so you'd better not start now. This is not who you are, Melody. This is not who *we* are."

"I'm not lying," she desperately pleads.

"Melody, I'm a fucking actor." I pull my hair, desperately trying to find a way to make her tell me the truth. "You can't fool me, and I don't understand why you would do that. When did you decide it's a good idea to stop being honest with me?"

"I am honest, I promise."

"Don't fucking make promises you can't keep, Melody!" I shout. "Don't make another promise you can't keep!"

"Another one?" she asks in a confused voice.

"You promised you'd never leave me after my parents died," I remind her. "That's a promise that you definitely didn't keep. But I forgave you for that. The only thing I'm asking is for you to not break another promise and to not force me to forgive you for doing it again."

"I would never force you," she says, giving in to the temptation of hugging me. She's hugging me so tight I feel out of breath. Then again, I'm not sure it's because of the hug itself, but because of how feeling her body so close to mine makes my lungs stop functioning. "I would never force you to do anything, Lucas! Not you! I swear!"

Despite wanting nothing more than to keep her close to me, I gently push her away. She flinches again. She fucking flinches again and I can feel my heart shattering and screaming in pain. I have no idea how to help her come back from this, or if she will even let me do that.

"I will ask you again and, I swear to God, Melody, if you don't tell me the truth, we are done. I don't want to hear from you ever again because I don't want to be in contact with people I can't trust," I tell her, even though I have to force myself to make those words come out of my mouth. "So, tell me, Melody. Who is responsible for planting all that fear inside you?"

Her chin trembles and her eyes are begging me to take back what I said. But I won't. I want her back in my life more than any-fucking-thing in the world, but I can't keep somebody who doesn't trust me or who I can't trust. Not even if that someone is the only woman I ever wanted.

"So?" I ask again, lowering my face so it's closer to hers.

"I'll tell you." She nods eagerly, looking around us. "I swear I will tell you the whole story. But please don't make me say it now. I can't do it now."

"You can do anything you want, Melody. You were meant for greatness, but settled for mediocrity."

"You sound just like Yonathan!" She bites the words out, pouring venom on them.

"Well, somebody had to raise me when you and Sandra decided that your lives can't fit me anymore!"

"That's not fair," she says, looking at the table where Manon and Yonathan are having a heated whispered conversation.

"It's more than fair, but that's a discussion for another time." I slowly put a hand on her face, making her look back into my eyes. "Assuming that you will tell me the story at some point, will you stay afterward? Or are you just going to pull another Melody classic and get out of my life without having the decency of offering me an explanation?"

She raises her chin and takes a step back, looking at me from head to toe. She shakes her head and when her eyes meet mine again, there's so much pain in them that it brings tears to mine.

"I didn't think you were the same."

"The same?" I frown.

"The same as most men," she clarifies.

"Most men wouldn't have asked you to stay with them five years after you fucked them only to abandon them," I say in a disdainful voice. I'm fucking hurt by a wound that never healed and she was the one who caused it. I'm not looking for an apology now, but I am looking for the slightest sign of commitment from her side. "I want you, Melody."

"How could you possibly want me, Lucas? You're young, famous, and have the world at your feet."

"So let me lay it at yours," I say, closing the distance between us and this time it's me who hugs her fiercely.

"I don't need the world, Luc," she says, burying her face in my chest. "At least, not this one."

"We'll build the perfect one, then." I give up fighting and I rest my face on her hair, inhaling her smell. I'm addicted to this woman like a junkie who was sober for a while, but remembered that the temporary happiness that drugs offer is better than the constant numbness that sobriety holds. "We'll do it together, but let me in, Melody. Just fucking let me in."

"I need time, Lucas. I can't trust anybody. I'm so fucking broken." I feel my shirt getting wet with every word she utters and I frown. I want to find out who broke her so I can break them ten times worse.

"I don't have time, Mel-Mel," I say, hoping that the nickname I gave her so many years ago will make her walls crack. "I'll be gone for the next six months. And if there's something I know, it's that fate brought you here, to this bar, when the sun just rose, only because it wants to give us another chance. But I don't want to force fate's hand." I try to soften my voice and calm my rage. "I can't go without knowing I'll come back to you and for that I need you to take a leap of faith and prove to me that this time it will be different. That I can trust you wholeheartedly and that I can spend my time in Romania daydreaming about seeing you waiting for me in the airport when I come back!"

She cries hard and hugs me even harder. I don't know if that is a yes or a no.

"I won't wait for you in the airport Lucas." Of course she won't. "Because I'm part of *Dysfunctionally Perfect*'s PR Team. I'll be right there with you for the next six months." Of course she will.

Chapter 5
Melody

This is home. I have never felt more at home than I do now. And I can't help but wonder what that says about me. Why do I feel so much peace in the fact that I will spend the next few months so far away from the city I know the best in this whole world?

I think I'm either dreaming, or have gone completely insane. There's no other explanation for me being so excited to leave everything behind and flee the country with the boy I somehow raised and his two best friends.

His two best friends who are complete strangers to me, one that I despise and one that I feel sorry for. I never thought somebody with an exterior as strong as Manon's could have so many demons haunting his soul.

Manon's story is more similar to mine than he realizes. The only difference is that my monster has a name, a face, and a body, whereas his is lurking in the shadows of his soul. But we both are forced to face them and live with them. We are cursed to live our lives feeling the worst kind of fear. People fear villains only because they don't know that monsters are the ones who choose their victims at random. It can be the prince, the witch, or the seamstress. Monsters never care. Monsters are the only ones able to eat everybody alive.

I wonder if he can read me the same way I do him. I wonder if I could ever be brave enough to open up to him or Lucas and tell them my story. I wonder if they will judge me or mock me.

I'm afraid that they won't understand why I didn't leave Bart sooner.

Why I stayed with him, hoping that one day he will go back to being the man who took me out on dates and complimented me every time he saw me. The thought of them all perceiving me as weak is petrifying. I don't want to be weak, and on some level I think I'm more than brave to accept that I made some mistakes, but I'm ready to move on and leave the past behind.

"So, I'll be able to see you every day from now on until we come back?" Lucas asks in his boyish voice.

I look into his dark green eyes, taking in all the feelings that are pooling in them. There's a roughness in them now that I didn't see before and I'm sure that's Yonathan's imprint on his soul. Despite how much I dislike Yonathan, I feel completely grateful to him for taking care of Lucas when I couldn't. Or, better said, when I wouldn't. When I was too self-absorbed to realize that he needed me more than he let on.

"Only if you want to. I can stay away and ask somebody else to take the pictures or videos I'll need to post on social media," I rush out. "And regarding the events, I'll be able to work on them from the hotel I'll be staying in and not join them.'

"So you'll be my stalker?" he jokes, and I notice he still has his arms around my waist.

"Better said, I'll be one of your stalkers." I laugh. "I'm sure you have an army of groupies waiting to catch a glimpse of you in the airport."

"At least you'll have a contract as an excuse for stalking me. You're legally bound to stalk me, Melody Byers," he says and I lose my smile when I hear him calling my name in that excited voice. I'm not Melody Byers anymore, or, at least, I'm not the Melody Byers he used to know. That girl is dead and buried, replaced by an empty shell.

"You forgot to add *ex-Trello*," I correct him, although I would love nothing more than to travel back in time and make the right choice.

"Why would I do that? You don't need that constant reminder, and you definitely won't get it from me," he replies. "And Italian suits you only when it comes to clothes."

Play My Part

I feel my cheeks turning red, so I bury my face in his chest again, looking at Yonathan and Manon with genuine curiosity. I would love to get to know more about their dynamic and about how their friendship started. Manon looks back at me and gives me a reassuring smile and a nod, signaling that he thinks both me and Lucas are doing the right thing. My heart is swelling witnessing this act of kindness. I wish I could have a friend like him, rooting for me even if the future is uncertain and that my choice has as many chances to be the best thing I ever did as it has to become a complete nightmare.

I feel bitter when I realize how much I need to tell Lucas. How many things have happened in the past five years, things that I never told him about. Because I was a coward and because a part of me always waited for her knight in shining armor to come and save her. And I can't stop listening to my heart whispering that my hero is currently hugging me to his chest.

"I need to go. My colleagues are, most probably, waiting for me so we can go," I say, putting my hand on Lucas's beautiful face and giving Yonathan a hateful look.

He quickly notices it and lets out a long exhale. "He might be a tough pill to swallow, but he means well, I swear." He sighs and cups my face.

"I apologize for his crudeness, beautiful Melody."

I shake my head and I feel my smile growing bigger when I hear his compliment.

"It's not you who should apologize. And given the fact that he never will, let's just leave it at that."

He lets me go and grabs my hand and the gesture scares me. Any sudden move scares me these days. Even if I'm on a walk and somebody around me suddenly takes a left, my heart starts beating faster and it takes me a couple of minutes to realize I'm not in danger. I know that feeling safer on the streets than in your own home isn't normal. I know thinking that sleeping under a bridge is better than sleeping on your Egyptian cotton sheets isn't normal. I know that not a single fucking thought that crosses my mind is normal, yet it's not something I can control. There are very few things I still have control over.

Lucas stops dead in his tracks and looks at me with a mixture of pity and anger in his eyes. I don't need pity, but I could use that anger. I could use it so I can mold myself into a version I could actually be proud of.

"Listen to me, Melody, and listen to me good," he says, and I sense that anger being reflected in his voice, too. "You will tell me one day who turned you from a wolf to a deer. Who killed the hunter in you and made you their prey. And when that day will come, I will make sure to kill their soul the same way they killed yours."

I give him a single nod. I don't want him to kill Bart's soul. I want somebody to kill his memory so I can live the rest of my life without having to permanently look over my shoulder. Because even if I would move to the other side of the world, I would never be able to have a peaceful life. I would always be afraid of both him and the horrible things he put me through. There are times when I think that death might be easier than to keep fighting to recover. That the only way of healing from this fucking trauma is to purely stop breathing.

"Are you ready, baby Temple?" Yonathan's voice interrupts my train of thought and for the first time in the last hour, I feel grateful for something he did. Death comes to my mind more times than I would like to admit, but deep down inside I know that those thoughts are not a reflection of my wishes. I don't want to die, I want to kill the woman I've become. I've got so much life in me, and I can't seem to find an outlet for it. I want to feel alive and to shout it to the world. I want to make the world scowl because of how loud I'm laughing. Fuck, I just want to be happy!

"As ready as I can be, given the circumstances," he answers, looking at me like I'm the most precious thing he could've ever found.

"Oh, circumstances," Yonathan replies. "If only the odds were in your favor. Unfortunately for you and completely fortunately for me, they aren't. Now chop-chop."

"What exactly is your problem with me, Yonathan?" I ask the man who grates on every single one of my nerves. "You can't be so cruel just because my interaction with that waiter disrupted your peaceful conversation with Manon, so what is it, huh?"

"Oh, sweetheart." He gives me a menacing smile. "You haven't seen the cruel side of me yet. And don't tempt me to show it just yet. Now be so kind and fuck off my friend's life!"

"And what if I don't?" I challenge.

"Then maybe you have a death wish. Because crushing someone's soul to pieces is one of my favorite things to do. I've done it before and I would do it again. And nothing would bring me more pleasure than to take the one belonging to the person who mistook Lucas's kindness for weakness and smashed it into small pieces." He comes closer and wraps a strand of my hair around his index finger, keeping that smile on his face. "You have no idea how deep my loyalty or my taste for vengeance goes. The pain of the people that hurt me or my brothers is my favorite dish, Melody. And I would eat yours for breakfast, lunch, and fucking dinner, and I would still be asking for dessert. Do. Not. Tempt. Me."

He lets go of my hair and I release the oxygen that got stuck in my lungs. Yonathan might've said that he feeds off pain, but it's clear to me that he feeds off weakness, too. And there is no way I would let another man see me as weak. I am my ex-husband's victim for all the wrong reasons, but I would never allow another man to treat me the same way.

"Then you'd better be ready to starve to death," I hiss. "Because you will never get my pain. And you will never witness my suffering. You're not worthy of seeing me at my lowest point."

"So you're telling me you can stoop even lower than you do right now?" He half laughs. "How desperate are you really, Melody? If you want to have a taste of a circumcised dick, all you need to do is ask!"

He takes a step back and unbuckles his belt. I stare at him in disbelief, but I don't stop him. I am genuinely curious how much of this is a bluff that he hopes I won't call. But I refuse to let him win this hand. If he wants to play poker, then poker he will get. He has no idea that I have nothing to lose, so there's nothing stopping me from going all in.

"Fucking stop already, Yon." Manon stands up and pushes his best friend. Yonathan looks at him in disbelief and I can hear Lucas groaning on my left.

"Why did you stop him?" I ask Manon. "If he thinks that showing off his cock in a crowded place is the best thing to do right before he starts filming a movie, then you should've let him!"

"Because sometimes he doesn't know when to stop," he replies in a hurt voice. "And that's when he needs me or Lucas to step in and remind him how much of a great person he actually is."

"I don't need either of you to stop me," Yonathan deadpans. "And I honestly don't understand why both of you keep protecting her like she's fucking made of glass and she deserves to be placed on a pedestal."

"She's a fucking woman, Yonathan," Manon retorts. "And this," he motions his hand around Yonathan, "is no way to treat a woman. You know better than this."

"Are you serious right now? She just fucking came here, making an entrance, and expects all three of us to fall at her feet just because she fucked Lucas once?"

"No, not because of that!" Manon screams. "But because she deserves our respect. You don't know shit about what she went through or what she has on her plate. You just think that everybody is out there to get us, harm us, or make us suffer." He takes a step closer, giving him a challenging look. "But maybe sometimes that's not the case."

"It's not the case now, Yon," Lucas confirms. "You know that Melody and I go way back. We have history and a story just waiting to be written."

"And did you think about how that story ends, my dear younger brother?" Yonathan snaps. "Or did you jump directly to the conclusion that you'll live a fairy tale for the rest of your lives?"

"That's none of your fucking business!" I get closer to him, willing to show him that I don't care about what he thinks of me or about how my story with Lucas will end. "So maybe you should focus on your life instead of living vicariously through your best friends!"

"Tread carefully, Melody Byers," he says in an irritated voice. "Tread very fucking carefully, because I have anything but limits. And once I'll make both Lucas and Manon see you for who you really are, you'll run as fast as your feet can go!"

"Why not go ahead and ask me instead?" I sarcastically laugh. "Why do you need to threaten me with showing everybody who I really am? As you just said, *all you need to do is ask*."

"Because you already lied." He sounds indifferent. "And that told me more than you think. You're a fucking liar and I'm a sucker for the truth. Two sides of the same coin, one preferring to live in the shadows while the other is bathing in the light."

A shiver runs down my spine when I realize how strongly he believes that I'm willing to pursue something with Lucas because I want his money. And what scares me more is that I know he is conniving enough to build a narrative that his friends will believe. A narrative that would make Lucas leave me because he would trust his chosen brother more than me. And he would be making the right choice. Because while I kept things from him and ignored him in the past, Yonathan was there for him every step of the way.

"Is this the moment where you expect me to shit my pants and run away?" I ask him.

"I have no expectations from you, Melody." His voice sounds like thunder announcing a devastating storm. "You'd never meet them anyway, so why set myself for disappointment?"

"Maybe I'll surprise you," I challenge.

"There are few things that could surprise me in this life. And you're definitely not one of them!"

He turns his back to me, grabbing his bag from the floor, and heads toward the exit. I don't know how to handle this situation because a part of me is scared of Yonathan's thirst for finding out the truth. And another part of me wants to stay by Lucas's side and have his hand in mine while walking on the path that waits for us.

"I'm sorry for putting you through the pain of listening to that horrendous dialogue," Yonathan says looking first at Manon and then at Lucas. "Now that this shitshow is over, can we just go?" he says, brushing his jacket sleeve.

I look at Lucas while grabbing my bags from the floor.

"I guess I'll see you on the other side of the pond."

"Come with me. You can fly with us, there's plenty of…"

"Absolutely not!" Yonathan interrupts. "As long as I'm the one paying for our means of transportation to and from Romania, I get to call the shots. And there is no way your long-lost crush will step foot on my plane."

I grit my teeth, biting back all the ways I want to tell him to go fuck himself. I hate him so fucking much. I hate how he's making me feel like the dirt on his shoe and I hate how he always dismisses me like I'm nothing more than a burden he doesn't wish to carry.

"I wouldn't want to get chlamydia, anyway, so you don't have to worry about me stepping inside your precious plane," I retort.

"I'm sure you already know the cure for it since you sucked all the c—"

"Yonathan!" Lucas shouts, bringing the tension to a new higher level. "I asked you nicely once, but I won't do it as nicely the second time. Just stop already with all this shit. Where do you think it will get you, huh?"

"As long as it's far away from…" he waves his hand around me, "this, I'm up for any destination."

I chuckle and start turning my back to the triumphant trio.

"Then I'm sure you'll enjoy me being so close to you while you're on set."

Play My Part

"Oh, sugar, I think you read my calendar wrong. Assuming you know how to read, which, let me tell you, is a complete surprise for all the people here, I'm not on my way to Whorelania. Have fun in your motherland, though." He starts laughing, but I'm happy none of his friends join him.

"I'm going to be part of the movie's PR team." I act braver than I feel, but I don't want him to know that.

"Like fuck you will!"

"There are children around you," Manon says, clenching his jaw.

"Not my children, thank fuck for that." He laughs again. "So, not my monkey, not my circus. If these people want to protect their spawns from hearing all these nasty words, maybe they should go live in a bubble. Effective, but utterly boring."

"Or you should finally accept that we're living in the twenty-first century, and manners are definitely trending!" I say.

"So is eating Tide Pods. That doesn't mean I should do everything society tells me to do." He starts walking again, but stops suddenly, looking back at me. "I don't want you on the set when I'm there, which is most of the time. I don't care where you get your materials from, but if I see you there once, I'll make sure to never see you a second time."

"You're insane," Manon says. "This is her job, Yonathan. Just fucking stop with the threats and with this whole superiority act."

"I've been called worse." He shrugs. "And threats? I didn't even start with the threats."

"I'll quit!" Lucas booms. "If you do something, anything to make Melody's life difficult while we're in Romania, I'll quit the movie. You know I have enough money to pay the sanctions, so don't think for a second that's going to keep me from leaving."

"The puppy has teeth," Yonathan mocks. "Pity he shows them to the wrong people."

"Or maybe I just realized who I was supposed to show them to since the second they started growing."

Something passes between them, judging by the look in their eyes. I look at Lucas, whose nostrils are flaring and whose breaths are shallow. He might say that he changed or that he learned things from his *brother,* as he calls that scum of the earth, but I know him. Deep down, behind that rough exterior that he so proudly shows to the world, lies the sweet boy he once was. He's probably happy with the woman I used to be and I find myself wishing that we can bring our alter egos to the surface and let them take the steering wheel instead. God only knows we would be so much happier than we are now. At least, I would.

"I should go," I whisper, taking Lucas's hand on instinct, because I'm afraid of Yonathan's reaction.

"You shouldn't," Lucas insists. "You'll fly with us, Melody." He gives Yonathan a threatening look and the crack on Yonathan's resolve is visible. I'm not sure that's happening because of him not wanting to upset Lucas or because he just decided to put this battle on pause.

"I don't want to bother you," I say, not wanting to add more tension between Lucas and his friends.

"Nonsense," he retorts. "You won't bother any of us. Come with me, beautiful Melody. Let's start this adventure together."

I want that so much. Every piece of me is craving to be next to him now, on our way to Romania, for as long as possible. I want to be with him, to feel his hand on my skin, and I want to know what his lips taste like. I want to whisper sweet nothings in his ear while he grounds me with his mesmerizing eyes. I want all of him, even though I'm still not ready to give him all of me.

I'm sorry that at the moment I can only give him scraps of myself. I feel nothing but regret and self-judgment because I want him to give me everything while I can give him a piece at a time. But I told him I needed time and he accepted. I need time to put my thoughts into words and tell him everything he needs to know, hoping that he will still want me after I'm done.

Play My Part

"I'm not sure if that's a good idea, Luc," I say. "I will only make everybody feel more uncomfortable in a confined space."

"You're the only one who could make me feel comfortable, Melody," he says, kissing my knuckles. "You're my peace now. And I don't like feeling uneasy."

His words go directly to my heart because he's my peace, too. He's the only one who can make me feel like there will come a day when fear and numbness will stop being all the things I'm able to feel. He's the past that was stubborn enough to turn into my present and a possible future.

I exhale and drop my head in defeat. But I never felt less defeated than I do now.

"I want to go back to writing our story as soon as possible, Lucas." I smile.

"We have more stories to finish, Mel," Lucas whispers, pleading for what, I don't know. "I can't wait to get to the next chapter with you. I can't wait to read a particular story with you by my side."

"And what story would that be?" I ask, getting closer to him, unable to fight the invisible pull I feel toward him.

"I'm not sure it has a title yet, but we can work on that. We can do everything as long as we're together, I promise."

I feel my knees weakening and when I feel his hand coming around my waist again, I need to fight as hard as I can to stop myself from putting my lips on his. I want to feel the velvet of his lips embracing the poison on my own. I want him to heal me and to promise me that everything will be fine.

"When we get there, we're getting a dog," Yonathan deadpans while buttoning his jacket. "Since I see you're both inclined to pick up strays, at least we can choose a loyal one next time."

"He'll change, I promise," Lucas whispers, grazing his lips over my ear. "When he sees how hot your soul is burning, he'll have no other choice than to let you melt his."

"I don't care about his soul, Lucas," I whisper back. "It belongs to the devil, anyway. And I would rather melt the one belonging to the angel that is now holding me to his chest."

"Angels are only doing God's work. And I would love nothing more than to be the messenger of the goddess that is kind enough to let me hold her."

And I know now that I will fall in love with Lucas Temple like I never did before.

Chapter 6

Lucas

"We need to talk, baby Temple," Yonathan says after I come back from the bedroom where Melody is currently sleeping.

"Of course we do." I roll my eyes and take a seat next to him on the leather couch. "I suppose this is about Melody."

"Smart boy." He chuckles, leaning back and watching the whiskey swirling in the glass he's holding. "I need to know what your game plan is."

"My game plan?" I frown. I don't have a game plan. I just want to make her see me as a grown-up man who wants her. I want her to never leave me behind again and I want both of us to build a new world for us. One where we'll be happy, carefree, and do everything we want.

"Yes. Your game plan. Or, better said, your endgame. What do you want to do about her?"

"I want her back in my life." I sigh. "I missed her so fucking much and I can't handle her leaving me behind again. And I don't care what you or the world has to say about that."

"Luc, are you sure you aren't rushing into things?" Manon joins the conversation, sitting across from us. "You met her, what? Three hours ago?"

"I met her fifteen fucking years ago, Manon," I bite the words, hoping to make the message as clear as possible. This is not a crush and what I'm feeling for her is anything but lust or just physical attraction. Do I want her screaming my name when I make her come? Yes. But I want to kiss her right after. I want to play with her hair and keep her in my arms as she falls asleep. I want every fucking piece of her.

"Exactly. You met her when you were a kid," he says back, and I grunt, shaking my head. They can't understand all the emotions that are running through my body and all the thoughts that are running through my head. "I think you might be a tad confused. Back then she was your savior. She was your friend, who also protected you when your sister couldn't or wouldn't. Your feelings are all over the place and that's normal, so maybe you shouldn't do or say something you will regret later."

I stand up and take a seat next to him, forcing myself to keep it together. I really need to make them understand that Melody isn't going anywhere and that she's here to stay. I'm sick and tired of people abandoning me and if I can do something to prevent that, I will.

I know that Non is right. I am a mess of emotions, but not because I'm confused about what I'm feeling for Melody. That's clearer than the blue sky on a hot summer day. I'm angry with my friends who, instead of supporting me, treat me like a fucking child who doesn't know right from wrong or love from hate. And I fucking had enough of this shit.

"I know what I'm feeling for her, Non." I sigh. "Please believe me when I say that my feelings are completely clear. I feel happy because I found her again, yet confused about the future. I feel my heart beating faster when I look at her, yet stopping when I realize that a lot of things have happened since we last saw each other." I pause and look at both of them. "I know all these things. I know passion, I know lust, and those are far from what I feel for Melody. I know that I'm already falling for her. Or, better said, I know that I never stopped doing it. I fucking know, Manon. I've known since I first had an erection that Melody is it for me."

"And if you had to choose between us and her?" he asks in an aggressive voice that I never heard coming from him.

"Why would you ask me that?"

"Because I feel like she could take you away from us," he answers in a voice that expresses nothing but sincerity. "And I need to know if I should get ready to lose my brother or not."

"She won't."

"Let's talk about it in five days, when you'll be mesmerized by the fact that she decided to grant you access to her pussy." He dismisses me.

"What the fuck is wrong you?" I scream. "I thought you're on my side. On our side."

"I'm on her side when it comes to Yonathan treating her as trash, but don't think for a second that I'm a fan of your infatuation!" he screams back. "I've seen this happening a million times. We're all friends until you realize that getting your dick wet is more important than people who actually care about you."

"Fuck off, Non." I turn my back to him, looking outside the window. "If it never worked out for you, it doesn't mean it won't for me!"

"Right, because the woman who fucked you for her own entertainment and then went to get married to another man is definitely worth a ring on her finger. Your father is fucking rolling in his grave witnessing this."

It takes me a second to realize that I had turned around and grabbed the collar of his shirt, but I don't regret it.

"You don't talk about my father," I say through gritted teeth. "Not about him, not about my mother, and you don't talk that way about Melody."

He gasps and pushes me hard. When I fall from my seat onto the floor, he mirrors the gesture I made earlier and grabs my shirt, throwing me back next to Yonathan.

"If you ever do that again, I swear you'll eat with a straw for at least a month after I'm done with you," he screams in my face. "What the fuck are you trying to prove and, more importantly, to whom? To us?" He moves his index finger between him and Yonathan and lets out a laugh without a trace of amusement in it. "We fucking raised you, you ungrateful piece of shit!"

I've never seen Manon so angry. I might have exaggerated a bit, but his actions aren't justified. They aren't a normal response to what I said or did. And that makes me wonder if there isn't something else bothering him or causing him to react like this, something that has nothing to do with me or Melody.

I don't know as much about him as I do about Yonathan, and that's not because I'm not interested in finding out about his past. It's because he told us that he had a family and now he doesn't anymore, asking us to leave it at that. I don't know if that means he left them behind like Yonathan did, or if they died like mine at some point, but I'm sure that his OCD and his panic attacks are rooted in the actions of the people he doesn't have anymore. And despite the fact that I'm sorry for him more times than not, now is not one of those times. Now I'm not a huge fan of either of my best friends.

"Back off, Manon!" I scream back.

"Or what? You'll hit me? Punch me? Harm me because I dared questioning your feelings for your fucking childhood crush?"

"Nah, I'll just give you both the middle finger and live a happy life without all these complications," I say, faking indifference. But I don't feel that way. I feel like I want to crawl into the dark and cry, because I'm sick and tired of things being more complicated than they should be.

Manon hurt me with his words. He hurt me so fucking bad, and I want to see him in pain, too. I need my words to cut as deep as his.

"Complications?" Yonathan, who was silent until now and watched our altercation with amusement, intervenes. "So, now we're reduced to complicating your existence?"

"Well, since you behave like you're the only adults in the room, I guess this kid," I say pointing to my chest, "doesn't want to make your life harder with his infatuation." I air quote the last word. "So, yes. You are complicating my existence at the moment."

"That's because we are the only adults in the room!" Yonathan roars,

Play My Part

throwing his glass at the wall. "Can't you fucking see that you're behaving like a spoiled brat who found his favorite toy after losing it so many years ago? What you fail to remember, Lucas, is that so many people already played with it. And, eventually, they grew tired of that toy and threw it away."

"And that only worked in my favor!" I scream back.

"Did it?" Manon says, towering over me. "Or there's a reason for people leaving her behind? Did you ever consider that *you* are her toy, not the other way around? That she'll fucking play you like a fiddle and then throw you in the garbage?"

"She won't do that," I say, clenching my jaw.

"Well, excuse me if I beg to differ." He dismisses me and leaves the space going God knows where.

I look at Yonathan and frown when I see how clearly disappointed he is with me.

"You're pathetic," he says, taking Manon's seat from earlier.

"I'm anything but. I'm fighting for what's mine."

"Weak," he continues.

"Calling me all the names you can think of won't change how I'm feeling, Yonathan."

"The fucking disappointment of the century."

"Fine. Have it your way. I'm pathetic, weak, and the fucking disappointment of the century! There. Are you happy now?" I ask, standing up and going to the mini fridge to grab a bottle of water. I see all the shelves filled with Dr. Pepper cans and let out a small laugh. For a person incapable of feeling anything, Yonathan sure walks the extra mile to make sure that his friend has gallons of his favorite drink throughout the duration of the flight.

"I'm afraid happiness isn't a familiar feeling for me." He pinches the bridge of his nose and takes off his glasses, like he usually does when he feels frustrated.

"I'm wondering whose fault that is." I say in a sarcastic tone.

"Mainly yours, if you ask me." He shrugs, and I hate how honest he sounds. I can't believe he actually thinks that I am the person responsible for him being so miserable.

"Mine? When did your happiness become my responsibility, Yonathan?"

"Oh, I don't know! Maybe when I found you in the gutter, and fought for making you the greatest version of yourself?" I stay silent, because I completely disagree. I wasn't the one who came asking for help. He was the one who volunteered to help me. He was the one who gave me that speech about how extraordinary I'll be. "You did nothing to pay me back in all these years."

"I didn't know you were expecting a reward," I say in an exasperated tone. "Silly me. I thought you actually gave a fuck about me and your help was unconditional. And I'm sorry if my happiness brings you sadness. I'll just go back to being a miserable shell of a man only so I could make you feel better about yourself. Maybe this way Master will give Dobby a sock when the time feels right and Dobby will be a free elf," I continue in the same sarcastic tone.

"I fucking saved you, Lucas!" he screams. "I found a lost, broken boy and I shaped him into the best version of himself. I took care of you. I provided for you. I gave you every fucking thing you asked for. Fame? You have it. Fortune? More than you will need in this lifetime. Fun? I took you everywhere with me. I fucking healed you, Lucas." He continues screaming, and I can't do anything but be quiet until he's done with his speech. I know it would be useless to try to reason with him now. He doesn't listen to people in general and when he's angry, he completely blocks everything around him. "And this is how you repay me? This is how you repay both Manon and I? By turning your back on us when that fucking slut comes back into your life?"

"Stop offending her." I sound completely unhinged which I find very comforting, because that's exactly how I feel.

Play My Part

"Why don't you make me? Come on, you're a big boy now, right? Grab my shirt the same way you did Non's and show me how much of an adult you are. Because violence is always the adult answer to being hurt, isn't it?" It's his turn to be sarcastic and I can't fucking take it anymore. I turn around, deciding to go to the bedroom to check on Melody.

"Fuck you, Lucas," he says when my back is facing him. "Fuck you and your lack of loyalty. Fuck everything I've ever done for you. Fuck the moment I decided you're strong and capable of facing the world. Fuck you and mostly, fuck the life you want to build with her. And I honestly hope she will dump your ass again, because I want to see you crawling back to me. But, keep in mind, Lucas, that when you do, the only answer I'll give you will be my spit on your face."

"Really, Yon?" I ask, feeling my heart break. I want to fucking cry because his words hurt me so much that I can't handle it. "Is this where we are now?"

"It's where you brought us," he deadpans.

"No, Yonathan. It's your need to control me that brought us here. It's your fucking thirst of having everything, every detail going the way you want it to go. And when it doesn't, you panic and become an even worse person than you usually are. I'm tired of defending you and I'm fucking exhausted of believing that at some point you will let the world see that you are not as bad as they think you are," I say, forcing myself to swallow the lump in my throat. "I'm so fucking tired of you behaving like a Neanderthal and me always being there, trying to explain your arrogance and excuse your spitefulness to all the people you hurt intentionally or not."

"Funny," he says, pouring himself another glass of whiskey. "I don't remember asking you for any of those things."

"Funny. I don't remember asking you to save me or to make me famous." I half laugh. "But you did. Because this is what we fucking do, Yonathan. This is what we've always done and will forever do. Save each other when we don't know we need saving. Together, we clean the mess one of us made. We stay united and tall. We face the world and everybody in it."

"Well," he takes a sip from his glass and grimaces, "I hope Melody will do exactly that for you."

"You don't get to throw me out of your life, Yon!"

"I think I'm the one who decides if I take out the trash or let it rot in my life's kitchen, Lucas." Lucas. Not baby Temple and not Luc. "And, as I always do, I decide to take it out and burn it, just to make sure it won't find its way back."

"You don't mean that," I say, blinking back the tears that are flooding my eyes.

"Have a nice life, Lucas Temple."

"You don't mean that," I say, louder this time.

"Please don't embarrass yourself more than you already did. Just go and check if your precious Melody is comfortable between my sheets and just let me be," he says, looking out the window.

"Take that back, Yonathan!"

"I'm not sure what part of what I said you wish I'd take back, but either way, I won't. I don't regret anything from what I said. You made your choice so go and face the consequences. I'm sure now that you're all grown up, you know that every action has a reaction. Every decision you make will have some consequences that you'll have to suffer," he says in an indifferent voice. "You made your bed, now lie in it. At least have a good fuck, since you're there!"

"Yonathan, I'm sorry if I hurt you," I say in a pained voice. "I'm so fucking sorry."

"It's cute that you think you could ever be able to really hurt me. I don't need your apologies, Lucas." He sighs. "Actions speak louder than words and your actions from the past couple of hours are disappointing to say the least."

"Why can't you be happy for me, Yon?" I ask with resentment. "Why the fuck is it so hard for you to accept that I want her in my life as much as I want you and Manon?"

"Oh, I can accept that you want her in your life just fine!" he hisses. "What I can't accept is you wanting to hit one of the people who would do any-fucking-thing for you. That is why I can't agree with your choices, Lucas. Did I make myself clear or do you need a fucking Pictionary round?"

"I'm sorry," I say again. "I'm so fucking sorry, Yon. I didn't mean to…"

"I don't care about what you meant. I care about what you did. And what you did is fucking disgusting!" he cuts me off. "We did so much for you! We would cut a fucking limb for you and you are just an entitled piece of trash who takes us for granted!"

"I'm sorry." I will say this until he'll forgive me. I can't imagine a life without him and Manon in it, so I will do everything necessary to keep them close, even if that means I need to apologize for something I don't feel guilty of.

"Just fuck off, Lucas."

"I'm sorry," I say, getting closer to him.

"Don't you understand English anymore? I told you to fuck off." He pushes me, but I don't do anything except look at him with determination in my eyes. If he wants to hit me just to recreate the balance we had, then I'll take it.

He pushes me again and this time I take a step back. The next time he does, I realize my back hit the wall, so I stand there, waiting for him to make his next move.

"If you ever do something like that again, we're done, do you understand?" he asks in an angry voice. "We are fucking done." He punches the wall next to my face. "Fuck!" he screams. "I can't believe you did that, baby Temple! Why the fuck would you do that to begin with?"

"I'm sorry." I keep standing there and look at him.

"And to Manon, of all people. To the man who would never hurt a fly, least of all you. Why would you do that to one of the few people who genuinely cares for you? Do you know how rare it is to have somebody trust you wholeheartedly and love you unconditionally?"

"He does," Manon says, coming back and wiping his hands on a paper towel. "I'm sure he does." He gives me a wink and goes to grab one of his sodas.

"I do." I clear my throat and look at both of them. "I do, because as you both know, I had my portion of people leaving me. You are the only two people I trust to stand by my side through thick and thin."

"What about Melody?" Non asks in a curious voice.

I shake my head. Melody doesn't trust me enough, which leads to me not trusting her either. Not until she fully opens up to me and lets me get to know her darkest thoughts and her deepest desires.

"I hope that one day we'll get there." I sigh and pull my hair. "God, you have no idea how much I want that. But she won't tell me what's wrong with her, so that means I can't let my guard down. Not yet."

Manon offers me a can of soda, but I point to my water that I haven't touched yet.

"Why is that relevant?" he asks, grabbing some peanuts in his fist and putting five of them in his mouth.

"What do you mean?"

"Why do you need to know who hurt her to lower your guard?" he asks in an honest tone.

"Because I can't lower my guard when she won't do the same for me. And before you ask, it's not about tit for tat or about show me yours and I'll show you mine. It's because I don't want to give the whole me to somebody who is willing to give me half of them."

"Atta boy," Yonathan says in a proud voice and I give him a smile, telling him without words how happy I am that we've moved past our first serious fight in over seven years.

I know the fact that Melody was the reason for that fight should ring some alarm bells in my head, but it doesn't. Not because I'm blinded by the feelings I have for her, or at least, not only because of that. But because I knew for a long time that whenever a woman comes into our lives, the ocean of tranquility we are swimming in will suddenly form a tsunami.

But, like it happens after every storm, we regroup, evaluate the damage, and start rebuilding. I just never expected that I would be the first to fall in love out of the three of us since I am the youngest. But love doesn't have a timeline. It just has chaotic moments.

"In my humble opinion, and I hope you won't be violent again when you're hearing this, you don't need her to lower her guard or to tell you who hurt her."

"I do, Non." I sigh. "I really do."

"You need to show her that you're different from the one who hurt her. You don't need to know who they are, you just need to prove to her you're better. What difference does it make if it's a friend, her ex-husband, or a random stranger? Would that contribute to your relationship?"

I take a minute to consider what he said. And I realize he's right. It doesn't matter.

"It doesn't make any difference, you're right. But I still can't trust her, Non. There's something stopping me, I can't put my finger on it, but it's there," I say in a frustrated voice.

"Then you'd better find out what it is and kill it before it lays eggs. Because you can't build something with her if you doubt her or don't trust her, regardless of how much you want her. Regardless how much you love her." He gives me another wink and I laugh.

"Just so we're clear, my silence doesn't mean I like her," Yonathan says, and I give him a half-smile.

"The fact you stopped calling her a whore or a slut is still progress and I'll take it." I shrug. "And now, if you'll excuse me, I'll go start building that something with the woman I'm ready to fall in love with."

"Just choke her so I won't be forced to hear her moans!" Yon screams behind me and I can't help but laugh when I hear him talking in the voice he usually has when he isn't serious.

"That's your thing, Yon. I'm more into biting and scratching."

"Such a good little puppy," he teases. "Make sure to lick her clean while you're there."

Some things will never change. And the imbecile jokes I make with my brothers is one of them.

Chapter 7
Melody

"Time to wake up, beautiful Melody!" Lucas's familiar voice interrupts the best dream I've had in years.

I was free in that dream. Free as a bird is from the second it flies away from the nest that offers it warmth and nurture. People usually cry when they leave that safe haven, but not me. I was always curious about the world and what it has to offer. I wanted to explore and to get to know cultures, places, and people. To live in all the corners of the world while having two or three people close to me that will share my joy and join me in my adventures.

I was more awake in that dream than I feel now. I want to go back to sleep because I want to live in a place where Lucas is kissing me in front of the Colosseum and telling me to hurry because we need to leave for Paris.

I give him a smile that doesn't reach my eyes, because I'm not sure I can face reality yet. I don't know what I was thinking when I accepted getting on this plane with a man that hates me, one that pities me and one that I desperately want while knowing having him is close to impossible.

"What time is it?" I ask in a panicked voice when I realize it's dark outside.

"It's ten past eleven a.m. in Austin and ten past seven p.m. in Bucharest." He checks out his watch and lies next to me on his side, cupping my face with his hand.

I can't help but lean into his touch and get closer to him. I feel like I have no control over my body and my movements, like there's a higher power that is directing my body to his, without allowing me to have a say in this. And I don't want to. It's easier to blame it on something else than admitting that I'm more than willing to let the man who holds my heart in his eyes touch me less than a week after getting divorced.

"I'm sorry," I whisper. "I'm sorry for barging into your life this way and creating all these complications. I know I can be a handful and Manon doesn't have to…"

"Manon will fall in love with you if I'm not paying attention," he cuts me off. "He lives for protecting innocent souls and taking care of them. That's his greatest flaw and what makes him a perfect human being at the same time."

"Still…"

"Still nothing, queen," he says and I feel my cheeks turning red.

"Oh, I'm far from being a queen." I brush it off, like his words didn't go directly to my heart and made it melt.

"You are meant to be one." He shrugs. "Always have been, always will be."

"Did you run this decision by all the other queens in the world? I'm sure that they has some other heirs in mind." I laugh while getting a bit more lost in his forest green eyes.

"I don't have to." He grazes his lips over mine and I freeze. There's less than an inch separating our lips and less than a fraction of a second to turn my life upside down, with no way of getting back. And I don't know if I'm ready to take that leap of faith. "Because only one person can rule over my world and the throne already has your name carved in its golden headrest."

"You need to stop saying things like this, Lucas." I move my head, so his lips reach my left cheek. I hate myself for doing this, because it's getting clearer by the second that he wants the same thing I want. That he wants me the same way I want him, or even more.

"What I need to do and what I'm willing to do are completely different things, Melody," he says in a determined voice.

"And what are you willing to do?" I ask him in a hopeful voice.

"For you?"

I nod.

"What do you want me to do?" he asks.

"I don't want you to do anything, Lucas." I shake my head vigorously. "You already did more than enough."

"I didn't do shit, Melody!" he booms and I watch him in utter shock. I wasn't expecting him to get angry, nor do I know this side of him. I think there are a lot of things that I don't know about Lucas Temple anymore.

I try to keep my tears at bay, but my traitorous mind won't let me. Every time I hear somebody screaming, my eyes start watering and I fall into a state where I can't do anything but cry and try to isolate myself from the raised voices around me. I always fail, but God, would I love to be able to be normal.

"Fuck!" he yells even louder. "Melody, my beautiful, gorgeous Melody," he pleads, cupping my face with both hands, forcing me to look at him. "Please don't cry. I'm begging you, Mel-Mel. I didn't mean to scare you."

"It's fine, I-I-I just need a minute," I say between sobs. "I need to be alone."

He hugs me and inhales deeply, burying his face in my hair.

"You will never be alone again." But he doesn't know that having people around you isn't enough to stop being alone. "I don't want to leave you alone because I'm afraid that if I let you out of my sight for more than a second, you won't be here anymore when I come back. Please don't put me through that again because this time I don't know how to get back from it, I swear."

"What are you even talking about, Lucas?" I frown. "You can't say things like that only because we just happened to be in the same place at the same time."

"As a matter of fact, I can." He sighs. "Can't you fucking see that it isn't just about being in the same place at the same time? It's about us traveling for the same amount of time to the same destination while spending every waking hour together."

"It's called a coincidence, Lucas," I say in a dismissive voice, because at the end of the day, I need to accept my fate.

I need to push him away, so I can heal properly and learn how to be on my own. I need to take care of myself and learn how to land on my feet, especially since I don't know how Lucas will react after I open up to him. I'm dreading that day, but I know it has to happen sooner rather than later. I need to let him see the true me, the one wearing battle scars and the one that is hideous on the inside.

"A coincidence," he repeats. "Well, fine by me, Melody! Call it whatever you want because I actually don't give a fuck about labels. Those are meant for lunch boxes, not relationships." He shakes his head and moves to a sitting position.

"I think *divorced* is a pretty important label and that doesn't belong on a lunch box! I was married, Lucas. I was married to a successful man, and our divorce was on the front page of multiple papers. I can't just start something with another famous man. Can you imagine what the whole world would say about me?"

"Because what the world has to say is much more important than what you feel right now. Than what I felt for fucking years, from the second you hugged me when I found out my parents were… not here anymore," he mocks.

"You were fourteen. You would've fucked and fallen in love with every woman older than you." I scoff.

"Really?" he cocks an eyebrow. "Then how come after the wake was over and we were the only ones left in that house I felt like my life just began? That I don't want any other woman except you? How come every fantasy, every dream, was about you and having everything I want only to share it with you, Melody? Are you so fucking shallow that you can't see that what I feel, what I always felt, for you is as real as it gets?"

I sit up, mirroring his position and give him a hateful look.

"I'm starting to grow tired of being offended so much in less than twelve hours," I clench my jaw and grit my morals, "and while I expected nothing more from that son of a bitch, I did from you. I guess I was wrong, because, let's face it, the great Yonathan Friedmann shaped you exactly the way he wanted. And who he wanted you to become isn't who I wanted you to become!"

Lucas stands up from the bed and when he reaches the door, he locks it, making my body shiver.

"First of all, I meant what I said. If that's what you think, you're fucking shallow!" he screams. "Why can't anybody believe me when I say that I'm ready to own up to my feelings and do something about it? God!"

"I'm just saying that we need more time, Lucas. I'm mature enough to know rushing into things is always a bad idea."

"Rushing into things? I've known you for fifteen years. You came to my house and fucked my brains out after ten of them. I've waited for you ever since. I never gave you shit about leaving me. I've never asked you to not marry Bart or to do whatever you fucking wanted with your life. I. Have. Always. Waited. For. You." He keeps screaming and this time he is completely indifferent to the tears running down my cheeks. "So tell me, Melody, how does it feel to witness somebody twelve years younger than you being more mature and smarter?"

"You're so fucking mean," I whisper.

"And you should thank yourself for that." He takes his eyes off mine, like looking at me brings him pain.

"Me? No, Lucas. I'm not responsible for the person you turned into. You know damn well who it is."

"But you are!" he roars. "You fucking are! Because I would've never let Yonathan turn me into this fucking resentful human being. Not until you came back and led me to believe that you were back for good. Do you have any fucking idea how it felt to wake up smiling because I was sure I would find you sleeping next to me, only to start crying afterward because you left. Leaving nothing but a trace of your perfume behind?"

"I do!" I scream back.

"You fucking don't, Melody! Don't pretend that you feel the same pain I do, because your pain is completely different from mine." He goes back to looking at me and only now I can see how much I actually hurt him. "I'm not saying you're not going through shit, but you don't get to invalidate my feelings just because you have similar ones. You don't get to take that away from me, too. God only knows that you took enough."

"Then you can have everything back because I don't need it anymore," I say, feeling my heart stopping. "Because I've never meant to rob you of something in the first place. It was you who gave it to me. You were the one who put his soul on a silver platter in the middle of my dining table without even asking me if I wanted it or not. Well," I sniff, "it looks like it's no use to me, since the man I thought you were is dead and buried in Yonathan's cemetery. I hope he at least gave you a nice funeral!"

"I guess you'll never know since you couldn't be bothered to attend." He dismisses me.

Neither of us says anything for some excruciating moments, my sobs being the only sound that fills the room.

I can't understand how the sweet boy, the cute teenager, and the considerate man I once knew turned into the devil's spawn, but I do know one thing: I despise Yonathan more with every second that passes. Not only is he rude and has sociopathic tendencies, he's pure evil. He's the devil and he won't rest until he will turn everybody around him into his humble servants.

"Why did you lock the door?" I ask, wiping the tears from my cheeks, only to make place for new ones.

"Because I didn't want my brothers to hear you screaming and that's the only way to make this room soundproof," he says, raising his eyebrows, like a veil just came down in front of him, revealing something he wasn't expecting to witness. "But that wouldn't be the first time somebody wouldn't hear you scream, would it, Melody?"

I look at my hands, chipping the red nail polish from my thumb. I can't lie to him anymore. My heart is tired and my soul is drained. I can't stand behind this fucking curtain anymore, waiting for the final act to end, so I can breathe easily because I managed, yet again, to keep my face away from the public's sight.

"Answer me," he says in a choked voice, gently grabbing my chin between his thumb and index finger. "How many times did you scream for help without getting an answer?"

I shake my head, because it's the truth. I never screamed for help, because I knew nobody would. I always screamed *stop*.

"Don't lie to me, Melody."

"I'm not. I never did."

"But you did scream." A statement, not a question. "If somebody would've walked into your house. If the maid would've come earlier. If my sister would've called you."

All his statements make my heart beat like it's going to tear my skin and jump on the floor because they're completely true. I can't remember the number of times I begged God to send somebody, anybody, when Bart was beating me or raping me.

"If one of those things had happened, they would've heard you scream. Am I right, Melody?"

His grip on my chin tightens and I instinctively slap his hand away. He moves it immediately and I can't help but feel surprised by how good it feels when a man stops hurting you when you ask him to.

"I'm going to ask you this once, Melody. If you give me the truth, you will finally find out the answer to your earlier question. You will find out what I'm willing to do for you." He kneels in front of me and scoots me closer to the edge of the bed with his muscled arms. "But if you lie to me,

I will consider this as your way of telling me to get away from you and never look back. I want to save you, Melody, and I'm begging you to let me do that."

I look at him and nod, feeling my flesh starting to hurt. I never told a soul except my therapist about the abuse I was suffering, and it's hard to take off the mask that I expertly wear since so many years ago. They say that the wearer of the mask becomes the mask, but this isn't a mask I'm willing to become.

"Was Bart abusing you, Melody?" He puts one hand around my waist and with the other one, he gently grabs the back of my neck, keeping my head in place.

"He was," I whisper, and I feel like the greatest weight has just been lifted from my chest.

I feel like I just found the key that opens the door of my cage, and that there's so much light cutting through the darkness I've lived in for so long.

He gives me a nod and before I can figure out what he's doing, he starts unbuttoning my shirt. I don't say anything when the top button opens, nor when the second one does. When the third one suffers the same fate, I recover from the shock and put my hands over his.

"What are you doing?" I ask in a scared voice.

It's not that I don't want to sleep with him, it's that there's a voice inside my head screaming that I shouldn't. That it's wrong, depraved, and disgusting. That if I take this step, there will be no difference between me and Bart, because I would become a monster, too.

"Do you trust me?"

"I do, Lucas. Otherwise I wouldn't have told you this secret I've been keeping."

He finishes his task, looking at me instead of the buttons, and that makes me terribly jealous, thinking about all the women he undressed before. I know I have no right to feel like that, but the heart is never the organ to try to reason with.

Play My Part

"That's just about the change," he says, determination dripping from his voice.

"What is?" I frown, not knowing what he's referring to.

"I will be your secret. For now, at least." He chuckles and pops the last button of my shirt. "One day I will be the thing everybody knows about you. Now ask me again what I am doing."

"What are you doing?" I breathlessly ask when he takes off my skirt, leaving me only in my underwear and my bra.

"I'm closing all your wounds." He kisses my left knee. "I'm turning on the bright lights because your soul forgot how to." He takes my palm and puts his tongue on the scar on my wrist, making me whimper. "I'm healing you, Melody. I'm going to kiss it better until your skin will be covered in love marks and make it forget all the other bruises it suffered."

"Lucas..." I moan and immediately feel ashamed of how good I feel.

"I'm going to bathe you in love and devotion, Melody," he moans, too, putting his lips on my neck. "I'm going to make you feel like nobody else ever did. I'm going to worship every piece of your beautiful body. I'm going to cherish you and I'm going to appreciate each and every one of your limbs." He stands up again and takes his T-shirt off, making my mouth water when I see his chiseled chest and stomach. "I'm going to make you come, not only because I'm desperate to feel your skin on mine. I'm going to make you go over the edge because I want to replace all the moments of pain with excruciating pleasure."

"I don't know if I'm ready for this, Lucas," I say, feeling miserable for rejecting him. "Not because I don't want to, but because I'm afraid. I'm afraid that I will see him instead of you, and you don't deserve that, Lucas," I whisper.

What I said doesn't seem to stop him. On the contrary, he looks at me with the same determination and takes off his pants.

"Do you still love him?" He threads his hand through his blond locks.

"I did," I reply.

"That's not quite accurate, is it? And, just for the record, the deal with you not lying is still in place. But I asked you a yes or no question. So, do you still love him?"

"It's not fair, Lucas," I say, trying to cover my body with my hands, but failing when he takes my wrists and pins them on each side of me.

"Do you or do you not still love him, Melody?"

"I don't, Luc. That isn't what's keeping me from sleeping with you. I already told you what I'm afraid of. And besides seeing him instead of you, I'm afraid that if we take this further, there's no way the world won't destroy me."

"Then let it destroy you, Melody. Let it destroy us. We don't need other people to decide what's right or wrong for us. Fuck the world and everybody in it." Determination is dripping from his voice, convincing me a bit more to give in to him. "Choose to live instead of letting yourself suffer a long and painful death. Accept that you found somebody who will make your heart beat while making your body explode, not the other way around. Not beating you until you feel your heart explode."

He unclasps my bra, but leaves it in place.

"The choice is yours, Nightingale. Do you want me to help you live or do you want to allow him to make sure you keep dying more and more with every day that passes?"

"Nightingale?"

He nods and kisses my forehead before speaking. "Nightingales are the symbol of melody and beauty. Of darkness and mysticism. And you're beautiful, Melody. Your darkness can only write symphonies. You're a mystic beauty," he whispers, putting his forehead to mine.

"Does that make you the beast in our story?" I put my hand on his face and kiss the top of his nose.

"Only when it comes to keeping you from being hurt again. By that motherfucker or by anybody else. I swear to everything I hold dear that I will protect you like my life is depending on it. On second thought, it

Play My Part

actually does," he says, gently biting my ear. "I swear to you that I will never make you suffer. That I will give countless kisses to all the places he bruised." He kisses my neck again. "That I will replace his slaps and punches with the gentlest of touches my fingertips and tongue can provide." He proves that by licking the column of my neck. "That I will turn your pain into pleasure and your screams for help with screams for more."

He grabs the back of my head and kisses me. It takes a second for me to decide to kiss him back. When I open my mouth to allow him more access, he groans and devours me like a man who just found a spring after climbing the highest mountain.

He takes his lips from mine and I whimper, missing him already. "I'm going to do all of that and more even if those are the last things I do on this earth. But only if you let me!"

"I want to try, Lucas! I don't want to promise you that I'll succeed, but I want to try!" I say, allowing my bra to fall in my lap.

He inhales deeply when he sees my breasts and spends several seconds taking me in, a mix of adoration and hunger pooling in his eyes.

"Then sing the song of the night between my sheets, Melody Byers."

He pushes me on my back and I want to cry because of how gentle his touch is. Not compared to Bart's, but compared to the way a man should ever touch a woman.

"I'm going to fall in love with you, Melody, and I'm going to do it like you deserve it," he says while taking my panties off. "I'm going to love the fuck out of you until you'll beg me to stop because your heart can't take it anymore. I'm going to love you like a madman and I'm going to make you fall in love with me like the stars fall in love with the night sky. Like you depend on me to live. Because I'm going to do the same."

"I'm broken, Lucas. I don't know if I'm able to love madly. Not anymore," I say in a sad voice.

He crawls above me and places his index finger on my nipple, making my body shiver.

"Then I'm going to love all those broken pieces until they come together and make a new version of you. I'll bring you to perfection, my beautiful nightingale."

Chapter 8

Lucas

The fact that Melody is lying naked next to me is bringing me on the verge of insanity. It takes every ounce of self-control to keep me from grabbing her hair and thrusting inside her as hard and deep as I can. A part of me says that I deserve that. I deserve it as a reward for all the years I kept waiting for her, and I fucking deserve everything she has to give because my soul was hers even when my body wasn't.

I slept with a grand total of ten women and all of them sucked my cock like their lives were depending on the quality of that blowjob. I never appreciated women that wanted to sleep with me only because they fell in love with the sweet teenager that made his big brother feel love for the first time in his life. If they only fucking knew that behind the scenes, the big brother was the one who was changing the little one—not the other way around.

But because sometimes thinking about Melody became overwhelming, I indulged myself and picked a random woman from one of the parties I was forced to attend by my agent and took her home. Unfortunately, every single time I slept with them, I ended up hating myself and the way they moaned like they were having the best orgasm of their lives from the second I started touching them.

I hated their whimpers, their whines, and how they let me do everything I wanted with them. Every time I was fucking one of them I felt sorry for her and scared at the same time. Because seeing somebody completely at your mercy only because she can later brag to her friends that the great Lucas Temple shoved his cock down her throat is scary, trust me.

None of those women slept with me for me and who I am. They slept with me for fame, for leverage, or for any other fucked-up reason their small, limited brain conjured. They were never interested in finding out what's my favorite ice cream flavor, what makes me smile in the morning, or if I like coconut in my cookies.

Contrary to Yonathan, who I'm sure is fulfilling every dark fantasy he has with the women who are patiently waiting in line in front of his apartment, I was always a gentleman with them. Yes, I used them as a means to an end, but I always took care of them after I was done. I always fed them, and let them use my shower, and paid for their Uber ride home. I was a nice guy even though they didn't want the nice guy. They wanted the half-naked hotshot who was killing the bad guys while they were eating popcorn and drinking low quality cola. They wanted all the characters I ever played, but not a single one of them wanted Lucas Temple. And that's fucking sad.

I could've slept with a number of women most third graders don't know how to pronounce the names of. I could've had threesomes, foursomes, orgies, and I could've shared dozens of women with Yonathan if I accepted his invitations. However, the fact that my parents lived in the same world, had access to the same opportunities, and managed to stay loyal to each other, only made me decide that I could be loyal to the woman I wanted to spend my life with since I was a teenager. Those two angels respected and loved each other, and their spawn should follow the example they set.

"I don't know how to do this," she whispers. "I don't remember how it feels to have sex with someone and enjoy it. I don't even remember how it feels to have sex with someone and consenting to it."

I try to stifle my anger, but I fail. The fact that Bart fucking Trello not only beat the shit out of her, but also raped her, makes me want to go find him and bash his head on the sidewalk until the matter of his deranged brain is spread around me.

I punch the headboard and I hear Melody gasping. The second I see tears falling again on her red cheeks makes me hate myself even more. I would do anything for this woman, except hurt her.

Doesn't she know how much I fucking care for her?

Doesn't she see that my chest is ripped open and my heart is there for her to take and do whatever she wants with it?

I lean down and wipe her tears with my thumbs. For some particular reason, her tears make my cock even harder than I ever thought it could be. I've never been so aroused in my life and the fact that my soul feels sorrow while my body feels craving and longing is confusing to say the least.

"I would never hurt you, beautiful Melody," I say right before I kiss her again, and this time I'm not taking it easy. It's a violent kiss, one where I'm sucking her tongue, making spit dribble over her chin. It's messy, just like what's going on between us.

My lips leave hers, only to find her neck. I want to kiss and lick every single part of her body. I want to taste her skin and I want her to come on my tongue, to feel that fucking sweet taste of her in my mouth again.

I know that making her body feel pleasure is only the start of this. I know the wounds that will heal the hardest are the ones on her soul. It's going to be a long process, so it's a good thing that I'm not a quitter. Not only will I help her heal them, but I will make sure the only way for her to get new ones is for me to be dead. And I'm not so sure about that either, because I will go to unfathomable lengths for her even in the afterlife.

She moans when I bite her shoulder on my way to her nipples. I can't fucking wait to put my tongue on those sharp brown buds that are the perfect addition to her large, full breasts.

"Do you like what I'm doing, Melody?" I ask her in a deep voice.

She nods while she bites her lower lip, and that's when I realize her eyes are closed.

"Look at me, Nightingale. Look at your man when he's making your pussy wet," I command, and she obeys. "Good girl," I chuckle and flick her left nipple with my tongue.

When I take her whole nipple in my mouth and start sucking while gently grazing her skin with my teeth, she whispers my name, and I groan because I need to feel her pussy as soon as possible. But I remind myself that I need to be patient. My queen needs her king to take his time with her. Besides, I want to give her a taste of her own poison and make her wait for me since I waited for her for so many years.

"Tell me again," she says in a determined voice right when I start swirling the tip of my tongue around her belly button. I look in her beautiful hazel eyes and laugh internally when I see how dilated her pupils are. She's turned on and I'm the reason for it. And that's just the greatest fucking feeling in the world.

"What do you need me to say, Melody?" I continue kissing and licking her stomach, doing my best to keep myself from thinking that, at some point, this perfect skin had black and blue spots around it. I wish I could've been there for her when it happened. I wish she would've called me and asked me to come and help her, and I would've done it in an instant. I feel so fucking sorry for her, but now is definitely not the time to think about that. I don't want to miss the show my beautiful woman puts on for me. And the best part of it? She doesn't fucking fake it. Every reaction she has is natural. Every jolt of her body, every moan that comes out of her mouth, is an honest reaction to what I'm doing. She's the only one who wants Lucas Temple, the boy who doesn't want more than to feel loved. She wants Lucas Temple, the man who wants her back. The man who will hold her hand while she remembers how to turn from a scared little hatchling to a majestic nightingale.

"You know what I want you to say," she says in a timid voice. And I do. I know exactly what she needs to hear, but the fact that I couldn't wait for this to happen doesn't mean that I'll go easy on her. She needs to remember who Melody fucking Byers is. And Melody Byers is a strong woman who asks for exactly what she wants.

"I'm not in the business of reading minds, Mel. So, tell me. What is it that you need to hear?"

"Arrogant bastard," she sighs, and I let out a small laugh.

She doesn't say anything, challenging me to give in. Little does she know that I won't. I stand up from between her legs and get out of bed to find my phone, so I can connect it to the audio system. This room might not be too spacious, but it's perfect for two people who want to get lost in each other while being thirty thousand feet away from the ground.

Yon always said that fucking during a flight is completely different than fucking in your bedroom, and I couldn't agree more. The adrenaline of flying contributes to the adrenaline caused by the tension that's filling the space. The fact that she has no place to run. The fact that even if she does, I will catch her. All these things make this experience completely different than anything I have ever felt. And the fact that Melody is the one I'm sharing this with can easily make me feel like the luckiest man on the planet.

When I hear a small gasp behind me, I turn around and see Melody's lips moving while her fingers are covering her eyelids. I try being as silent as possible when I get closer, because curiosity gets the best of me. I want to hear what pep talk she is giving herself.

Only it's not a pep talk. It's the cruelest thing I've ever heard.

"See, Melody? You're not good for him. What were you thinking when you spread your legs like a whore for him?"

My heart is in fucking shreds. I don't know if or when I will be able to help her change that speech inside her head. The speech that her shit of a husband, the media, and even Yonathan slowly but surely put there, because that's not my Melody talking. My Melody would never tell herself such horrible things.

I pick up the phone from my slacks' pocket and, after various attempts, I finally manage to turn on the Bluetooth. I'm not technologically challenged usually, but now I'm so fucking angry I can't see straight.

When "Flames" by Donzell Taggart starts coming out of the speakers, Melody's mouth stops moving and she looks at me with fear in her eyes. I sit down on the edge of the bed and slowly, so slowly, crawl my index finger over her stomach. I barely touch her, but goosebumps are covering her skin.

"So responsive," I whisper in her ear when I lie down next to her. "Do you like it when I touch you, Mel?"

"Yes," she instantly answers, arching her back.

"Where do you want me to touch you?" I stop moving my hand and she whimpers.

"Wherever you want." She looks at me, and I smile when I see that fear being replaced by what I think is hope.

"Tsk." I pause. "That's not how this will go. When you're with me, you decide what I do and where I touch you. You have full control over my body, even when you won't have it over your own. So, where do you want my finger, my beautiful queen?"

She gently takes my hand in hers and drags it toward her lower abdomen, but freezes when it reaches her pelvic bone. I give her an encouraging look, and she swallows, gathering the courage to make my hand cup her pussy. The heat that is radiating from it only makes me think of how good it will feel when I'll bury my tongue in that warm, wet hole of hers.

"Do you want my finger inside you, Melody?" She nods, licking those plump, luscious lips. When I put my middle finger inside her, I let out a breath because I can't believe this is finally happening again. I can't believe that I finally get to feel how the most intimate part of her feels like it did that night.

I start moving my finger in and out of her, all the time while making

Play My Part

sure my palm grazes her clit at the same pace.

"More," she moans and I gather her breasts with my free hand, putting those fucking beautiful nipples one next to the other so I can lick and suck them at the same time. "More," she says again and I add my index finger and speed up my movements. When I feel her pussy throbbing, I let go of her breasts and put my mouth right above my fingers, sucking her clit hard.

"You taste so sweet, Melody. Your pussy tastes like gods' fucking nectar."

"Please," she says between the loud moans coming out of her that are covering the song that's playing on repeat.

"What do you want, Melody?"

"I don't know," she desperately whines. "I want more. I want it all. Please, please, please."

My sweet nightingale wants to come and she doesn't even know it. And whatever she wants, she fucking gets. I take my fingers out and replace them with my tongue, thrusting her pussy with it while rubbing fast circles on her clit with my middle finger.

"Fuck, Lucas!" she screams when I feel her pussy clenching around my tongue so hard that I think she'll rip it from my mouth. But it would be worth it. Everything would be worth it for her.

"Such a good girl coming for me while screaming my name," I say, kissing her and making her taste herself. She moans loudly in my mouth and I can only imagine that happens because she likes her own taste as much as I do.

"I think…" she hesitates and looks at me with a new set of tears in her eyes.

I hug her to my chest and begin rocking her, kissing her hair, her forehead and her cheeks.

"We don't need to do this, Mel-Mel. But do know that feeling your cum in my mouth is the best thing that ever happened to me," I say. "You're so beautiful when you come, Nightingale. You're the most beautiful, the smartest, the kindest woman on this planet."

"I think I'm ready," she says, putting her hand on my cheek, and I give her a chaste kiss.

"Are you sure?"

"I want to do this. I need to do this, Lucas. I need to replace all those horrible memories with a new one. With a great one." She sounds so determined that it makes my heart swell. "I need to have this with you and I don't care if I'm selfish, a whore, or whatever the world wants to call me. I'm doing this for me as much as I want to do it for you."

She licks my chest and I can't help but grab her hair, pulling her close to my face so I can kiss her again, letting her know that I'm right here, next to her, and that we'll face the world together. The world be damned! We don't need anybody else other than the people who could help us grow and who would be happy for us. The rest of them can go fuck themselves because they could never understand what we have. Nobody could fucking understand that we were never star-crossed lovers, but the best kind of fated mates. "I want you inside me. I need you so much, Luc-Luc," she pleads and I can't be happier to oblige.

I take a condom out from the nightstand and rip the foil with my teeth. She sighs in relief when she sees what I'm doing, and I frown.

"Don't worry, Melody. I will put a baby in this beautiful body when the time comes. I will fucking breed you until we'll have a family bigger than the ones in those sextuplet reality shows. But not now."

"It's not that," she says with a trace of regret in her voice. "It's that Bart…"

"You don't say that name when I'm fucking you." I thrust inside her hard and deep, feeling like I could come on the spot. Hearing that name coming from her mouth makes me lose my mind. "You don't say any name except mine when your tight pussy is wrapped around my big, thick cock."

"I'm sorry." Her back arches so much that it looks like she's levitating.

"Never apologize to me when I'm inside you, either," I pant. "Just tell me what you want me to do to you. Tell me what you want from this thick fucking cock. Be a good girl and tell me. Please tell me," I say, clenching

Play My Part

my jaw.

I stop my movements and look at her. I can't take my eyes off her. She's absolutely stunning and the fact that her eyelids are hooded and her lips are parted enough so she can let out all those beautiful moans makes me want to be at her mercy even more. With all the other women, I had to play the alpha role. Dominate them, make them obey each and every one of my commands. But with Melody I can be my true self. I can let her know that nothing turns me on more than a woman who knows exactly what she wants and takes it from me. A woman who uses me for her own pleasure is the only type of woman who can make me come so hard I see stars.

"Tell me, Melody."

"Fuck me, Lucas!" she screams when I pinch her clit. "Fuck me with everything you have. Just bend me and fuck me."

I grab her knees and force her to open her legs as much as possible, bringing her calves close to her ears.

"That's it, Melody. Spread your beautiful legs for me," I say as I move faster in and out of her. "And you're spreading them because you're taking what's yours, not because you're a whore. So take me, Mel. Fucking use me and get what you deserve." I pant. "You deserve the moon and the sun in your palms, and that's what I'll fucking give you. I will give you every." *Thrust.* "Fucking." *Thrust.* "Thing!"

Her screams are becoming raspy and that makes me fuck her harder. I lied earlier, because it's me who can't control his body. I feel like I died and went to Heaven. I push her knees even closer to the bed, never dropping her gaze. "What do you need, Melody?"

"You," she moans.

"What do you need from me? Harder, slower, faster, deeper?"

"Deeper," she whispers, and I see her cheeks turning even redder.

"That's a good girl. Do you like it when you control what my cock does to you?"

She nods and I slightly slow down my pace, doing my best to go even farther inside her.

"Is this deep enough, Nightingale?"

"I feel so fucking full." She grimaces and whines, her eyes rolling to the back of her head.

"Do you like it when I'm balls deep inside you?" I put my palm on her stomach, paying extra attention to keep it right above her pelvis. What I'm planning shouldn't hurt, it's supposed to bring her to climax again.

"Fuck, I love it," she groans, and her eyes come back to mine.

With my other hand, I start rubbing her clit up and down as fast as I can. She whimpers and screams so loud I'm afraid that not even the soundproof system will keep my friends from hearing her. But I don't care. I'm a man on a mission and I'll be damned if I don't get what I want.

"Lucas, I'm gonna come," she says in a panicked voice. "I'm gonna come so fucking hard."

"Do it, Melody," I moan. "Spread that fucking cum all over this thick cock that's railing your hot, dripping pussy. Be a good girl and do it."

I don't get to finish my sentence because I feel the warm liquid on my hands and on my abdomen. I make a mental note to thank Manon for teaching me about that spot that brings a woman so much pleasure. From the second he told me about it, I had this replayed in my mind for thousands of times, and I couldn't be happier than I am now, seeing that I succeeded in making her feel so fucking good.

When she keeps repeating my name like a prayer, I can't help it and let go. When I come, I do it while roaring her name and looking in her eyes, telling her how fucking beautiful she is and how much I waited for this moment.

I pull out of her and use my last remaining strength to crawl next to her.

When I hug her to my chest, I realize that the whimpers I heard earlier weren't caused by the pleasure she felt. She's crying. Fucking sobbing.

And I hate myself so fucking much for not noticing and letting myself get lost in that perfect moment that was a nightmare for her.

Chapter 9
Melody

"*Can you feel my cum leaking out of you, slut? Stop crying and answer me, you fucking disgusting whore!*"

"Yes," I whimper, trying to close my legs, but failing when Bart kicks my knee.

"That's right. Who owns you, Melody? Who's the man you belong to?"

"You are." I rush out, only to make him stop and leave me to go and lick my wounds.

"Good! Now go and clean up. You're fucking filthy and no one will love you except me, right? Nobody could love a pathetic, dirty whore like you." He grabs my cheeks and squeezes them with one hand and he wraps his other one around my neck, applying pressure on my airway.

I nod and head toward the stairs and freeze when I hear my name coming from his mouth. "Melody!"

"Yes?"

"Melody!" he screams louder, and I take a step back, knowing that I will be punished for not answering when he called me the first time.

"MELODY!"

I blink, and all of a sudden, Bart's hateful look changes into the kindest one I've ever seen. His face slowly morphs into Lucas's and I remember where I am and what just happened.

I let him down. I wanted to give myself to him so much, but I failed. I couldn't even give him a complete experience with me, and that makes me feel like a failure yet again. I realize now that Bart was right. Nobody could love me because I'm broken. Torn into pieces that no entity, higher or lower, could put back together. Not even Lucas, the angel that God himself sent to Earth to protect me. I failed him, I failed myself, and I've let Bart control my life even when he's not in it.

"Mel-Mel," he breathes, and hugs me to his chest, "fuck! Don't ever do that to me again, Melody." He squeezes me harder, making it almost impossible to breathe. He lets me go and cups my face in his hands, brushing my cheeks with his thumbs and looking into my eyes. "I'm so sorry, Mel. I'm so, so fucking sorry. I was fucking stupid. Please forgive me. I'm begging you to forgive me, my beautiful queen."

I hug him with the same strength. He shouldn't apologize for anything. It was me who, instead of enjoying the best experience I had in so long, went to that fucking dark place that haunts me unexpectedly.

"I'm sorry, too," I tell him, holding his gaze. "It happens sometimes."

"What do you mean?" He frowns and turns me on my side, brushing his lips over mine. "What happens sometimes?"

"It's just," I clear my voice, "I do this shit and," I inhale deeply, "fuck! When I feel happier than usual, my brain decides to remind me of all the shit Bart put me through."

He grimaces, like I just slapped him, but then he says in a determined voice, "We'll fix this, Melody. Together, we will fix this. I shouldn't have let myself do th…"

I put my fingers to his lips and bury my face in his chest, because I'm not brave enough to look him in the eye when I'm saying this. But he needs to know. He said earlier he wants to bathe me in love and devotion, but before doing that, he needs to know who will be at the receiving end of all these feelings. He needs a chance to change his mind before choosing me.

"I'm damaged goods, Lucas," I whisper. "I'm not able to give you what you need, obviously. So maybe it's better to let me go before picking me up."

Play My Part

He groans and slowly pushes me back, and my soul is shaking when I see the pain written all over his face. He looks like somebody is performing surgery on him without any trace of anesthesia, and knowing I'm the surgeon makes me want to die. Why am I bringing so much suffering in the world? Why am I forced to suffer so much in the first place? God, what did I do to deserve this fucking horrible life?

"You might think that you're damaged, but for me? For me you are mended. You are fucking pristine, Melody." He lets out an exhale before continuing, "Can't you see that it breaks my heart seeing you like this? Can you even fucking imagine what I feel now, when I can't see any sparkle in your beautiful hazel eyes? If you're damaged, then I'll be damaged with you. I can't be complete without you, Melody."

I nod, because I understand completely how he feels. I can't be complete without him either, because he's my lifeline. I am sure now that if there's a person out there who can help me go back to being who I was before or an even better version of that person, it's him. Maybe it isn't fair to put so much hope in somebody. Maybe it isn't fair to expect somebody to heal you when you can't heal yourself, and maybe letting myself care so much for him in this particular moment is wrong. But I don't care. I took his words from earlier and let them flow around my body and go through my blood. I will burn this world with him and I will build a new one where we can be happy, even if that means I have to kill Bart myself.

"I don't know how to love somebody else, Melody," he confesses. "I tried so hard all these years. I kept telling myself that you're happy, that I should let you be happy and forget about you." I shake my head because after everything that just happened, hearing this makes me feel dizzy. "I fucking tried, Melody. But do you know what happened every time I did it?" I shake my head again. "I tried finding a piece of you in them. In every woman I ever slept with, I tried to find something that reminded me of you. And when I found it, I started looking for another one. And another one, and another one, until I couldn't find any more and decided to leave them. Sometimes their hair didn't smell like yours does. Sometimes they didn't have your kindness, sometimes they didn't understand my jokes, and some-fucking-times they didn't live up to the fantasy I was trying to bring to reality."

"That sounds like an awful lot of women." I try to hide my jealousy, but based on the way he smiles I clearly fail.

"Could've been one, ten, a thousand, or a trillion. None of them was my Melody. None of them knew how to make my heart skip a beat. None of them could have made me feel the same way you did."

He gets closer to me and grabs the back of my head, making my whole body shiver.

"Is this okay, Mel?"

"This is more than okay, Luc. If anything isn't, it's what I'm doing to you. I'm the one whose brain is damaged. I'm the one who has so many stories to tell you." I sigh. "I want to tell you everything, I do. I want to let you in, but I don't know how. I don't know if I can!"

"Why?" He frowns, clearly not expecting these words to come out of my mouth. "If you're afraid something will happen to you, you don't need to worry about that. You can live with me, Mel. I have tons of people guarding my house day in, day out. I can't make a single step without a dozen people forming a wall around me. You won't just be protected, you'll be fucking guarded better than the Mona Lisa is!"

"I'm not afraid of that, Lucas." I thread my fingers through his soft hair. "I'm afraid of something never happening to me. I'm afraid I'll always take one step forward, and three steps back. I'm afraid that I'll always end up crying when I feel happy. I'm afraid these memories will haunt me for the rest of my days. That I will never be able to breathe and sleep properly. I'm scared of a lot of things," I finally admit.

He stands up abruptly and heads to the adjacent bathroom. He crooks his finger, signaling me to join him, and I stand up from the bed, wrapping a sheet around my body.

Play My Part

"Are you going to take a shower with that thing on?" He laughs.

"I'm not a huge fan of my body," I whisper.

"Well, I am. I am its biggest fan." He gently tugs the end of the sheet and I allow it to fall to the floor.

He moves his fingertips all over my body, like a sculptor adding the final touches to one of his statues. I close my eyes, putting my forehead to his shoulder.

"You're so beautiful, Nightingale," he says. "You're one of God's greatest masterpieces."

"You're biased." I laugh.

"I don't care," he says in a reassuring voice. "I know I am, but I don't care. If I could give you my eyes only for a couple of minutes to make you see yourself the same way I see you. So beautiful, yet flawed. So fantastic, yet human. Fucking phenomenal."

He drags me to the shower, kissing me when the water starts falling on our bodies. He never takes his lips off mine, not when he puts some shower gel in his palm, and not when he ever so gently rubs it all over my body.

He finally breaks the kiss, making me turn around so he can wash my hair, too. I have never been so taken care of in my life. I never felt like this before and I never want to stop feeling like this.

Lucas makes quick work of washing himself, too, and before I can say something, he wraps me in a towel, takes me in his arms, and seats me on the bed. Putting on his clothes and throwing mine on the bed, he takes my hand and pulls me fast in his arms. He gasps and takes a step back.

"I'm sorry, love." I have no idea what he's apologizing for, but I let him continue. "I'm behaving like a fucking Neanderthal with you and keep forgetting that you're sensitive to every touch." His voice is sad and thoughtful, and my heart keeps swelling until I'm afraid it will pop like a balloon. I smile and put my other hand on his clean and soft face.

"I trust you, Lucas Temple. I trust you to heal me instead of causing me pain. I trust you to take care of my body that only got destroyed by others. I trust you fully, completely, and wholeheartedly." I put my lips on his, feeling proud of how brave I am to do this. "I trust you with all the pieces of my broken soul and I don't need you to treat me with kid gloves. I need you to teach me how to live and burst this bubble of pain I've been living in for such a long time."

He looks at me through his long eyelashes and I feel my knees weakening again. I can't help but wonder if I will ever stop feeling like this every time I see all that care and determination in his eyes.

"There is nothing I wouldn't do for your happiness, Melody. If you want me to take off my gloves, that's what I'll do. If you want me to put them back on, I will. I want you to use me, Melody. Play me like an instrument and use me like a toy. Let me make you happy, Mel."

He unlocks the door and before he opens it, he kisses me again with the same passion from earlier.

"This is what's going to happen, my beautiful queen. We're going to go out there as a team. We went in this room separately and we're going out of it together, and there is nothing that will separate us from now on. Is this what you want?"

I nod and give him a smile. I am absolutely sure that this is what I want.

"Last chance, Melody. Because if I go out there holding your hand, I won't ever let you go. You will be mine until the end of eternity, and even then I will fight all the gods willing to end this world only to spend another second with you."

I feel my vision getting blurred because of the tears that are threatening to fall, but I blink them away, because I want him to see that I can be as determined as him. I need him to see that I'm as sure as he is that we will find a way to get out of this fucked-up situation and live happily together for as long as we can.

I know now that even if life decides that we can't be together for some reason, I will always feel grateful for what he is doing for me now. For his will to help me and for his dedication to the mission of saving and healing me.

Play My Part

"I'm not as good with words as you are, Lucas," I say in a choked voice. "But do know that I want to play on your team. I don't want to be in any other team except yours."

"Then let's play this game together, Melody Byers. And when we'll get to the end of it, our names will be the first ones on the leaderboard. There is no way we lose, love."

I don't know if he realizes that it's the second time he called me *love* in a span of a couple of minutes, but I don't want to correct him. We've always loved each other, even though it's the first time we do it in this way. It's clear to me now that his obsession with me started a long time ago, but what he doesn't know is that I was as haunted by the what-ifs as he was.

Every time I was at Bart's mercy, Lucas was my happy place. The young man I first saw one sunny Saturday afternoon and his sister were the only memories that made me want to go on with my life. Sandra and Lucas Temple saved me several times and they have no idea that they did.

I promised myself many times that I would reach out to them at some point in my life and thank them for existing and for being such an important part of my life. I never found that suitable moment until now. And I will gladly spend the rest of my life showing Lucas how grateful I am.

When we get back to the lounge, I see Yonathan laying on the leather couch, his eyes covered by his arm. Manon is looking at something on his phone on the other couch, laughing like he's having the best time of his life.

The contradiction between their two stances is completely ridiculous and I can't help but laugh.

"Oh, good. The rotten mother and the prodigal son return." Yonathan stands up and takes Lucas by the arm, forcing both of us to sit down in the same spot he occupied earlier. "I have a question, baby Temple."

"Shoot." Lucas relaxes and puts his hand on my thigh, giving me a coy smile and a wink that makes me melt.

"Did I ever lead you to believe that I want children?"

"No," his question is completely weird, but knowing him, this is just the beginning of a long interrogation.

"Good. Did I ever show love, compassion, or interest, for that matter, to a person below the age where you can fuck in the US and drink in the EU?"

"Y…"

"Besides you."

"No." He sighs and leans back and I try to understand what the fuck he actually wants.

"Good. Did I ever say that I want to save the planet, make this world a better place, or help the ones in need?"

"Are you practicing for your next audition for the role of a villain in a superhero movie? I heard *The Batman* franchise has an opening for the *Joker*!" Lucas laughs, but when Yonathan's eyes narrow, he abruptly stops.

My nemesis refills his glass. I'm wondering how the fuck he's not completely wasted yet. But then again, maybe not even alcohol could make this man loosen up.

"I don't think I'm ready for that role just yet," he hisses after taking a sip. "Not insane enough. But you know what? If I spend another fucking minute listening to 'there was a farmer who had a dog and Bingo was his name-o' or to the PG-13 version of Cinderella sucking the prince's cock, I might get there!"

"Jesus Christ." I exhale and Manon frowns.

"You do know that *Cinderella* is a story for children and that porn movie is an adaptation, not the other way around, right?" Manon asks, not taking his eyes from the phone, where he watches the *Cinderella* cartoon.

"What do you mean?" he asks in a confused voice.

"Jesus Christ," I say again

"I think he's a bit busy to come and save you, Melody, but please feel free to try again. Maybe he's like *Beetlejuice* and shows up only if you say his name three times in a row." Yon sneers.

"Shut the fuck up, Yon." Manon laughs. "It's not my fault that the Wi-

Play My Part

Fi installed in your precious airplane restricts playing anything meant for people older than four."

"Can somebody do that?" I ask, frowning. I've never heard about this before.

"Only the best developers." Manon replies. "And that's exactly who Yonathan hired to make his precious baby the best of the best."

"I'm sure it's an honest mistake." Yonathan picks some invisible lint from his jacket and straightens his glasses, sitting next to Manon.

"Or they just can't fucking stand you," I retort. "I wonder why."

"Okay, cut it," Lucas says and gives my hand a gentle squeeze. Yonathan frowns, probably surprised by this turn of events. "I need you to listen to me. Both of you."

"Sure," Non says right when their other friend opens his mouth. "What are we listening to?"

Lucas looks first in my eyes and then at his chosen brothers. His smile when he's watching all of us together might make an outsider think we've all known each other for years.

I cover my face with my hands, embarrassed by having all these pairs of eyes on me. I can feel myself blushing, because I don't know what his friends will say when he finishes telling them that we want to give us a chance to make each other happy. I try to bury deep down inside me the unsettling thought that he'll never want me after hearing what I have to say. I want to live in the moment and be happy. I want to put the future on hold, even if it's only for a couple of hours.

"You're brave, queen," he whispers in my ear. "You're braver than anybody I know."

"I'm not," I say, slowly raising my chin and looking at Manon. I don't have the courage to look at Yonathan just yet. "But I can try to be."

"So, here's the thing." Lucas's voice turns serious. "Melody and I are together now."

"Together how?" Yonathan asks, typing something on his phone and putting it back in his jacket pocket.

"Together. A couple." Lucas sounds like he is addressing a child. "Two people who kiss and spend time together."

"Fuck, suck cock, eat pussy, anal, praise, degradation, bondage." He waves his hand, encouraging Lucas to continue. "I know what a couple does. Although I would recommend trying a throuple! Completely different experience."

Manon finally stops the children's song playing in the background and leans forward in his seat, crossing his hands in front of him.

"So you asked her to be your girlfriend, I take?" he asks.

Lucas laughs, and puts his hand on the headrest, stretching it until his elbow is on my shoulder.

"I think we're a bit past that. But if you think that's necessary, then," he gets closer to me, his lips slightly touching mine, "Melody Byers, would you make my greatest dream come true and accept being my girlfriend?"

I nod eagerly and he grabs my face, kissing me with patience and care. Our tongues meet and I have to fight the urge to climb on his lap and ask him to fuck me like he did earlier.

"See, Manon? We have porn, after all." Yonathan breaks the spell between Lucas and me.

Lucas lets me go, giving me a wink before going back to look at his best friends.

"Happy now, Non?"

He doesn't answer, so Lucas continues, oblivious to the fact that none of them seem happy for us. That honestly makes me feel like shit, because I don't know how I will ever find the energy to keep myself from blurting out everything I want to say to Lucas in one go, and fighting to make these two men see that I genuinely care about him. To make them understand that I'm done hurting him, or at least I hope I am. That I want to heal myself, to help him heal, and to heal together.

"We'll take it slow," he continues. "For some time I would like to ask you to be discreet and not tell anybody else about this."

"Who the fuck would we tell, baby Temple?" Yonathan rolls his eyes. "You two are the only friends I have."

"I don't know, Yon," Lucas shakes his head, "Joanna, the media?"

"The only things I tell Joanna are *such a fucking slut desperate for my cock,* and *ass up, face down.* And the media? When did I ever talk to the media without being forced by the circumstances?"

"Don't worry, Luc," Non says in a cold voice. "All your secrets are safe with us."

I don't know if he refers to some things that Lucas hides from me, or to my own secrets that he might have found out. I try to calm myself, realizing there is no way either of them could have found out about what happened in my past, but my heart begs to differ.

I feel scared again, but for the first time in a long time, Bart isn't the cause of me feeling like that.

Chapter 10
Lucas

"And here is the living room! This is suitable for dinners with a lot of guests, or gatherings, and if you want to take out some furniture, we can definitely do that," our whatever-staff-member-she-is says in a chirpy voice and a perfect American accent. It feels odd being so many miles away from home, but hearing so many people speaking your native tongue. And the fact that they speak it better than most of the people I went to high school with makes this experience even weirder.

"We'll keep all the furniture," Manon rushes out. "We don't want to make any changes since we'll be only living here for six months, give or take." He gives her his signature smile, the one that makes every woman's panties drop. My brother isn't beautiful in the traditional way. He most definitely doesn't look like a pretty boy or like an alpha man ready to rail you at any point during the day or the night.

Manon's beauty lies in the mysterious aura that always seems to surround him. You feel him before you see him entering a room. It's like the man has tendrils made of dark smoke that grasp your whole body, choking you and making your soul dance with his. Once he sets his black eyes on you, you have no choice but to drown in them and beg him to blow some oxygen into your lungs, just to be able to hold his gaze until the end of time.

Play My Part

His tanned skin is filled with tattoos in more than ten languages, out of which only one is in English. The one that says *If by my life or death I can protect you, I will*. And he didn't get that only because he's a fan of J. R. R. Tolkien. Both me and Yonathan know he is obsessed with a lot of things, since his disease has the word in it, but his greatest one was and always will be to protect the ones in need. And the ones who don't need it, if you ask me. At first, it seemed ridiculous when I saw him fighting with people who were keeping their dog's collar too tight around their throats, but now that I know that it's his soul demanding to do that it's just, I don't know, sad, maybe?

"Oh, okay, Mr. Toussaint!" She giggles like a teenager and adjusts her red skirt. Threading her fingers through her blonde hair and wrapping a strand of it around her index finger, she looks at Manon and continues, "Should we continue with the bedrooms?"

"Did she say *in* or *with*?" Yonathan whispers in Manon's ear, making him let out a laugh.

The woman, whose name I can't remember to save my life, blushes and starts analyzing her green high heels. I take two steps toward her in an effort to show some compassion and make her relax, but she still stays quiet.

"I would love to see the bedroom where my girlfriend and I will spend the next months," I tell her in a kind voice. That brings her back from the place her mind traveled and she gives me a nod. I don't know if it's a sign of gratitude, but I'll take it as long as she stops feeling uncomfortable because of Yon's crudeness.

When we start walking down the hallway behind the wooden staircase, I hear Yonathan's voice from behind me. I knew for a fact that he won't let what I said go unnoticed and that he will have something to say about it, but I find myself not being able to give a fuck about his thoughts or feelings.

"Manon, do you happen to know a good otolaryngologist here? I know you haven't visited this country in a while, but maybe you still have some connections here."

Miriam Rosentvaig

"Why is that, Yon? Did you finally decide to take your nose out of my business and you need a professional to make it happen?" I counter while continuing walking next to the tall blonde.

"No, I actually need him to teach you how to stop gagging the next time you're going to suck my cock," he says in that tone that could make the sun freeze. "You know I'm the face-fucking rather than sloppy blowjobs type."

The poor woman trips hearing his crass words, and despite my best efforts to try and catch her, she falls to her knees on the gray marble tiles.

"I was talking to baby Temple, but since you seem more eager than him, hell, I'll take it," Yon says, looking at her from above. "I would need your consent first, given the fact that my friends here will watch and this might turn quickly into the next scandal on every tabloid's cover. Even better, I think I have an NDA somewhere around here. Hold please." He lifts his index finger before bending and rummaging through his Armani bag.

"I'm so sorry! It was an accident, I swear," the woman cries, but Yonathan pays no attention to her. A part of me wants to believe he's joking, but I quickly remember that he's completely unhinged and has the social filters of a snail. So, I extend my hand to her, helping her to stand up.

"He sometimes forgets to take his pills," Manon says. "The doctors told him several times to stop listening to the voices, but when he's tired, it's getting hard for him to tell the difference between reality and the vivid images in his head."

"Oh, I didn't know he's sick," she says in a sad voice. I guess our talent is helpful off the film set too.

"Yes, very sick," Manon continues, a set of unshed tears pooling in his eyes. "It was terrible to be forced to see him lie in that hospital bed for so many months, you know?" He presses his index fingers on his eyelids and dramatically puts his hand over his mouth. "I will never forget the day when he woke up and started sobbing when the physician told him that his body is fully recovered, but he will always suffer from erectile dysfunction. Such a tragedy."

The woman gasps and looks at Yonathan, whose eyes are shooting flaming arrows in Non's direction. I give Non a nod, letting him know that I'm with him this time and that I'm willing to keep this up as long as he is.

"We still love him, you know?" I say in a soul-crushing voice. "But sometimes, especially when he wakes up screaming *I want cock* in the middle of the night, it's hard for us to realize he's talking about his own." I sigh and look at the ceiling, mimicking fighting tears, when, in reality, I can barely contain my laughter. "He needs constant supervision since the last time he had an episode he came into Manon's room with a butcher knife in his hand and screaming that he will cut his penis because if he can't have a functional one, his brothers won't either."

"What a horrific night," Manon adds.

"Oh, look!" Yonathan screams. "It's Beavis and Butt-Head, kids! You can recognize them by the fact that they're the only people laughing at their jokes."

He drops his bag on the floor and comes to stand next to me, giving me a look that says that this isn't over. I know that, Manon knows that, and nothing could make us happier. It has been a while since we pulled something like this.

"Care to help me prove them wrong, honey?" he asks the flustered young lady.

"I'm engaged." She raises her left hand, pointing with her other one to the huge diamond ring.

"That's not a no."

"It's not a yes, either," she says in a timid, yet determined voice.

"So, a maybe?" He raises one of his dark eyebrows.

"So, a never!" She turns her back to him and resumes walking. "Now, gentlemen, please follow me so I can show you the master bedroom and get this tour done."

Before I can mentally congratulate her for standing up to him, Yon shouts, "You were willing to fuck Manon five minutes ago."

"As you can see, this room is mostly decorated in light tones, since the owner's wife was the one in charge of decorating it and spent several nights here," she says to no one in particular, since all three of us are still in the hallway while she's alone in the bedroom.

"With who?" Yonathan shouts again, as we make our way to where she is.

"Of course, whoever will use the room for the duration of your stay could change things around. As long as it doesn't affect the house's structure or the paintings on the walls, I think you're good," she continues, completely ignoring Yonathan's question.

"This would be perfect for me and Melody!" I say in an excited voice. "It's the only bedroom spacious enough for two people and has its own private bathroom! We could have her beauty products on that vanity, and I can use the desk for reading scripts."

"Non, I definitely need you to find me that doctor. I keep hearing things, like Melody living with us, but that can't be right." Yonathan scoffs, and right when I open my mouth to tell him off, Manon starts talking.

"Yonathan, Melody and baby Temple are a thing, and that's happening whether you like it or not!" He takes a seat on the bed and looks at the woman who is tapping her foot on the floor, a plea written in his eyes. "Could you give us a moment?"

She nods and leaves the room, probably going to the bathroom to try to keep herself from having a mental breakdown after everything that happened since we entered this house.

"Now, the sooner you'll accept that, the faster we can move on with our lives. We can sit here and argue, you can try to pour venom in Lucas's ear, but all you'll manage by doing that is to make him want to get as far away as possible from us. If you're willing to let that happen, well," he shrugs, "I'm not. So, what's it going to be, Yonathan? A life without us or a life with us and Melody?"

Play My Part

"I love it when you just make things seem as simple as that woman's mind," Yonathan replies, pointing with his thumb in the direction his poor victim went earlier. "However, I would like to refresh your memory, since both of you clearly went through a lobotomy on the plane. One," he raises his index finger, "she was fucking married. And not only that, but her ex is one of the most famous gynecologists in the US of A. Don't ask me why a man who sees so much pussy on a daily basis decides to tie himself to Melody's" he shrugs, "but I'm completely against kink shaming, so to each his own."

"You have no fucking idea who he is," I say clenching my jaw. "You can't even begin to imagine what he put her through."

"Why don't you enlighten me, then?"

When I stay quiet, trying to control my breathing and fighting the surge of anger that makes me want to fly back to the US to find that piece of shit and beat him to death, Yon decides it is the best moment to continue. "Let me guess. She wanted the newest Valentino bag and the bad man didn't give her his black Amex?"

Melody confided in me and I know how hard it was for her to utter those words. I don't want to disappoint her, by telling her story to third parties, but I don't think Yonathan would judge her or think less of her if he found out what Bart did to her. Not that it would be possible for him to think even less of her as he does now.

For a second, I consider telling them Melody's secret, but decide against it, because I'm not sure how she will react if she finds out that I couldn't keep it.

"What was it, baby Temple? A new car? A new dress?" Yonathan continues, pissing me off more and more with every word that comes out of his mouth. I've never felt more inclined to beat the shit out of my best friend than I do now. I hate how he belittles her. I hate how he thinks that she's just a spoiled housewife, who only has a job because she got bored of staying at home and hanging out with the other women in their secluded community. If only he fucking knew why she loved her job that much. If he only knew the truth.

"Or maybe is it because the man actually has a career and doesn't fuck her like an animal day in, day out? Is that why she fucked you? Because you're younger and your dick is better than the vibrator she uses on that old, wrinkled, used pussy?"

That does it. I stand up and push him the same way he pushed me in the plane. It's the second time I get in a conflict with him in less than twenty-four hours and I can't wrap my mind around the fact that the man who I called *brother* for so many years is nothing but a vile, fucked-up human being who is not only lacking empathy, but any positive emotion on the spectrum. Maybe he actually is a fucking psychopath.

"If you ever speak like that about her again, I will fucking rip your throat." I grab him by the collar, forcing his back to the wall. "Stop underestimating me, Yonathan. You have absolutely no fucking idea what lengths I would go to for this woman."

He pushes me off him with what seems to be all his strength. I fall with a thud on the bed, my whole body jumping from the mattress from the impact. I don't have a chance to land back because he grabs the hem of my T-shirt while I'm still in midair and throws me to the floor.

"What did I tell you the last time you did something like this, Lucas?" he shouts while grabbing me again, pinning me to the wall. "Did I or did I not tell you that we're fucking done if you ever do this shit again?"

"You did," I roar in his face. "So, I guess there's no better time than now to tell you to go fuck yourself and continue your miserable existence as far away as possible from me."

My jaw hurts from the second I feel his knuckles on it. Feeling a copper taste in my mouth, I give him what I'm sure is a blooded smile, hoping like hell that seeing the proof of what he did will make his vicious blood boil. Maybe there's no other way to cleanse it and make him become a better friend for the poor people who will come into his life from this point on.

He lets me go, covering his mouth with his hands. Even though I still feel the pain from his punch, there's no comparison between that and how happy my soul is to see shock written on his ridiculously beautiful face.

"Now that you got that out of your system, can we talk like normal human beings instead of behaving like cavemen, gentlemen?" Non interrupts the invisible war we're fighting.

"There's no talking, Non," Yonathan says, not dropping my gaze. "Didn't you hear what he said? We are done."

"No!" I scream. "Don't put this shit on me. You were the one who threatened to punish me if I didn't play by your rules, while you weren't willing to respect any fucking rule whatsoever. Not even the ones required by basic common sense."

"I respected every single rule of our friendship," he hisses.

"Oh, is that right?" I mock. "Well, excuse me for missing the memo saying that it's okay to call the woman your brother," I emphasize the last word, "loves a whore!"

"Big words for a small mind," he spits. "Love? What do you know about love, my dear Lucas?" The fact that he went back to calling me *Lucas* doesn't go unnoticed, but I don't give a fuck about that at the moment.

"I may not know a lot, but please don't make a fool of yourself and tell me that you can teach me that, too. You wouldn't know love if it hit you in your fucking forehead," I continue screaming, pulling my hair from its roots in frustration.

"There's a fine line between love and obsession, you fucking delusional imbecile!" he screams back. "You don't love her, you're obsessed with her. The unrequited love that you just want to force and bend to your will. You always dreamed about being with her and now that she gave you another taste of her pussy you think that she is yours. Just fucking wake up, Lucas. She's not yours and she never will be." His voice is so loud that I'm sure our bodyguards are hearing him despite being at the gate, which is four miles away from the mansion. "What your thick skull refuses to understand is that she will dump your sorry ass the second you make her come for four times instead of five! She's nothing but a spoiled cougar and you fell right in her trap!"

"You have no idea what you're talking about!"

"Just shut the fuck up already," he says in a disgusted voice. "I have no interest in hearing your sob story again. I listened to it more times than I can count. And you fucking forgot that. You forgot I," he points to his chest with his index finger, "was the one who wiped your tears when she left you. I was the one who promised you it would get better despite not believing it for a second. I was the one who you turned to when you were just a miserable pile of shit."

"Oh, behold the mighty hero on his fucking white horse," I say, spitting the blood gathering in my mouth on the plush carpet. Fuck that! I'll buy them a more expensive one.

"I never intended to be your hero. You were the one who portrayed me like one."

"You know that's not true," Manon says in a detached voice, lighting a cigarette, standing next to the *no smoking* sign. Guess I'm not the only one destroying this house.

"Oh, thank you for your intervention. It's uncalled for." Yonathan dismisses him.

"And who exactly do you think you're talking to now?" Non asks him. "I'm sorry if I ever let you believe that I'm one of the women you're fucking and that I will allow you talk to me like that."

"Oh, so now you're siding with Lucas?" he says in a disappointed voice. "I should've known better, I guess." He half laughs. "I was a fucking imbecile to believe for a second that you two can actually care about me, right?"

I frown because his words sound completely weird. I cared for him the same as I did for my sister. Hell, I still do, because feelings aren't something written on a blackboard that you can easily erase with your jacket sleeve. But he never seemed to give a fuck if we care about him. He always made me believe that he will be the same with or without me in his life and that he was doing me a favor by sticking with me.

"It was always you two against the world with poor Yonathan just tagging along, right?" he says in a pained voice. "Always pretending like you know better, like you're somehow superior just because you experienced love and affection, even though we all know that it ended up in pain and disappointment."

"What the fuck are you even talking about, Yonathan?" Manon lets out an exhale filled with blue smoke, taking another drag from his cigarette right after. "It was always the *three* of us against the world. The fucked-up boys who fought to become better men. The ones who suffered, who cried, who felt the worst kind of pain. But what you fail to understand is that your pain isn't greater than the one *we* felt. Our pain doesn't get canceled out by yours just because you perceived what you went through as the greatest injustice in the world."

He approaches Yonathan with caution, like you would an animal that came out of the jungle and faced civilization for the first time. And he's not wrong because that's exactly what Yonathan was when he was sixteen. I feel my soul cracking when I remember his life story, but I quickly force that memory away. I'm still angry as fuck because of what he said and the fact that he went through that heartbreaking shit isn't enough to make me forgive him.

"I'm not saying that your life wasn't a nightmare. I'm saying that maybe you should wake up from it and enjoy the dream we are currently living in."
"I can't!" he roars, making me jump, because Manon's thick, soothing voice made the tension easier to bear up until now. "I'm stuck in that fucking nightmare and that's where I will always live! I'm not you, I'm not Lucas, I'm me. And if you don't want to put up with me, just take a lesson from Lucas's book and leave."

"We're not going anywhere," Manon says in a determined voice. "We're here, Yon. We're right there with you in that nightmare, but don't push baby Temple away just because he woke up from it."

"He's more than happy to go and live in the fantasy world he built." Yonathan's voice drops an octave, making me shiver. "He doesn't need us anymore. He used us as a safety net, but now he prefers to free fall!" He straightens up and re-arranges his silk tie. "And I can only thank him for not forcing me to catch him anymore."

He starts to leave, but I know that I can't let him walk out of my life. I'm drawn to him on an inexplicable level, and the connection between us is absolutely unbreakable, no matter how hard he tries to convince me and himself otherwise. We are not blood brothers, we are soul brothers. And, indeed, blood is thicker than water, but both Manon and Yonathan are running through my veins.

"He raped her," I choke, deciding to come clean. I've never lied to them. I've never hidden something from them, and despite the fact that I love Melody more than words can tell, I won't let this love cancel or be greater than the ones that I feel for them. I've wanted her my whole life, but I had them for the same duration. And there's a great difference between wanting something and having something else. "He beat her close to death! He threatened her, hurt her, he did every single hideous thing a man could do to a woman."

I raise my chin and look at both of them. Manon looks like he's on the verge of crying, while Yonathan looks angrier than I feel.

"Say what now?" my blue-eyed brother asks, his voice carrying a trace of denial.

"I don't want to say it again." I swallow back the lump in my throat. "I can't."

Everybody falls silent, Manon's long exhale being the only sound that cracks the unbearable quiet around us.

After what has been a minute, but felt like a year, Yonathan asks me,

Play My Part

"And what are you going to do about it, baby Temple?"

"Honestly? I want to kill him." I shrug because it's true. "But given the fact that I'm neither an assassin, nor a vigilante, I want to find the legal means to keep him as far away as possible from her. From us."

"She does have a restraining order against him, right?" Non asks, hope filling his voice. "That should be enough."

I shake my head in disappointment and look at both of them, my chin still touching my chest.

"It's a temporary one. She isn't ready to tell the world about this, so she barely could get this one, and it expired anyway, now that her divorce trial is over." I blow out a breath. "She'll kill me if she knows I told you this. But I need to help her. I need it both for her and for me."

"I'll call my lawyer. He'll know how to deal with this kind of shitshow," Yonathan deadpans, going out of the room. "And before I forget, if you ever tell a woman that I'm suffering from erectile dysfunction again I will punch you harder!"

I let out a laugh and give him a questioning look.

"We're fine." He nods. "We've never been better."

I swear I see a shadow of a smile on his lips, but it goes away as fast as it came.

Chapter 11
Melody

Shutting down my laptop after sending Charlie the agenda for the upcoming week, I exhale and bury my face in my palms, trying to wrap my mind around everything that happened in the past five days. And it's a fucking lot to take in.

An image of Bart's sadistic smile when our divorce was finally pronounced comes to mind, but I quickly send it away, remembering how I met Manon and Yonathan in that coffee shop. What were the odds? Close to zero. Maybe Lucas was right when he said that fate is stubborn enough to always bring us together, no matter how far we try to stay away from one another.

And God only knows how much I tried to keep him only as a memory and how many times I had to stop myself from reaching out to him. I didn't lie when I told him I missed him. I missed him so fucking much, more with every day that passed. But we never stood a chance, and I'm not completely sure that we do now.

I slept with him. I had sex with a man whom I haven't seen for so much time, and I don't know what jumping in bed with him two hours after we met again makes me. A part of me tells me that it was the right thing to do and that it would've happened sooner or later. I needed to sleep with him again, not because I needed validation or because I needed a confirmation that *I still got it*. I needed to sleep with him because I needed to remember how it feels to have sex with somebody that actually gives a fuck about making their partner feel good. I needed to sleep with him because no matter how hard I tried to deny it, that soft spot I always had for him turned into lust, then into something greater than I can describe.

Do I love Lucas Temple? Maybe I do. I know that I've always loved him in some sort of shape or form. Because what is love if not a piece of clay that two people mold together, turning into what seems fitting at the moment?

I slept with him and I can't find it in me to regret it. I asked myself if I will ever be able to forgive myself, only to realize that there's nothing to forgive. I'm not married anymore, so I didn't cheat on anybody. And even if I were to still be married to Bart, he isn't a sweet, devoted man whose trust I would've taken advantage of. I don't have a caring husband whom I took for granted. I was married to an animal who took every opportunity he had to belittle me, make me believe that I'm not worthy of unadulterated love, and fucking destroyed me.

I decide to try and get some sleep. I'm completely exhausted, since I still didn't manage to get used to the night becoming the day and vice versa. The eight-hour difference between Romania and Austin, US is taking its toll on me and even though I feel depleted, my brain seems to refuse to shut down. It keeps playing on repeat the same bad memories it usually does, refusing to enjoy how much I found pleasure in Lucas kissing me during his breaks in the dark corners of the sets, where nobody could see us. How every time he had a heartwarming line, he looked at me for a second before delivering it. Even if he had to take tens of takes, he did the same thing, making me smile and making it hard for me to focus on doing my job.

I can't seem to enjoy what's happening to me in the present because of everything I did or others did to me in the past. And I start wondering if this isn't another shape of the slow, painful death Lucas talked about on our way here.

Everything is quiet around me. This hotel, despite being populated by most of the film crew, is always quiet during the night. Because people go out for drinks and dance their worries away, while I stay here, all by myself, staring at the white ceiling and thinking. Just thinking, letting the silence speak volumes. I let the silence envelop my brain, like a long-lost lover, hugging it and kissing every single part of it. And I succeed. The quiet moment, when even my mind is silent and doesn't judge me for my conflicted feelings, is interrupted by a knock on the door. I frown because I didn't order room service, and it's too late for someone to come and change the sheets.

I don't want to get out of bed. I want to lie here for a couple of minutes more to take advantage of this break my mind is kind enough to grant me. But when the intensity of the knocks grows, I sigh and realize I have no other choice than go and see who wants something from me at nine p.m. on a Wednesday.

When I open it, I feel my jaw falling to the floor because Yonathan was the last person I expected to see standing on my doorstep. Looking impeccable as always, dressed in a black three-piece suit, his dark hair looking like somebody spent hours combing it to perfection, and his blue eyes piercing me from behind his black-framed glasses, he analyzes me from head to toe.

"Shorts and a ripped T-shirt? Who are you? Britney Spears before her meltdown?" he mocks.

I slam the door in his face because while I was forced to tolerate him during our flight, if the sadistic imbecile came here only because he was bored and had no one to pick a fight with, then he can go fuck himself. Unfortunately, my plan fails because Yonathan puts his foot on the threshold, slamming the door to the wall.

"You almost broke the door from its hinges!" I shout.

"Yeah, that's how strong and cool I am! I am man, hear me roar!" he says in his classic sarcastic tone. "Now start packing." He gets inside the room, grimacing when he sees it. "I didn't know the staff sleeps in the stables. You live and you learn, I guess."

I gasp when he goes to the dresser, picks up my bag, and starts throwing my clothes inside it. It takes me a minute to recover and when I do, I take the bag from his hand and take a step back.

"What do you want, Yonathan?"

He offers me a pitied, yet patronizing look before speaking.

"Me? The world and everything in it." He keeps throwing my clothes on the bed like he's a robot who was programmed to do that task. "It's Lucas who wants you living with us."

"So what? You suddenly decided to be his lapdog and bring the stick to your owner, hoping he'll play with you more and throw it away again and again?"

"Oh, how I would love for him to throw you away." He laughs mockingly. "However, the moron lives under the impression that he loves you, so I find myself in the uncomfortable situation of having to help you. Oh, how the mighty have fallen." He sighs, crossing his arms on his chest.

"He loves me?" I ask in a choked voice.

"Oh, is this the part where you play the virgin whore and I'm supposed to fuck your ass or your throat?"

"What the fuck does that even mean?" I mirror his stance and give him a hateful look.

"That you pretend you're shocked he loves you, and I say *But, Melody! Of course he loves you! How could he not? Such a lucky guy!*" He rolls his eyes and pinches the bridge of his nose, making his glasses go up on his forehead.

If this man would've had a soul, he would be perfection on a stick. Unfortunately, the only way I can see him is as a rotten heart dressed up in church clothes. Such a shame. "Now, can you please pack your shit, so we can leave this hotel already? I don't have all night. I mean, I do, but not for you! I have a redhead and a brunette salivating on my sheets as we speak. Don't inconvenience me more than necessary, Melody."

"Inconvenience you? You are the walking definition of an inconvenience, Yonathan. You barged in here like you fucking own the place." I stomp my foot on the floor and the movement doesn't go unnoticed by Yonathan, judging by the chuckle he lets out.

"If I buy the hotel, would it make you move faster?" he challenges, cocking an eyebrow.

"Get the fuck out of my room," I say in an angry voice, putting my discarded T-shirts back in the dresser. "I don't want to deal with pieces of shit like you and my ex-husband ever in my life. And if that means I can't live with my boyfriend until we all are fucking done here, then so be it."

"I'm nothing like Bart Trello," he says in a calm, detached voice.

"You're exactly like Bart Trello," I retort.

"Well," he darkly chuckles, "If I'm exactly like him, then I guess I should rape, beat, and gaslight you! When would you be available to start?" he asks in a condescending voice.

"How do you…?"

"Don't you fucking dare compare me again with that piece of trash of your ex-husband," he says before I get to finish my question, "because while I am a lot of things, a man who physically abuses women is not one of them. Got it?"

I give him a single nod. I don't know if he expects me to apologize, but if that's the case, he should be ready to wait for a long, long time. I don't know if I should believe what he just said, but something in me tells me that there's more to Yonathan than he lets on.

"Good girl. Now, chop-chop. The clock is ticking and those tight pussies are waiting to wrap my cock."

"Why are you so crude?" I ask him with genuine curiosity.

"Why shouldn't I be?"

"I don't know, don't you want to be a good person?"

"No," he deadpans.

"You're not bad either," I offer.

"Thank you, random character from the *Desperate Housewives*. Are you done?"

"Talking or packing?" I laugh.

"Both."

"Did Lucas tell you?" I ask after a long pause.

"Yes." Not a single word more.

"I asked him not to."

"And I asked him to."

"If this is another game of yours, just to show me that Lucas does what you tell him to, then you can already stop. I know that's the truth," I shrug, "and I'm not planning on stopping him from doing that."

"You're talking like you could actually be able to."

"Maybe I would," I resume packing and taking out the T-shirts I just put back, "but we'll never find out. I promise you, Yonathan, I'm not against your friendship and I don't want to see it ruined. Despite our differences, I know how much you three care about each other."

He nods his head, and I take that as a *thank-you*. Because that's the furthest his gratitude can go.

"Are you going to change?" he finally asks me. I don't think he's really interested in my outfit, but he just needs to go back to his comfort zone, where we talk about shallow things.

"I take it you're not a Britney Spears fan?" I laugh.

"Define *fan*." He smiles, and this time it's genuine. I don't know why, but knowing that I made this man smile does something to my heart. It makes me feel good about myself. It makes me proud of myself.

"I don't know, were you obsessed with her at some point?"

"Define *obsessed*." He smiles again and I smile back, closing the zipper to my bag.

"How should I know?" I drag my suitcases from behind the curtains and place them in front of the bed. "I was never obsessed with someone."

"But Lucas was. Is," he says in the same cold tone from earlier, and this is when I know that whatever temporary peace we made just went back to being a war.

"Most probably," I whisper.

"Listen to me, Melody, and listen to me good. I don't like you. I don't like you for Lucas, and I don't like you in general," he says, clenching his jaw and taking his glasses off. "I think you'll only bring him heartache and I find you weak and terribly lacking a spine. I have this gut feeling that you're keeping things from him, things that will only bring him heartbreak and will make his pain reach unknown levels!" He raises his hands, letting out a frustrated sigh. "But if my brother is stupid enough to fight for you, then I'm right next to him on the battlefield. However, mark my words, Melody, if you do something, anything that will make him suffer, I will pay you back tenfold. I have no fear, no filters, and no fucking care in the world. I've had enough of seeing him suffering and he had enough of suffering to last for two lifetimes."

I scoff in dismissal, trying my best to not let myself be intimidated by him and his presence. I start walking to the door and I'm surprised when he takes the bag from my hand and picks up my suitcases, too. I really can't understand this man.

"Just for the record, that goes both ways, Yonathan," I say, walking down the hallway, ignoring the scowl on his face. "If you ever hurt him again, I will do my best to end you. Don't underestimate the connections I have and the power the media has over every single famous person. You might be a respected actor today, but it won't take me more than fifteen minutes to end your career. So you'd better not test me either."

He gives me a different look this time. I wouldn't say his eyes are filled with pride or admiration, but they're not full of hate either, so I'll consider that as progress.

When we go inside the elevator, he pushes the button for the lowest level of the parking lot and takes out his phone.

"There are going to be three gray SUVs. You'll get on the backseat of the one in the middle and your bags will be in the last car's trunk. Any questions from the audience?" He smiles coldly.

"Is this all necessary? We're pretty close to your mansion."

"Welcome to the glamorous life, dearly beloved. Enjoy the party."

The ride to their mansion takes half an hour. Situated in the northern suburbs of Romania's capital, its garden is bigger than most parks from the city Lucas and I grew up in. Even though it's dark outside, there are so many streetlights that it's easy to notice all the details on every flower around us. It looks like Heaven, but I'm not sure I'm ready to step inside yet. Walking on the path that leads to the mansion I abruptly stop, trying to realize what the fuck I am actually doing. Yonathan takes a few more steps before noticing I'm not walking next to him anymore and without turning to look at me he says,

"It's now or never, Melody. You either walk inside the house, own the shitstorm you started and do whatever needs to be done, consequences be damned, or," he takes a deep inhale before continuing, "I tell Lucas you refused to come and that you changed your mind. I will pay you double of what you you'll earn in these six months and you can go back home. It would sting a bit, but I will help him get over it. Unlike you, I've always done it and I won't stop now."

When I don't answer him, he resumes walking, waving a hand in the air.

"Being always right is so fucking disturbing. I knew from the second I first heard about you that you're pathetically weak. Good riddance, Melody. Have a fantastic life."

"Wait!" I scream. "I never said that I don't want to get inside the house. I just needed a second, for fuck's sake. I need a second to realize what's happening to me. My life is moving on fast forward, twist after twist, and I don't know how to keep up."

Finally, he turns around and looks into my eyes.

"Do you want him or not, Melody?"

"I do," I whisper. "I want him in so many ways, but..."

"But nothing," he hisses. "If you want him, then go in there and have him. It's as simple as that. I don't understand what the fuck is your problem. Are you suffering from Stockholm syndrome? Did that man train you so well that you'd rather sleep in his doghouse than in Lucas's palace?"

I open my mouth to say something, but he raises his index finger. "I know that sometimes the Hell you know is more comfortable than the unknown territory that Heaven is. But if these two worlds coexist, wouldn't you like to spend eternity in pure bliss rather than being burned constantly in the largest cauldron?"

"I would, Yonathan," I sigh, "I most definitely would. It's just a lot to take in, that's all. I have known Lucas since he was a child," I sigh, "innocent, pure, everything I wasn't. And I just wish he would've stayed the same. I wish I could've found a way to keep him from going through so much. Instead, I only made him suffer more. And I don't know how to forgive myself for that."

"Children shouldn't be protected at all costs, Melody," he says, piercing me with his blue eyes. "I think it's better to let them know as early as possible that the world is shit, disappointing, and unfair. They need to know that they are expected to fucking fight even for the smallest amount of happiness."

I frown, taking into consideration what he said, but I can't agree with him. Children need to live a carefree life until they're hit by the reality of adulthood. They need to keep their innocence, to be happy and not traumatized by the events happening in their parents' lives. They have plenty of time to learn how sadness feels, how disappointment guts you, and how crying can be cathartic.

I decide not to answer him, choosing to start walking toward the house instead. I have to agree with Yonathan on one thing. This is a monumental step I'm taking. Me walking inside that house means accepting a higher commitment to Lucas than what we have now and I know, I fucking know we will need to fight tooth and nail to finally be able to live in peace.

Play My Part

Maybe we will succeed, or maybe we won't. Maybe Bart will kill me at some point for leaving him and making him look like a fool. Maybe Lucas will decide I'm bringing too much drama on his doorstep and he won't be able to forgive me. Maybe, maybe, fucking maybe.

But, deep down inside me, I know that both he and I deserve a chance. And how can we ask the universe to give us one if I wouldn't? So I will step inside that house and I'll do my best to remember how to be a fighter and how to take what I want from this world.

"Just remember what I told you," Yonathan says, climbing the four marble steps that lead to the huge wooden door.

When he pushes it and walks inside, I grit my teeth and nod to myself. I follow his suit, gasping when I see the huge hallway leading to the even bigger living room illuminated by crystal chandeliers. There are paintings on every wall around me and all the furniture except the huge yellow couch in the center is brown and made out of wood. I feel like Yonathan wasn't exaggerating when he said that Lucas lived inside a palace, because this is exactly what this house is.

"I would've chosen a smaller one." The sweet, yet masculine voice that drives me mad says from behind me. "It didn't feel like home at all when I walked inside a couple of days ago."

"And now?" I turn around, and as soon as I do I get lost in his dark, green eyes.

"And now I feel more at home than I ever did in my life," he chokes out. "I've missed you so much."

He wraps his hands around me, holding me to his chest. "I've missed you so, so much, beautiful Melody."

"You just saw me a couple of hours ago." I laugh.

"But a couple of hours ago you weren't in my arms, but talking to Manon about his plans for the future." He laughs back. "How did you get here?"

"Your bestie kidnapped me from my hotel room." I playfully roll my eyes and hug him tighter, inhaling his scent and imprinting it on my brain.

"I never got to thank him for that."

He gently pushes me back and looks at me with shock written all over his face.

"Yonathan brought you here?"

"Didn't you ask him to?"

He frowns, looking around the room. I turn around to see what caught his attention, and I notice both of his friends looking at something on the laptop that sits on Yonathan's lap.

I squint my eyes, trying to see what's written on the document they have open, but the letters are too small for me to be able to read from such a distance. When Manon notices that we are looking at them, he quickly closes the lid, making Yonathan jolt.

"You almost hit my fingers, Non," he tells his friend while wiping his glasses. "My hands are needed later on."

"I'm sure you'll find other things to insert in those women's pussies." He laughs. "Be creative, Yon."

"You know? I always had this fantasy of fucking somebody with one of my awards. I think it would be a boost of self-esteem to say the least." His voice is so serious that an image of him doing exactly that comes to mind, and I shudder.

"Melody, welcome," Manon says, louder than necessary. "I would say it's our humble home, but this monstrosity is anything but humble." He grimaces.

"You don't like it?" I don't understand what's not to like. Sure, I wouldn't spend the rest of my life here, because it's too flashy and too cold to be called a home, but I could see myself spending my holidays here.

"I'm not a fan of luxury," he replies. "I come from poverty, but my childhood, despite being eventful, was the happiest period of my life. Well, some of it at least." he looks outside and I can notice how he slowly gets lost in the memories. And again, I can't help but realize how much we are alike.

Play My Part

I know that haunted look. I know those glassy eyes every time you think what would've happened if you did better. If you chose differently. If you walked on another path. I take a few steps, kneeling in front of him, making all three men give me surprised looks.

"I know," I tell him, taking his hands. "I live in a similar world, too."

He doesn't say anything, but his look says more than words can tell. He feels understood and seen. I know that his two best friends are always willing to help, but neither of them can fully understand neither him, nor me. It takes one to know one. It takes being a victim haunted by your past to know a victim haunted by his own.

"Maybe one day we can talk about these worlds? See if we can help each other escape?" he asks in a hopeful voice that would've brought me to my knees if I wasn't on them already.

"I would love that," I whisper. "I would love to help you escape."

"Okay, Michael Scofield and Lincoln Burrows, playtime's over." Yonathan puts his hand on Non's knee and stands up.

"Did you just make a *Prison Break* reference?" I ask him.

"I did. I don't know why you seem so surprised about it."

"Didn't take you for a guy who spends his free time watching trending series, that's all." I stand up, going back to Lucas's arms and kissing his cheek.

"And I didn't take you as a woman who can function without Prozac, yet here we are."

"At least he's not calling me a whore anymore," I whisper in Lucas's ear. "Although I'm not sure if mentally unstable is worse or better."

"Better." He laughs. "Much, much better."

He takes my hand and leads me down the huge hallway with doors on both its left and its right. I feel like we've been walking for days and we still haven't gotten through half of it. Besides the fact that it's absolutely enormous, all the portraits on the wall give me a feeling of being watched, and not in a good way. I don't know who was responsible for decorating this house, but I think they could've done better. Much, much better.

Finally, we reach a hardwood black door that Lucas can barely pull. When I get inside the room, I finally feel that I can breathe, seeing that this is as modestly decorated as possible. Well, if you can consider a four-poster bed as modest.

"Do you like it, Nightingale?" he asks me, hugging me from behind. "It's ours if you do."

"I love it, Luc." I smile. "How did you manage to make it so… feminine?" I point to the beautiful vanity that's decorated with all sorts of stickers in the shape of stars under the small bulbs that illuminate the room in white light.

"I didn't do anything. This is how the owner's wife decorated it. I didn't want to change anything because I dreamed about this moment as soon as I stepped inside this room. Also, Manon said the colors go well together." he smiles back, making me feel like I'm melting. "Since he's also a painter, he knows more than me about how purple and yellow go together, but purple with green is blasphemy."

"I would love to see his paintings one day!" I say, cupping his face and kissing his soft lips. "I think that's a very healthy way to let out your demons. Also, a good opportunity to know more about him."

"You like him," he says without a trace of jealousy in his voice.

"I do." I nod. "I feel connected to him somehow. Like our souls met each other before. I don't know how to explain it better."

"But ours met before, right?" Now his voice does have a small shadow of jealousy in it.

"I don't know about before," I whisper, "but I know they never let go of each other since they met."

Apparently, I gave the right answer to his question based on the passion he puts into the kiss he's giving me. He kisses me like I'm an oasis in the desert and he's a dying man who lost all hope. I wrap my legs around his waist and kiss him back, pouring all my longing and love in the kiss.

Play My Part

"I missed you," he tells me again, and this time I realize what he meant. He didn't miss seeing me. He missed being with me without any restrictions.

"I missed you, too, Lucas. So, so much."

"I want to be inside you so badly, beautiful Melody," he pants between kisses.

"And what are you waiting for, Lucas?"

He nods and puts his hands on my ass, making me grind against the bulge I feel through his jeans. He groans and shoves his tongue farther in my mouth.

The madness and the passion come together in the hungry kiss we share. We both put in all our regret, all the longing, and all the moments we didn't get to share in so many years.

When I take my hand from his face and grab his cock through the material, rubbing it, he breaks the kiss and gives me a look filled with lust.

"I think we should take it slow," he says in a pained voice.

"Why?" I ask, feeling braver than I felt in so many ears. "Do you regret what happened on the airplane?"

"Do I regret it?" he laughs. "I jacked off thinking about it. Twice."

It's my turn to laugh and playfully shove his shoulder, swallowing when I feel his muscles through the green T-shirt he's wearing.

"I wasn't joking, Melody," he whispers in my ear. "But I want to take it slow because I don't want you to be scared of me. I don't want to make you go to that fucking dark place again."

"It's not your fault," I say in a serious voice. "I don't think it's mine either. I would like to blame it on fate, but how could I talk bad about fate when that's what brought me back to you?" I lower my face, licking the left side of his neck, slowly grazing my teeth on it. "What brought you back to me. And I'll be damned if I ever let you go again. I need you, Lucas. I need you now and I will need you as long as you'll have me."

He closes his eyes and lets his head fall on the wall behind him.

Swallowing, he says,

"I need you more than my next breath, Mel. But, still…"

"Still nothing." I put my index finger to his lips. "I want to be yours, Lucas Temple. I made that decision when I walked inside this house and I won't change my mind. If you'll have me, I want to be yours," I plead.

"You were always fucking mine, Melody." He kisses me like my mouth is the answer to all the questions humanity ever asked. And I kiss him the same way. I don't know how I could've ever believed that Lucas and I are anything but two halves of the same whole, two pieces that fit together in life's puzzle.

After several minutes, I take my lips from his, gasping for air.

"I don't want to take it slow, Lucas. I want to be yours, even if there are still things between us. But now? Now I need you to fuck me like I was never fucked before."

He lets me go and rushes to the door, locking it. I start taking off my clothes, but he puts his hand on mine, stopping me.

"I want you to savor this, Melody," he whispers, gently biting my chin. "I want you to enjoy every second of it. But trust me, Nightingale, I will fuck you like a madman. I will make that pussy throb and clench, and I will make you come as many times as you want." He continues drawing circles with his tongue on my neck, making a small moan escape from my mouth. "I'm going to obey every single command you give me, only to have the chase of seeing you come undone. I will do every single thing you want me to the second you let it fall from your beautiful lips. You know why, my beautiful queen?"

"I don't." I moan loudly when he takes my breast in his hand, pinching my nipple through my bra.

"Because I'm fucking obsessed with you, Melody Byers. And because you deserve to be fucked properly by a man who was always yours."

Chapter 12
Melody

"Do you want me, beautiful Melody?" Lucas asks me in a raspy voice, getting down on his knees.

"I think you already know the answer to that question." I let out a shaky exhale when I feel the tip of his fingers grazing my calves.

"Maybe I don't." He stops moving, giving me a questioning look from below. "Or maybe I do, but I need to hear you say it."

"I want you," I say the words so fast I don't think anybody else would've understood them. But he did. He always understands me.

He resumes moving his fingers all over my legs, teasing me, making my blood boil and my skin too tight to hold everything I feel. My breaths become shallow, feeling like a pair of hands is squeezing my lungs and I whimper when his thumb grazes the back of my knee.

"Please, Lucas," I barely manage to get out.

"What are you asking for, Nightingale?" he says in a low voice. "I will do anything you want me to. God, I can't wait to make you mine."

Suddenly, a feeling of dread fills my whole body. I don't know what caused it, but I know I need to get out of here as fast as I can. I can't do this. I can't fucking do this. I just can't!

I turn around and fumble with the lock on the doorknob. I'm too slow because one of his hands is pushing the door, and with the other one he grabs my chin and forces me to look at him.

I hate the frown on his face and the way his lower lip trembles because of rage or sadness, I don't know. I was never good at reading people, and apparently, I still suck at it since I can't figure out what the man I'm slowly but surely falling desperately in love with wants to say.

"What's wrong?" he asks in a sweet voice. "What did I do to upset you?"

I take lying to him into consideration for a second, but I know that would be wrong. I won't lie to the man who showed me nothing but kindness and who for some reason wants to fight for me. Not more than I already do, anyway. One lie is enough to keep us apart and another one would only lead us to ruin.

Lucas deserves better from me and, to some extent, I still think that Lucas deserves better *than* me. The fact that he chose me after all the shit I put him through and after bringing so much emotional baggage on his doorstep doesn't make me feel lucky. It makes me feel like I don't deserve it and that it's a matter of seconds until he and everybody else will share Yonathan's opinion. That I'm not worthy of him. That I don't deserve a happy life with Lucas because I need to reap what I sow. And what I sow is deceiving him for more times than I can count.

"I'm scared, Lucas," I say, fighting my tears. "I'm so fucking scared."

I lean against the wall and close my eyes. Clenching and unclenching my fists, I continue.

"I'm scared to be with you because I'm not able to give you what you need. I'm terrified of the thought that this will break us more than getting us closer." I pause, trying to structure the thoughts that are running around my head, screaming and wailing. "I'm scared that me moving here will change everything between us and I'm terrified of what the future holds," I say, looking into his eyes that express so much pain it would bring anybody to their knees.

"I have so many ghosts, Lucas. They're haunting me every waking hour." I swallow and grab my hair from its roots with both of my hands. "And I'm afraid that if we do this, there will be no way of keeping them from haunting you, too."

"And what if I open my door and dare them to try and scare me?" he asks me in a shaky voice.

"You don't want that, Lucas," I whisper. "There are some things that I would like to keep to myself and not share them with you."

He takes two steps back and it's the first time I see hate swimming in his eyes. My heart breaks yet again knowing that I hurt him for the thousandth time in this life, but after I left a piece of myself with Bart, I'm not sure I can fully open up to anybody on this planet. I don't want to open the pages of the book my tired soul has written over the years. I just want to keep them buried deep inside me because erasing them turned out impossible.

"You know what? You're right," he finally says after a long pause. "You don't need to tell me anything." He walks toward the other side of the room, looking to the beautiful garden. Half of his face is illuminated by the moon while the other half is covered by the dark. He was a beautiful child, but he grew up to be the most handsome man I've ever seen.

"I had many dreams throughout the years, Melody. I fulfilled most of them because I was determined and I worked fucking hard to turn them into reality! But do you know what is the only dream I didn't get to see happening?" he asks in an angry, yet calm voice.

"I don't."

"The one where we trust each other. The one where I first put a ring on that finger. Then a wedding band. Then I put a baby in you. Two babies. Three, four, five, as many babies as you fucking want!" he screams. "The one where we're happy, where you choose *me*. Where it's just us, living the best life in our home in the countryside. The one where I cook breakfast and you feed *my* child."

"I'm sorry." I try to get closer to him, but he raises a hand, signaling for me to stay away. This time I do manage to read him.

"I," he screams, "was the one who told you to take it slow! A fucking minute ago I told you that I don't want to make you feel uncomfortable and you," he points his index finger in my direction, "were the one who said that you chose me and that you want this. Did you lie when you told me that, Melody?"

"I would never lie about that," I scream back. "You have no fucking idea how huge this feels for me. The risks that I'm taking. The consequences I'll have to face if somebody else other than your friends find out about us. And you don't even care about that. You only care about the final dream becoming a reality. Congratulations, Lucas. You finally managed to cross everything from your bucket list. Hoor-fucking-ay!"

"I don't care?" he roars. "I fucking punched my brother for you."

"You don't even have a brother. Your only sibling is your sister, Lucas."

"Oh, right. My sister. How could I have ever forgotten about her?" he mocks. "My sister who doesn't give a fuck about me or about my well-being since the moment she left the fucking continent. My sister, who calls me on my birthdays just to make sure I'm still alive. My sister, who moved to the fucking United Kingdom without even asking me how I feel about it. You're wrong, Melody," he says in a bitter tone, "I used to have a sister. Now I have a fading memory and two brothers for whom I would die if they would ask me to. No questions asked, no advice needed. I would fucking die for them and yet I almost lost them because I wanted *you*."

"That's not fair," I say in a determined voice. "Your sister loves you. And the reason you fought with Yonathan isn't me. You fought with him because he's a narcissistic sociopath who eats cruelty for breakfast."

"You don't know shit about my sister, Melody, and don't pretend you do. You haven't talked to her in years, so for all you know she might be dead." He half laughs. "And don't forget to thank the narcissistic sociopath for calling his lawyer to find a way to keep fucking Bart as far away from you as possible."

My knees buckle so hard that I can't stand anymore. I take a seat on the cold wooden floor, trying to wrap my mind around what Lucas just told me. Why the fuck would the villain in my story suddenly decide to play the hero? What would motivate a man like Yonathan Friedmann to do a selfless grand gesture like this? Or maybe it wasn't selfless.

"What does he want in return?" I ask Lucas in a cold voice. "There's no way he did this because he decided that he wants to be a good person all of a sudden."

"He didn't do it for you." Lucas shrugs. "He did it for me. He did it because, as always, he was there to help me when nobody else was." He sighs. "I do want you, Melody! I never had a fucking second thought about that. It was always you!"

He turns around completely, looking me dead in the eye, and if I wasn't already sitting, I would've fallen to the ground when I saw that look in his eyes. "It was always you who was walking in my dreams, even the ones I had when I wasn't sleeping. It was always you who I imagined having a family with, and it was always you who I imagined waking up next to."

He sits next to me and takes my hand, interlocking our fingers. "But I need you to know that I will *never* give up on either Manon or Yonathan. Not even for you. So, if you can't accept that," he looks at our hands, "then I guess this is where our story ends. Because there's only one deal breaker for me and this is it." He goes back to looking at me, a silent plea written on his face.

"You don't have to choose, Lucas," I whisper, dragging my body closer to his. "I would never put you in that position."

He gives me a simple nod, relief clearly visible on his face. I smile and I can't help myself. I kiss his stubbled cheek, inhaling his scent until my lungs are finally filled back with oxygen.

"And about what you said earlier," he continues. "I want to know all your secrets, but I don't want to rush you." He cups my face, his thumb following the outline of my lips. "I want to find out another thing about you every day. I want you to write me a note every day with something from your past, so I can learn more about you." He brings his face closer to my ear, tucking the wild strands of my hair behind it, before whispering,

"I want you to be my queen and rule over the world with your king. Our world. The one we will both create according to our hopes, dreams, and hidden wishes."

"That sounds beautiful." I nod. "I think I would like that."

"I want to bring you so much pleasure, my beautiful Melody." He bites my earlobe, making me feel like thousands of volts are going through my body. "And you will be the one taking it from me."

I look at him and frown because I don't understand what he means by that. He gives me a smile that makes my stomach flutter and my muscles relax.

"Tell me what to do, Nightingale," he whispers, grazing my lips with his. "Anything you want, anything you need, I'll do it. My body is your tool, so use me for making yourself feel alive and give those ghosts a chance to rest."

"Okay!" I exhale.

"Be brave, my queen. Use your words and let your man make you come so hard you won't be able to remember your own name." He moans right before he kisses me slowly and deliberately.

"I liked it when you went down on me." I feel my cheeks turning all shades of red. "I really liked that"

He lies on his back on the floor after taking off his T-shirt, and he slowly drags me until my knees are next to his face.

"I can't fucking wait to taste this sweet pussy of yours again." His voice drops down an octave and his eyes suddenly darken. "Sit on my face, Melody."

"What do you mean?" I ask, trying to figure out what exactly I am supposed to do.

"I mean," he grabs my waist and lifts me up like I weigh nothing, making me straddle his chest, "put that pretty pussy on my face and grind on my tongue until you'll fill my mouth with your cum."

I moan, hearing those dirty words coming out of his month, ashamed of how aroused they make me. I look at him for a second and I see the same hunger in his eyes, like a predator who is ready to feast on the poor animal he prayed on.

I lower myself a bit and lift my dress until my panties are visible. He lifts his head off the floor and inhales deeply, moaning when his nose reaches my clit. With his index finger, he drags my panties to the side, leaving me exposed. The cold air I feel on my sensitive skin makes my pussy clench around nothing, begging to be filled. I don't remember being so turned on in my life.

"Be braver, Mel," he pleads. "I want your pussy all over my mouth and my nose, so I can inhale and taste you at the same time."

"Okay!"

"Okay!" He gives me an encouraging smile and that's all I need for gathering up the courage to lower my body completely. The second I do, I feel his tongue on my clit, flicking it in rapid movements and I moan his name. I can't help but to start moving my lower body at the same pace his tongue moves all over my pussy, his own moans muffled by my skin. He looks at me with hooded eyes and there's so much passion, so much desire in them, that I can't look away.

My movements are more rapid now and I feel the orgasm building in my stomach taking over all my senses.

"I need to come, Lucas. Make me come on your tongue, please," I whimper.

He groans and his tongue goes to my lips and then to my slit. When I feel his tongue inside me and his nose on my clit, I come so hard that I can see my cum dribbling on his chin and his throat. And he doesn't stop. He keeps fucking me with his tongue while I'm climaxing. And even after I gave him all I had to give, he keeps feasting on my pussy like he can't get enough.

"Fuck, Lucas. I don't know what I'm feeling, but it's so good. Please don't stop." I beg and he obliges. I close my eyes and I shiver when my brain pushes forward one of my many fantasies with him. I feel guilty for wanting that on some level, but then I remember what he said earlier. So I bite my lip and gather the courage to say the words out loud.

"I want to come on your face again," I say. I feel his hum of approval traveling from my pussy to my stomach. "But this time I want to do it while watching you stroke your cock!"

His tongue is still inside me when he nods eagerly and I feel like I can come again only from seeing how quickly and enthusiastically he agreed with my suggestion. I know now that I don't need to put any filter on my thoughts, not that I could, anyway. I can tell him whatever I want and I'm sure that he will happily do it for me.

The idiot lives under the impression that he loves you. Yonathan's words come to mind when I force my knees to stop shaking so I can lift myself up enough to turn around. Funny, I live under the impression that I love him, too.

He wipes my cum from his face and neck with his left hand and then he turns it for me to see.

"Such a messy girl," he teases. "I'm going to use this sweet cum as lube while stroking my cock for you. Are you ready to watch my cock getting harder for you while I'm feasting on your pretty pussy, my beautiful nightingale?"

"Do it," I breathlessly moan. "I want to see you palming your thick cock while you're eating my greedy, wet pussy."

"Your wish is my command, my queen." That's all he says before moving his hand down, lifting his hips so he can drag his sweatpants and boxers lower. I gasp when I see how hard he is for me. The purple crown and thick vein traveling from his dick to the base of his pelvis make my mouth water and I promise myself that one day I will be brave enough to ask him to fuck my throat while I'll be the one rubbing my clit until I make a puddle under me.

I feel his tongue inside me exactly when his fist wraps around his cock. His tongue and his hand move at the same pace, making me feel like

Play My Part

he's fucking me while putting on a show for me. Only for me.

"Fuck, that's so hot." I moan, taking off my dress and bra and throwing them to the floor next to us. I grab my nipples between my index finger and thumb, pinching them harder with every stroke of his tongue. "Faster," I urge, bucking my hips shamelessly, my ass covering his entire face.

I don't know which one of us moans louder now. We are a mess of sweat, whimpers, and moans. Seeing his precum leaking from the head of his dick and mixing with my cum from my earlier orgasm is making me even wetter and I can feel another orgasm slowly building.

"Faster. Please, Lucas, go faster," I say again and Lucas obliges. I pinch my nipples harder, rolling them to the side and then palming my breasts to soothe the pain. I repeat the movement for several times, not being able to take my eyes from that perfect cock that is now fucking his large fist. He can't control his movements more than I can, both of our bodies shaking from the absolute pleasure we're feeling.

His tongue is all over my pussy now. He licks my lips, my clit, and from time to time it goes inside me so deep that his lower lip is touching my clit and his upper one is close to my puckered hole. Another idea comes to mind and yet again I can't stop the words from spilling from my mouth.

"I want to feel your tongue in my ass, Lucas. Fuck, please do it."

"Fuck," he screams, taking his mouth from my pussy. "I'm gonna come if I do that, Melody," he whines.

"No," I say, looking at him over my shoulder. "Don't come anywhere else other than inside me, Lucas."

He frowns, a question written all over his face, and I smile, still feeling like I'm living in a dream.

"I need this, Luc! I need it so fucking much." I whimper when I feel his tongue back inside me. "Please do it! You don't need to worry about anything, I promise. You know I've been on the pill since I was eighteen and I had to get tested before traveling here," I say in a shaky voice.

"All of us had to get tested, Nightingale. And I'm clean, too," he groans, grabbing my hips and bringing me closer to his face. "And whatever my queen wants, that's what she fucking gets! Spread your cheeks for me, Melody. Let me eat that perfect ass while playing with your needy pussy and make you come again."

I do as he asked and when I feel his tongue at the entrance, my muscles clench on reflex.

"Relax for me, Mel-Mel," he coos. "I won't hurt you."

"I know you won't. Not now and not ever."

The second time I feel his tongue, I force myself to relax. He grunts, and pushes his tongue inside me painfully slowly, while rubbing my clit with the middle finger from the hand that's not around his cock. His nose is hitting the base of my spine and now I know that his tongue is all inside me. When I moan loudly, the finger on my clit goes inside my pussy and two seconds after, it starts thrusting at the same pace with his tongue and his other hand. I feel so full of Lucas and his cock is not even inside me.

"Deeper, Lucas. I need you to go even deeper. I want to come so bad." As per usual, as soon as I tell him what I need he does exactly that. He moans while licking me and I can feel the vibrations in my bones while his finger moves in and out of me so fast that my juices are smeared all over his throat and chest. His hips are bucking the same way mine are, hitting the floor with a thud at every thrust of his fist.

I know that he's holding back and that he wants to come by the way his cock is throbbing. When I hear him whimper, my orgasm hits me, the fact that I'm bringing him so much pleasure making my release inevitable. He moves his tongue to my pussy, slurping my cum and licking me clean for as long as my climax lasts. When I feel it's too much and that I'm too stimulated to bear another touch, I lift myself up and lie next to him, finally taking my panties off. It's only then I notice he didn't stop stroking himself and the grimace on his face.

"Does it hurt?" I ask him in a worried voice, but not telling him to stop.

He shakes his head, keeping his lips sealed and looking at me with

Play My Part

desperation in his eyes.

"Do you still have my cum in your mouth?" I don't know why, but that makes my pussy even wetter than it already is. He nods and grimaces again, his hand keeping the same pace I set earlier.

"Show me," I whisper. He slowly opens his mouth, letting me see all the white liquid he safely kept. I move from sitting on my side to lying on my back. "Pour it in my mouth. And don't take your hand from your cock."

He moans when he sees me opening my mouth and sticking my tongue out. My hand instinctively goes to my clit, starting to rub lazy circles on it when I see the rope of cum hanging from his lips and landing on my tongue. I grab the back of his head and kiss him, letting my cum and our spit mixing in our mouths and on our skin. I feel him rubbing his cock next to me, and I move closer, letting the crown touch my hip.

"Do you want to fuck me, Lucas?" I ask, pinching my clit. "Do you want to feel my pussy wrapped around your hard cock?"

"Please," he whines. "I need to be inside you so much, Melody. Please let me fuck your tight pussy. Please. Please."

I open my legs and bring my knees close to my face, putting my hands behind them for good measure.

"I don't want to be on top," he says in a scared voice. "I don't want this to make you feel like I'm overpowering you or dominating you."

"This is about what I want, isn't it?" I ask in a confident voice. He nods, exhaling and looking at my pussy, then at his cock that is still fucking his fist. "Then you'd better fuck me and come inside me, Lucas. I want to watch you from below when you shoot your cum deep inside my pussy."

He gives me a questioning look, and when I nod he thrusts inside me so hard that my body slides on the floor.

"Fuck. Your pussy feels incredible, Melody," he says through gritted teeth, fucking me in long, deep strokes, his balls slapping my ass. "I'm not sure I can last much longer. I need to come so bad. Fuck. I need to come."

"You can come if you make me come again!" I scream. "Make me come on your thick, hard cock that is fucking my pussy raw."

He leans down, taking my nipple in his mouth and sucking hard on it. His cock is so deep inside me that it feels like he's going to break me in half, but I don't care. My brain is completely empty and the only thing I can think about is how good I feel. How good it feels to have full control over what somebody is doing to and with your body. How good it feels to be the one saying what you want, what you need and to have somebody who respects that. I am in full control over this experience and I am the only one calling the shots. I decide where he comes, when he comes, and what he does to me. I am his queen and he is my king and we don't need anybody to rule over.

"I'm coming, Lucas," I say when my third orgasm starts building. "I'm gonna come so hard for you. I'm gonna come all over you and soak you! Fuck. Please, please, please, make me come."

His pace increases and if I thought he was deep before, now he's digging a hole inside me. He grunts, whines, and whimpers all this time looking at me and fighting his own orgasm.

"Come for me, Lucas! I want to feel your cum inside me so I can come, too."

"Fuck, Melody," he screams. "I'm going to spill all my hot seed in your fucking tight pussy."

"Do it, Lucas. Please. I'm begging you to come inside me. Please let me feel your cum coating my greedy, needy pussy."

When I feel his cock throb inside me, I look at him and focus on his beautiful face. I can do this. I know I can. I know I can keep the demons silent and allow myself to be completely happy. I feel the first spurt coming out of his cock and that's when my orgasm happens too. My body is shaking from all the pleasure I'm feeling and I'm screaming his name so loud that I'm surprised the windows are still holding. He's screaming my name too, time and time again. With every throb of his cock, his roars are louder.

Play My Part

We're looking at each other with love and adoration in our eyes. We don't know where we're headed, but we know that we're on this road together.

I chose Lucas Temple. And I'm fucking proud of it. Consequences be damned indeed, Yonathan.

Chapter 13
Lucas

It's been three weeks since Melody moved in with us. Three weeks and three days since I finally found her again. And zero nights since the last time she had a nightmare that I needed to wake her up from. Not a single night has gone by without me waking up in the middle of the night because Melody was crying and screaming that she can't do this. I have no idea what *this* is, because every time I wake her up she tells me the same thing. "I can't remember what I've dreamt of, but I know it's bad." Yeah, let me call bullshit on that one. Add that to the fact that I feel like she's slowly pushing me away from her, preferring to spend the evenings talking to Manon in the garden, and you can have an overview of my shitshow of a life.

I don't know what the fuck the two of them are always talking about. I asked them the first three times if I could join them, and they said yes just because they wanted to be polite. Because as soon as I sat down, they stopped talking. And that made me fucking uncomfortable so I decided to stop asking for her attention altogether. And each and every night when she comes to bed I'm fast asleep because I'm fucking drained. Drained from spending twelve hours per day on set and from waking up at least three times a night to calm her down and to promise her that she'll be fine.

I feel fucking lost because I don't know what to do to help her have a full night's sleep and how to make her nightmares go away. I feel utterly

Play My Part

useless, powerless, and like a ship that it's about to sink because it has more weight on board than it was supposed to.

"Maybe she needs another therapist," Manon whispers from my left while chewing on his weird sandwich during our lunch break. "You did everything you could do for her, baby Temple. But that kind of trauma needs to be healed by a professional, not by your new lover."

I want to agree with him, but a huge part of me tells me that if I won't be the one to help her heal her trauma, it would make her be disappointed with me. I'm afraid that if I fail to put her back together she will come to the conclusion that I'm utterly useless, that she wasted her time with me and that she deserves better. I'm so fucking afraid of losing her that every time I take that possibility into consideration, I feel my heart stopping and my soul aching and bleeding. I was never ready to lose her, and after that night when I had the best sex of my life I know that if she walks away from me again, I will never be anything but a hopeless wreck with no power left to smile.

I know this is not the healthiest behavior, nor the sanest way of seeing life. But I'm fucking afraid. Afraid of being abandoned again. Afraid of waking up alone with no one to love me or care for me.

Being with Melody has been my dream since I was a lost teenager, dreaming about the day when he will be reunited with his first crush. Finally getting the girl who told him everything there was to know about her during the all-nighters we spent in my room talking the same way she and Non talk now.

I was her secret keeper, and the thought that somebody else knows all her secrets now makes me fucking sad. I know that what's going on between Melody and him isn't anything more than an honest friendship. It's clear to everybody that they are not interested in each other in any other way. But I want to be the one who fucks her and the one she trusts with everything. I want to have all of her, but she always tells me to be patient because someday I will, whatever the fuck that means.

"I don't know what to do, Non." I pinch my lip, trying to think of something that I didn't do for her in the past three weeks. Maybe I missed something. Maybe I should stay awake and shake her as soon as the nightmare starts. Maybe I should suggest having sex with her again, but despite the fact that the last time it happened, on my bedroom floor, my world was completely and utterly rocked, I can't get myself to do it. I feel like she needs more time to recover. I think that since she was so bold and expressed what she wanted from me so loud and clear, if she wanted it to happen again, she would've said it. I'm fucking terrified of rejection because that's the first step to abandonment. And I know that I need to deal with that shit and heal my childhood trauma at some point, but first I need to help Melody heal hers. Because her wounds are deeper and more fresh. I've had mine for as long as I can remember, so what's a little more time in the bigger picture?

"I can't believe I'm going to say this," Yonathan breaks the silence, "but maybe we should go out with her!"

I look at him with my eyes wide open, trying to understand what the catch is. I'm sure there was a joke hidden under his statement, but the honesty on his face tells me he really meant what he said.

"Are you high?" Manon asks. "You? Going out? And suggesting to do it with Melody, no less?"

"Listen, all we did since we're here is being on this fucking set, then go home and sleep." He shrugs. "She also needs to squeeze in endless talks with my lawyer on the phone and the weekly session with her therapist. Not to mention the daily two-hour talks with Manon."

I groan because I didn't need to remember the fact that the woman I'm sleeping next to every single night talks to another man more than she does to me. And the fact that yesterday, when she made breakfast for all of us, she told Manon that she loves him made me fucking feral. Again, I know that her love for him grew because they can relate to each other from multiple perspectives, but the fact that she never told me those words hurts me on the deepest level. And what Manon is doing hurts me all the same. I was right there, next to him, for the past seven years. And he never opened up to me like he does to somebody he met a few weeks ago. I know that he and Yonathan go way back, and I know that their connection might be slightly stronger than the one I have with either of them. But fucking still. If he'd wanted to keep our friendship shallow, then he shouldn't have said he wants to stick with me through thick and thin during our stay in Philadelphia. He shouldn't have been there for me, giving me all those pieces of advice when I talked to him about how I feel about my parents. He shouldn't have fucking told me that I have abandonment issues and act like he was my therapist, helping me to process all that grief and rage I felt back then. He shouldn't have helped me become this kind, thoughtful man I am today at the same time Yonathan was trying to freeze my heart for the rest of my life because he thought I'd live a better life if I can't feel things. Needless to say, Manon won. But sometimes I wish he hadn't. Sometimes I wish I could be the person Yonathan told me to be. And I know that somewhere, deep down inside me, there's a ruthless man that Yon planted inside me. The good part is that I managed to bury it and never allowed him to see the light of day.

But right now? Right now, I hate the situation we are in. I hate that there's no way of convincing her to just open up to me and tell me what's on her mind. I despise the fact that I have no guarantee that she won't wake up one day and decide that she wants to go back home or anywhere else to start a new life without me in it. I hate the fact that instead of growing together, we grow apart and that I am more convinced with every day that passes that she is not the same Melody I met all those years ago. And the fact that confuses me the most is that I love this Melody more than the past one. We most definitely aren't the same people we were when we first met and we're not even the same people we were when she took my virginity.

I was determined to come clean that night and tell her that despite the fact that I was only eighteen at that time, I wanted her to be with me. I wanted to take my turn spilling all my secrets, even the one I kept hidden for all those years. I wanted to tell her that I love her. But when I heard all about her new job and how happy she was, how everything she wanted was to live life at its fullest, without a care or responsibility in the world, I decided that it was better to let her go. To let her be happy because her happiness was more important than mine. Because loving somebody means knowing what's best for them even if their best is your worst. Even if that means you need to let them go and be happy with somebody else but you.

"Don't groan, baby Temple. You know I'm telling the truth. It's fucked up, but it's your fucked up, so you'd better find the energy to fight for it," Yonathan says in a threatening tone. "It's too late to walk away now and you know it."

"When did you become a member of Melody's fan club?" I ask, opening a bottle of water and taking a sip from it. "Last time you two talked was when you thanked her for cooking dinner. That was a week ago."

"We talk." He takes off his glasses, wiping the lenses with a silken cloth he took out from his pocket. "I didn't know I had to give you a full report of my discussions with your coffin dodger."

"Oh, so now you moved from calling her a whore to making fun of her age?" I ask in an exasperated tone. "Very mature of you, Yonathan."

"Fucking an older woman is never a good idea, if you ask me," he says, putting his glasses back on his nose.

"Then it's a good thing I didn't ask you," I retort.

"I beg to differ, my dear baby robbed from the cradle! Not asking me was one of the worst ideas you ever had!" He throws the paper he was reading back on the small table in our dressing room. "Because if you did, I would've told you that fucking somebody you work with is a terrible idea. Fucking somebody who you work with who also happens to be your long lost almost-relative is even worse. And fucking your almost-relative work colleague who is also twelve years your senior and who clearly keeps shit from you is just another phrasing for *the Apocalypse*."

I stay quiet, because even though he said all those hateful things, I know he's right. I know it was a fucking terrible idea that would bring only complications, not only for me and for Melody, but for him and Manon, too. I knew that Manon would love her since their first interaction. I knew that he would do anything to make her smile because of his obsession with protecting people that life threw shit at the same way a lioness protects her cubs. I knew Yonathan would be hurt if she decided to leave me, to leave us, because if there's something he hates, it's weakness and betrayal. I have yet to find a person more obsessed with power and loyalty than Yonathan Friedmann. I fucking knew how complicated everything would be since the moment I brought Melody onto that airplane, and yet I can't find any trace of regret inside me. All I can find is a mix of determination, hope, and crippling fear.

"It's none of your fucking business who baby Temple decides to sleep with," Manon says in an angry tone. "None! None! None! None! None!" he screams. I put a hand on his shoulder, trying to calm him down so he doesn't have another episode where his OCD gets the steering wheel and takes full control of his actions and thoughts, but he brushes me off.

"That might be true," Yonathan nods, "but the fact that I'm helping her or chatting with her doesn't mean that I like her." His blue eyes are now narrowing, looking at Manon like he wants to challenge his demons to come out and play so he can burn them to the fucking ground. "She always looks like she has one foot out of the door, despite the fact that she said she won't leave you. But do know, baby Temple, I will fucking destroy her if she hurts you again."

"You will do no such thing!" I let Manon go and stand in front of Yonathan. "How many times do I have to tell you that I'm not a fucking child anymore and that you should stop treating me like one?"

"Aren't you tired already of giving that speech, Lucas?" He sounds bored and that makes my blood boil. "That's your fucking problem, you know? Whenever somebody sees things differently than you do, you throw a tantrum screaming left and right that you're not a child and you don't need people protecting you anymore? Do you know who throws tantrums? Children," he deadpans. "So maybe Melody, me, or everyone else would stop treating you like a child when you'll fucking stop behaving like one."

"Oh, so now that I take full responsibility for following my dream and being with the woman I dreamed about for my whole life is considered childish behavior?" I say in a condescending tone.

"You're not taking responsibility for shit!" he screams, standing up. "All you're thinking about is you! *Your* happiness, *your* dream, the woman that *you* love! You don't give a single fuck about her issues, you only care about what *you* could do to make her feel better. You care about what *you* fucking want and everybody around you has to solve *your* problems and deal with *your* shit while you blissfully live the dream!"

"It's called selflessness, you fucking moron!" I scream back. "I put myself on the line, willing to take a shot for the people I care about. Yes, I do want to make her feel better and come up with solutions to her problems because I fucking care for her."

"No, Lucas," he says in a deadly serious voice. "You do that because you want her to be whole, sane, and an open book because that would make *you* happy! You don't fucking care about the *how,* you only care about the result. I," he says, pointing to his chest with his index finger, "was the one who came up with the idea to talk to a lawyer and help her deal with that pig. Manon," he points his finger to our brother, "is the one who jokes with her, who entertains her when you're sitting like a lost puppy on the couch, feeling sorry for yourself. You keep saying left and right that you would do anything for her, yet you behave like she's fucking dead and you're mourning her."

I give him a deadly look, breathing heavily through my nostrils. That doesn't seem to impress him since he gives me a look that challenges me to say that he's wrong. But I don't know if he is or if that's the truth. I don't fucking know anything else than the fact that I do want Melody whole, sane, and an open book. Maybe I do want it for me or maybe I want it for her. Maybe I want it for both of us so we could finally be fucking happy and not having to deal with nightmares, sobs, *I love you*s to a different person and all these fucking emotions.

"I have the right to be happy," I say through gritted teeth. "I was miserable for more years than a child should be, and now I have the right to be happy."

"So fucking be happy," he shouts. "Or, at least, fight for your happiness. Don't expect the ones around you to do the same old dance and revolve around you only to save you. I did it once, but it's time for you to spread your wings and fly, not expect mama bird to come feed you," he says in a disgusted voice.

"Oh, right." I half laugh. "Because I need to follow your footsteps, right? Because if you left your family behind when they told you to get married at sixteen and spend your life begging God to take care of you and your people, I need to do the same heroic shit?"

"Better begging God to help me than the ones around me," he spits.

"Just go fuck yourself," I dismiss him.

"I'd rather fuck myself than fuck up my life because I'm a coward," he replies the second I finish my sentence.

"Enough!" Manon roars. "Just shut the fuck up. Both of you." He pulls his hair so hard that the cracking sound fills the room. "I'm so fucking sick and tired of your arguing, your reproaches, and how you both think you're better than the other. Spoiler fucking alert. You. Are. Not."

"Non, this is between Yonathan and me," I say in an apologetic voice.

"It's anything but!" he screams again. "Your fucking moronic fights hurt everybody around you. Melody, me, even your career, Lucas. You are shit on that set," he says, pointing his finger to the door.

"I am at my utmost best." I cross my arms over my chest. "I am killing it out there!"

Both Yonathan and Manon cock an eyebrow, making me feel so fucking small and even more useless than I felt before.

"Yon is right," Manon says in a low tone. "Your obsession of not letting Melody out of your sight isn't healthy and the fact that you're not beating her isn't enough to make you completely different than Bart."

"What did you just say to me?" I ask in an incredulous voice.

"The truth." He sighs. "You don't let her breathe, Luc. You're always on her tail like a fucking lost puppy that thinks he found a human who would scratch his ear. You want her to heal, yet you're not letting her do it on her own terms. You have no fucking idea what she went through and you just keep pushing her in the direction you consider the healthiest one. But what if your idea of health is the worst sickness for her? What happens then, Lucas?"

"Oh, and you know everything there is to know of how it feels to be sexually and mentally abused, don't you?" I let out a fake laugh.

When he remains silent and gives me a look filled with pain, I know I've fucked up. I never wanted to know more about his past because I wanted to respect his boundaries, but I now realize that maybe I should've insisted more in the rare moments when he opened up to me.

I swallow visibly and send him a silent plea to forgive me, but all I get in return is his back when he turns around to take a can of Dr. Pepper from the fridge.

"All I'm saying," he finally breaks the silence, "is that you should let Melody take the reins over her own life and, for some time, over your relationship. Let her explore, let her test the waters, Luc. Hold her hand and follow her, don't drag her through life on your own path."

I nod, despite the fact that I know he can't see me. It will be so fucking hard for me to let go because that feels like I'm opening the door for her and allowing her to leave me. I thought that maybe if I keep her close to me all the time she will need me the same way I need her. But maybe

Play My Part

Yonathan is right. Maybe I am keeping her hostage in a different way than her husband did, but a hostage nevertheless. Maybe my behavior will make her want to escape, while if I decide to go inside the cell and allow both of us to be fate's prisoners, we will survive and come out stronger.

"So, where do you want to go?" I ask Yonathan.

"What?"

"Tonight. You said we should go out. Where do you want to go?"

"Non?" he frowns. "You okay, buddy?"

"Perfect," he answers, but both me and Yonathan know he's not, by the way he's tapping his fingers on the can. I don't know what disasters he's trying to prevent from happening, but I'm sure they're heartbreaking.

"Since you know this city better than most of us," I tell him, "why don't you decide where we should go?"

"I didn't go to clubs much," he laughs, "but I know that Joshua goes out with a bunch of people from the filming crew every night."

"Joshua, our extremely untalented screenwriter Joshua?" Yonathan's brows reach his hairline. "I don't trust that man with putting his left foot in front of his right one and not tripping. I'm definitely not going where he is."

"I don't know," Non shrugs, "everybody seems pretty hyped about the club they're going to. It wouldn't hurt to give it a try, I guess."

"Fine," Yonathan sighs, "I'll bite. But I'm not the one talking to that moron. He's a fucking disgusting, ass-licking creep and I don't have any intention to talk to him more than necessary."

"I'll ask him," Non says. "Talking to morons and making them feel more important than they are is my guiltiest pleasure."

"I'll tell Melody," I say. "Ah, shit," I say, checking my phone. "The delivery of our new beds is coming tonight. One of us needs to be there to sign the receipt."

"I'll talk to Joanna." Yonathan rolls his eyes. "She's not the sharpest pencil in the box, but I trust her enough to not set the house on fire."

"You do know we have a fire alarm and several fire sprinklers in the house, right?" I ask him in an amused voice.

"Hence me trusting Joanna not to set the house on fire." He laughs. "And I'm sure she'll be there. She has this bad habit of doing any-fucking-thing I ask her to, that gets so boring sometimes, that I would rather watch a rock turn to dust than fuck her."

"So why do you keep sleeping with her?" Non rests his head on his left palm.

"Her ass is still tight enough." Yonathan shrugs. "Plus, the fact that she behaves like the perfect pet keeps getting my cock hard, even though she doesn't do it because she's naturally submissive and accepts me dominating her. She does it because she's, you know," he knocks his fist on his head, "not bright enough to be willing to find out more about what she likes, to put it mildly."

"That's so fucking wrong, Yon." Manon shakes his head. "You're taking advantage of the poor woman."

"I'm not taking advantage of shit," he says in a serious voice. "I always, absolutely fucking always, ask for her consent before I do anything, especially because of this. Especially because she has no fucking idea who she is, what she wants, and if she doesn't how could I?"

"What if she says yes and then changes her mind?" Non challenges.

"What kind of a fucking question is that, Non?" Yonathan sounds angrier than a second ago. "I would *never* force a woman to do something she doesn't want to, even if she agreed with it a second earlier and you know that all too well."

"Just making sure you still don't let your demons get the best of you when you're fucking someone, that's all." Manon raises his hand in defense. "I was just checking up on you."

"My demons," Yon clenches his jaw, "have no interest in hurting somebody other than myself."

"Now that we have that settled," Manon stands up, straightening his

T-shirt, and arranging the threads of his ripped jeans, "let's go to that debriefing meeting so we can shoot that final scene faster and go home."

When the three of us get inside the improvised conference room, everybody else is already seated. We're not late, but apparently all these people want to do their best to keep us happy, even if that means being fifteen minutes early to all the fucking useless meetings set by our PR team, our agents, or whoever the fuck involved in the filming of this movie decides we have more discussing to do. I care for Melody, I do, but all the talks about how well we do on social media, what hashtags are trending on Instagram, or how many retweets her posts get are completely draining me.

I take my seat between my two brothers, noticing that the one in front of me is still unoccupied.

"Where's Rah?" I ask no one in particular.

"There was an explosion in the building she was living in!" her agent answers immediately. "Nobody was hurt, thank God, but she needed to go there and see if there's anything left of her things or if they were all swallowed by the flames."

"Maybe I shouldn't trust Joanna that much?" Yonathan whispers in my ear, but I kick him under the table because that's not funny.

"Speaking of that," the engaged lady who gave us the tour of our house says, "I took the liberty of telling Rah she can live with you three until we find her a different place to stay."

"You can take the liberty to tell her that she can sleep in a hotel," Yonathan says. "We don't have any available rooms for her."

"That house has five bedrooms and three guest rooms!" she says back.

"All put to good use, I assure you." Yonathan gives her a wink.

"Then make one of them available because this is nonnegotiable." She leans back on her chair, writing something down on the notebook.

"Says who?"

"Says the head of logistics for this film crew." She points to herself.

So that's who she is. Not that I cared a lot, but at least now I have another name for her than *The House Lady*.

"What the fuck is a head of logistics? Does that imply you give good head? Because one of the bedrooms is perfect to put that talent in practice." He laughs, Non chuckles, and I snort.

"Really subtle, Mr. Friedmann." She rolls her eyes.

"Was I? Because I had no intention of being subtle. But, in case you didn't understand what I meant, I was asking you if you would be willing to suck my cock. Respectfully, of course."

"Of course." Non confirms, biting his lip.

"He was kidding." Joanna giggles from my left and I bury my face in my palms to keep from laughing. "He's always making these funny jokes that nobody understands."

I see Manon's body shaking on my right and this time it's him I kick under the table hoping to make him stop laughing, so I can keep myself from doing the same.

"Anyway," our head of logistics says, "I wasn't kidding when I said that Tzipporah will live with you. End of discussion!"

Yonathan groans next to me, but when I look at him, I see a mischievous smile on his lips and a glint of hunger in his eyes. That's when it hits me.

"It was all an act, wasn't it?" I ask in a low voice, so only he can hear me.

"I couldn't seem too eager to have that perfect ten in my house without raising any suspicions, could I?" he says, barely moving his lips. "The little bird just walked into my cage, baby Temple. And I can't wait to tie her to the bars and fuck her from behind."

I pat him on his shoulder and for the first time today, I look at Melody. She gives me a shy smile and I give her a simple nod, hating the fact that I can't fucking sit next to her and let the world know we're together. Yet.

When some accountant starts talking about the remaining budget for the movie, I take out my phone and text Melody.

Play My Part

Me: *We're going to a club tonight.*

Her phone pings on the table and I click my tongue loudly and roll my eyes faking annoyance. She rubs her eyebrow with her middle finger and I can't help but let out a laugh that I quickly hide behind a cough.

"It's the air conditioner," I say in a choked voice. "It always messes with my throat."

Several people stand up and run to the thermostat on the wall and I have to fight the urge of rolling my eyes.

"Leave it," I say in a gentle voice. "There's no need for all of you to suffer. I'll just drink a cup of tea after we're done here."

"Are you sure, Mr. Temple?" a woman who I think is Joanna's agent asks me. I give her a nod, and wave my hand, coughing twice for good measure.

Mel-Mel: *Who's we?*

Me: *You, me, Manon, and Yonathan.*

She looks at me with panic written all over her face, but I type faster than her.

Me: *Yonathan will behave. He was the one who came up with this, actually.*

Mel-Mel: *I hope the devils have jackets since Hell is apparently freezing.*

Me: *Forget about the devils. Do you have your earbuds with you?*

Mel-Mel: *Yup. Why?*

Me: *Because this is what I need you to do tonight!*

I open my Spotify app and send her the link to "<u>Trading Places</u>" by Usher. She puts one of the earbuds in her ear and her cheeks turn redder by the second.

Mel-Mel: *I don't think I can do this, Luc-Luc.*

Me: *Take me on a date, my beautiful queen! When we dance, whisper in my ear how bad you really wanna do me, take me home and get up in my pants. Pour me a shot and force me to the bed.*

I lick my lips after sending her the lyrics from the song and look at her, feeling my cock hardening in my jeans. She bites her lip and rubs her throat, the gesture making me even harder. She's so fucking beautiful that

Miriam Rosentvaig

I can't take my eyes off her.

    Mel-Mel: *Okay, let's do this. Also, I have a confession.*
    Me: *?*
    Mel-Mel: *I miss feeling you inside me.*

"Fuck!" I say out loud, making everybody turn and look at me. "It hurts when I swallow." I point to my throat, faking a grimace.

"All her cum?" Yonathan whispers in my ear, laughing.

I ignore him and look at my phone again.

    Me: *And I miss being inside you. I miss feeling your pussy clenching around my cock while I'm holding back my orgasm until you let me come.*
    Mel-Mel: *I miss your thick cock fucking me raw, Lucas. I miss coming in your mouth and my clit misses your tongue so much!*
    Me: *I can't wait to feel it swelling on my tongue right before I swallow all that cum you're so willing to give me.*

She mutters a curse under her breath, tapping her pen on the notebook in front of her. After a couple of minutes she takes the phone back in her hand.

    Mel-Mel: *I'm so wet for you, Lucas!*
    Me: *Show me.*
    Mel-Mel: *Are you insane?*
    Me: *Spread your legs under the table and let me see, Melody. Please let me see that damp spot on your panties. I need to see it so much, please.*

She sighs loudly and when I see her moving I drop a pen on the floor and kneel near my chair to pick it up. My beautiful nightingale is fucking soaked.

I go back to sitting on my chair and take my phone from the table.

    Me: *Jesus fucking Christ, Mel! Your pussy's dripping!*
    Mel-Mel: *I can't wait for it to drip on your long cock! I need you so much, Luc!*
    Me: *I need you too, Nightingale! So, so much! Can't wait for tonight!*

She blushes and lets the phone rest on the table, giving me a nod before going back to listening to what that accountant is talking about.

Play My Part

Several hours later, we're at the entrance of the club in the center of Bucharest. The streets are so fucking packed that you can't drop a needle without stinging somebody, and the fact that we have twelve bodyguards around us doesn't help.

Melody is wearing a yellow backless dress and a blonde wig, while I'm dressed in jeans, and a blue shirt. I have a cap on my head and sunglasses over my eyes, despite the fact that it's fucking eleven p.m., but at least we know that the club we're going to is rented only for the film crew.

Or, at least, that's what we thought because as soon as the bouncer lets us in we're hit by music playing at the loudest volume I've ever heard in my life and a huge mass of people.

We keep walking toward the bar, and I finally manage to take off my sunglasses and take a look around me. The people inside are most certainly not part of our crew. The men have their shirts unbuttoned all the way down, and the women wear nothing more than skimpy skirts and bras that are decorated with fake crystals and diamonds that remind me of those hideous chandeliers hanging from our living room ceiling. Huge golden crosses are hanging from all the men's thick necks and their tattoos look like they were made by a drunk petty thief who was serving his sentence in prison.

All the women inside this club look exactly the same. Their lips are swollen, they have absolutely no facial expressions, and their nails are much too long to be naturally grown.

"I think we're overdressed!" I scream in Yonathan's ear trying to make myself heard over the loud music.

"I think the problem is that we're dressed to begin with!" he screams back. "And what the fuck is this song, anyway?"

'It's called "La Inima M-ai Ars"!" Manon answers in a perfect Romanian accent.

"I beg your pardon?" Yon's voice is filled with awe and admiration for our best friend.

"*Luh eeneemuh mahee uhrse,*" he says, slower this time. "It literally translates to *you burned my heart.*"

"And I hope down in flames it goes so he will never be able to sing this obnoxious song again." Yon looks around him, a scowl on his face letting everybody know how angry he is about the circumstances we found ourselves in.

"Is this your people's music?" Melody asks in a genuinely curious voice.

"The low budget version of it." Manon groans in exasperation. "It's the one you would find if you typed *Roma traditional music* in AliExpress's search bar."

Suddenly, a high-pitched voice coming from behind us interrupts their conversation, making all of us turn around. We are met by a woman with long, blonde hair wrapped in a ponytail, wearing a silver dress that sparkles even though the club is almost completely dark.

She gives Yonathan a vulgar look, but she's so far from his type that I know this will end badly for her.

"*Ia zi, baiatu, dai si tu un pahar de vodka?*" she asks, her tongue slurring, making it easy to notice that she's completely wasted.

"Did she just address me?" Yonathan looks at Manon.

"Not only did she address you, she wants you to buy her a drink."

"Tell her that I won't."

"Can I at least be kind to her while giving her the message?" he smiles viciously.

"Just tell her to fuck off!" Yonathan screams in an exasperated voice and I can't help but to let out a laugh, making him frown at me. That only makes me laugh harder.

"I will fucking kill Joshua." Yonathan snaps his fingers and if looks could kill, our screenwriter would die where he's currently dancing next to a woman who rubs her ass on his too visible hard cock.

Melody scrunches her nose in disgust when she sees them and I put my hand on the small of her back, reassuring her that I'm here and nothing will happen to her. I've got her. I always will.

"Fucking Joshua," Yonathan says, gritting his teeth. "I don't think I despise somebody from our crew more than I do him."

"Same here," a raspy voice says from my left. "He's so fucking creepy and weird."

"What are you doing here, Rah?" Yonathan asks in a flirtatious voice. "Missed me already?"

"I came to spend time with my new housemates," she chirps. "Joanna told me where you were. After she had to go through tons of small papers in her bag." She laughs and that sound makes Yonathan's face lighten up.

"Will you let your favorite housemate buy you a drink, then?" Yon asks in the same tone as earlier.

Rah fiddles with her fingers and I swear I can see the same light on her face.

"I would love that, yes," she replies.

And that's when I know that this night has the potential of changing our planet's axis for Yonathan.

Chapter 14

Lucas

When "[Devil Inside](#)" by CRMNL suddenly comes out from the speakers, Melody grabs my hand and drags me to the dance floor. We barely take two steps before Theo, the head of our security, steps in front of her, giving her a pitied look. He may look like he just came out of prison, but behind that rough exterior lies the kindest man I've ever met.

"I'm sorry, Mr. Temple, but until we clear everybody from this," he pauses and shifts his weight from one leg to the other, "club, I would need all of you to sit in the bar area."

"We just want to dance, Theo," I say. "I'm sure there's nothing here that can put us in any danger."

He shakes his head and crosses his arms over his chest. I don't want to make his life more difficult than necessary, and the last thing I want is to be the spoiled brat Yonathan described me as earlier, but I really want to see Melody let loose. I want to dance with her and to feel her body close to mine, to get lost in the music while she grinds that perfect ass on me.

"That's okay, Luc," Melody says. "We'll dance where Theo tells us it's safe."

She turns around and puts her hand on my face, giving me a look that speaks more than all the words ever spoken. Her round, hazel eyes are a combination of *I'm sorry* and *I'm here*, and her face, God, her fucking beautiful face, tells me that she's scared. If she only knew how fucking crippled I feel, too.

Pushing that feeling back, I cup her face with both of my hands, leaning forward to kiss her. She pulls back the second my lips touch hers and that fucking stings. Not only the fact that she avoids my touch like it's burning her, but the fact that I can't let anybody, not even her, know how much I love her. How my heart beats on the rhythm that she sets, and how my soul begs me to surrender and let it fly in her chest.

I do my best to give her a reassuring smile, but based on her body language, I utterly fail. She wraps her hands around her and makes a beeline directly to where Yonathan and Tzipporah are sitting, him saying something that makes her let out a hearty laugh. I'm fucking jealous of how easy it is for them to interact. How the world would bow at their feet if they would ever be a couple and how many people would say *Oh, my God! They're so hashtag couple goals!* every time they would share a kiss in public.

But me and Melody? They would tear us apart for so many reasons, the main one being that we don't fit in the small boxes society has created. They would stare at us like we're a disaster waiting to happen. She would most probably be the gold-digger woman who left her husband because she had a midlife crisis. And, as per usual, I would be the sweet, naive little boy that didn't know better. Now, more than ever, I wish I had refused Yonathan's offer all those years ago. I wish I would've told him to go fuck himself and actually mean it, not trying to look strong, while feeling weak and in search of somebody who could just fucking love me. I absolutely despise the life that I once loved.

I watch her as she orders a drink and once the bartender offers her the cocktail, she wraps her lips around the pink straw, downing half the glass in one go. She might've drank it all if Manon didn't stop her with a gentle touch on her shoulder. Melody looks at him and something passes between them. He hugs her to his chest, resting his chin on her head and she crosses her arms around his waist, relaxing her muscles with every breath she draws.

I know I shouldn't be jealous, but I am. Out of my fucking mind jealous. Why can he hug her in such an intimate way while if I only want to give her a kiss she runs like I'm poisoning her? Why does she find comfort in Manon's embrace and not in mine? And, most importantly, why does he have to soothe her like I did something wrong? Like I'm solely responsible for the mess we're in or like she wasn't the one who wanted to dance with me.

I've been nothing but what she wanted. I promised her I would offer her the world and everything in it, and I did my best to give her exactly that. I accepted her, I was patient with her, I fucking listened to her telling me how her ex-husband beat the shit out of her and raped her. I did every single fucking thing that she wanted and this is how she repays me. By running from me the second I want to show her that I'm not afraid of admitting to the world that I'm hers. By going to my fucking brother, looking for comfort when things don't go the way she wants them to, in the rare moments when I do something *I* feel and what *I* need. I'm sick and tired of putting her first, only to be her close second.

I turn around and start walking toward the exit, not giving a shit about what Theo considers as safe. If people want to jump at me, so fucking be it. I'm not sure I care enough about my own integrity at the moment. Unfortunately for me, when I make the first step, I feel a hand grabbing the back of my shirt and pulling me back.

"Rah, please excuse my brother for being a dickhead," Yonathan says through gritted teeth, giving me an angry look, "he sometimes gets lost in his own thoughts. Luckily, I'm always there to bring him back."

He continues looking at me, challenging me to say differently. But I feel so tired, that the only thing I can do is to give Rah a polite smile.

"Yeah, I was thinking about the scene we have to shoot tomorrow." The lie falls easily from my lips, because I did think about it earlier. I was thinking how Melody would react when she would see me half naked next to this beautiful woman, faking that I'm having sex with her while I'm telling her she's a good girl and telling her to count her orgasms. I swear to God that this movie is a mixture of borderline BDSM and heartbreak, and I honestly hope that the final cut won't include half of the scenes in the script.

"Oh, don't worry." She laughs. "I'm sure we'll both do just fine. It's not the first time I have to act like I'm climaxing and being completely in love with the man next to me."

"Are we talking about movies or real life, little bird?" Yonathan asks, plastering that wicked smile on his lips.

Rah blushes so hard next to me that I think her cheeks will explode if she gets another question like that. She quickly recovers, shaking her head and making that long, copper hair move in waves on her shoulders.

"Could be one, could be both." Her voice is so smooth you can actually feel it wrapping around your brain, which, by the look on his face, is exactly what is happening to Yonathan. He looks at her like she's a mystery he can't quite figure out. I don't know what that means because I have never in my life seen Yonathan being puzzled or intrigued by something, least of all by someone.

"So, that's for you to know and for me to find out?" he finally says.

"So, that's for me to know and for you to forget," she corrects, giving him a wink before taking another sip of her martini.

I don't want to witness this shit. I'm not in the mood to see Yonathan getting all flirtatious with her, only to convince her to go to his bedroom and let him do God knows what to her body. I know the story from the first sentence up to the last letter. I don't need to watch it unfold again.

"As fun as this was, I'm heading home," I tell them, pushing myself off the bar. "I'll see you tomorrow."

"Nonsense," Yonathan says, louder than necessary, since the club is now half empty and the music is finally at a normal level. "Sit with us, baby Temple. Celebrate life and everything beautiful in it. Like our new housemate, for example."

I sigh, pulling my hair from its roots. I look at him, pleading with my eyes to just let me be, but he doesn't spare me a glance. His eyes are on the woman on my right, devouring her and, most probably, imagining how she looks naked and with her hair tangled by how much he'll pull on it.

"I do have other qualities, you know?" she sighs, like she's as tired as I am, and maybe she has a sob story of her own that makes her react like this when the most pretentious fucker on planet Earth pays her a compliment.

"That's definitely for you to know and for me to find out," Yonathan challenges. "Or am I mistaken, and this falls into the *what I should forget* category as well?"

"The jury is still out on that one," she muses, playing with the olive toothpick inside her glass. "Court is adjourned until further notice."

"Well, in that case," he gives a nod to the bartender who quickly refills his whiskey glass, "if you ever need an executioner, feel free to call me. I'm great at giving punishments."

I turn my head to look at Tzipporah, expecting to see her either all flustered, or clenching her thighs, but to my surprise, she holds her index finger in the air while she downs the rest of her drink.

"I'm completely innocent." She puts down her glass, and smiles at both of us. "I'm like a new student who just got her uniform and jumps up and down in excitement for starting school."

"Up and down you say?" Yonathan's voice is so low that I can barely hear what he's saying. "Can't wait to see that happening."

"Patience is a virtue, my friend." She playfully slaps his shoulder, resting her hand there for a second more than necessary. "And God only knows you'll need a lot of that!"

And there's the wrong button that was waiting to be pushed. Mentioning God to Yonathan is the equivalent of mentioning Lucifer to a nun. To my surprise, he says nothing. Well, the fact that he chugs the glass of whiskey does, but I was expecting a more violent reaction. Apparently, this night is full of surprises.

I dare to look again in Melody's direction, noticing both hers and Manon's somber faces. Not that any of them look in my direction. I am the fucking fifth wheel now, while I thought I was in the driver's seat when this evening started.

"I really need to go," I tell Yonathan, and this time he nods.

"Should we join him?" He extends his arm to Rah and if I wouldn't feel like I'm dying on the inside, I would've laughed seeing him doing something so chivalrous for the first time in his life.

I don't care if and what she replies, I'm just relieved that he won't be keeping me here anymore, trying to convince me that I shouldn't care so much or whatever the fuck he was trying to convince me to do.

I step out in the cold spring air, inhaling deeply. I would absolutely love this part of the city in any other circumstances. The careless laughter, the clubs that despite being one next to the other, are absolutely filled with people, and blasting music from different genres. I would love drinking in a club, eating at a restaurant afterward, and watching the sun rise behind the old buildings around us. I would give every fucking thing I own just for a night of being a normal person, who can kiss the love of his life without fearing that there will be a picture of us on the first page of every tabloid around the world.

But that's not all it would take, would it? It would take for Melody to want to kiss me back instead of going to cry on my brother's shoulder. My sadness quickly turns into anger because I fucking hate how weak she is. How she tells me she wants me, but lets me do all the work, like a life of missing her isn't enough. Like I need to work harder, better, only to keep her from leaving me all alone for the third time in her life. Like I am unworthy of her.

"*Mi-a furat berea!*" a male voice screams in pain from behind Theo. Panicked, I turn around to look for Manon, who is now keeping an arm around Melody's waist.

"What did he say?" I ask him, doing my best to keeping myself from punching him right in that fucking broody face for being the traitor that he is.

"Somebody stole his beer and he's upset about it." He rolls his eyes. "Could you please stop asking me to translate what every drunk we cross paths with says? It's the Old Town. People shout all kinds of obscenities and irrelevant things."

"Sorry for disturbing you from what's relevant for you, buddy." I give him a wink and turn around, looking at Theo's back.

"What the fuck is that supposed to mean, Lucas?" Manon shouts from behind me.

"I find it absolutely fascinating that a couple of square meters can hold so much mediocrity," Yonathan says. "I feel like I'm the lucky winner of a VIP pass to IdiotCon."

"Maybe you shouldn't judge them so hard." Melody's sad voice cuts through my heart. "They're only trying to have fun."

"Maybe you should change your definition of fun." Yonathan says in the most menacing voice I've ever heard coming out of him. "And maybe you should stop being a fucking parasite and move out of our house."

"Sure," she retorts. "I'll do that the second you'll stop being a fucking cunt."

"Good thing your ex bought you all those expensive clothes and bags to keep the appearance of having a bit of class. That mouth and those manners surely betray your peasanty upbringing," he sneers.

"Just fuck off, Yonathan," she says in a choked voice. "Leave me the fuck alone already."

"Happy to oblige. Should I call somebody to help you pack? Or is Manon already taking care of that for you?"

"Yonathan…" Non threatens, and I can hardly focus on my surroundings, knowing that every-fucking-body around me noticed the same thing I did earlier.

"Don't *Yonathan* me, Non," he sneers. "Do better!"

I climb inside the SUV and stretch my legs, closing my eyes just to avoid any curious gazes from the people around me. I don't want to talk to anybody, not that words could express what I feel anyway. I feel fucking disappointed, empty, and stupid for ever believing that Melody would want to give me a chance at some point. To give us a chance. I thought I could make her understand that I'm the one for her and make her see things the way I do. To make her see the world through my eyes and know that I don't give a single fuck about all the things that might keep us apart, and focus on the only one that truly matters. That we're meant to be. That when our souls were forged, they came out identical. Two flames of the same fire, resting in different bodies. Two constellations that dance on life's night sky. Two people that can do wonders individually and move mountains when they're together.

But, apparently, I'm the only one who thinks that.

"You need to talk to her," Manon whispers in my right ear, "and make peace with your past."

I open my eyes and I feel my jaw falling to the floor. I swear this man's audacity breaks every limit I have.

"First of all, when I need your advice, I'll make sure to contact you. And, of course, if you're not too busy hugging Melody, maybe you'll find the time to give me your two cents," I say in an indifferent voice. "Second of all, my past, her past, our past together is none of your fucking business, Manon."

"Trust me when I say that you have no reason to be jealous," he says in a pleading voice. "She just needs to feel understood and to connect with someone."

"Trust you?" I half laugh. "Okay, sure. Should I take a seat and watch while you fuck her into understanding? Since she clearly can't have that with the man whose cock she fucked herself with three weeks ago, maybe she can suck yours and finally reach that ultimate connection she wants?"

"I'm right here, Lucas." Melody leans forward so I can see her, looking like she wants to put an axe through my head. Little does she know that she already put one in my heart.

"Ah, perfect," I ironically exclaim. "So, let's get the show started, then. Non, can you put up the partition window? Of course, if you want our driver to watch, too, then don't stop on my account."

She slaps me so hard that my head hits the window with a bang. I start laughing like a maniac, rubbing the place she hit and giving her a disdainful look.

"Well, I guess Yonathan was right, after all. A main core of a peasant wrapped nicely in a flashy exterior."

Manon puts one hand on my shoulder and the other on Melody's. I slap his hand off me and that apparently hurts him since he's looking at me with pain written all over his face. In any other circumstances, I would do my best to cheer him up. Make the poor mentally ill man feel better about himself and reassure him that I'm here for him no matter what. But since nobody gives a fuck about my pain, why should I give one about theirs?

"You can discuss more at home." He finally breaks the silence. "This is not the time, nor the place to have this conversation."

"I'll make sure to knock before I come to your room to have that discussion with her." I wave my hand in her direction. "Of course, if the offer of watching you fuck her still stands, I'll just walk in. If you could do it from behind so I don't have to see her face, that would be great, but I don't want to add too much pressure on either of you."

Melody jumps at me again, but her hero is there to keep her from slapping me again or whatever she wants to do. I have to admit that she's strong, since Manon can barely restrain her. Too bad her spirit is fucking weak.

"You moron!" she screams while still trying to escape from Manon's grip. "You are such a fucking hypocrite. You say you don't care about labels and shit like that, but the first thing you do when something doesn't

Play My Part

go the way you planned is putting a label on it. You think I'm cheating on you with one of your best friends?"

"Cheating?" I laugh. "For you to be cheating on me, that would mean you accepted that we are an item. Did the letter get lost in the mail or was it that you're a fucking coward who wants to have me only when the lights are dimmed and people aren't watching?"

She stays silent, and I turn my head and look outside, realizing that we're almost home. I never wanted to not be home more than I do now. I'm stuck inside a mansion with the woman I love more than anything in the whole world, a man I love more than I love my blood sister, and both of them fucking stabbed me in the back.

I get out of the car and go directly to my room, feeling my blood boiling and getting angrier with each second that passes. I can't fucking believe they could do this to me. What were they thinking when they spent most of the night together having those heart-to-heart conversations and ignoring me, making me feel like absolutely nothing?

I kick the door to our—my—bedroom shut and I take out Melody's suitcase from the top shelf of our—my—walk-in closet. I frantically start shoving all her belongings in that suitcase, planning to throw it inside Manon's room and lock the door to my own so I can fucking cry myself to sleep like the miserable child that I am. I have now come to the realization that Yonathan was right. I am a fucking child, but not for the reasons he mentioned. I'm a child because I always thought people are kind and have good intentions. That the smiles they give me are genuine, and that Melody actually cares about me. And most probably she does. But not enough to keep her from hurting me the best way she can. Not enough for her to accept being with me, and not fucking enough for her to leave my best friends out of the fucking mess she made us go through.

I don't think she would've slept with Manon or that he would betray me in such a way. I know they have a genuine friendship and that's all there is. But God, did I want to hurt her. To force my pain down her throat so she could choke on it the same way I do whenever she tells me that she's not ready to fully give herself to me.

Every memory of her telling me to take it slow, to get to know who we are before we decide to have an official relationship comes to mind. She was never fucking ready and she never will be. And not because she's traumatized by her past relationship, or, better said, not only because of that. She was never fucking ready because she took me for granted and thought that I would be waiting for her until the princess finally comes down from her ivory tower and decides my fate. I told her she was my queen, but she can barely fit Cinderella's shoe.

"Are you seriously doing this, Lucas?" she asks me in a choked voice. "Only because I dared to befriend Manon and talk to him, you decided to hurt me, offend me, fucking rip my heart out and kick me out?"

I let out a laugh and keep packing her shit, hoping that she'll just leave me alone. Of course, my lucky stars aren't shining tonight because she continues.

"Do you want me to apologize for trying to find somebody I trust? Do you want me to beg for forgiveness because I finally found a friend?"

"I don't want you to do shit, Melody." I try to keep my voice as indifferent as possible, still not looking at her. "And if you think this is happening because you and Manon are friends, then you're shallower than I thought you are."

"Then what is it?" She comes next to me and pushes my shoulder. "What are you so jealous of, huh, Lucas? You're afraid that your brother," she air quotes the last word, "would love me more than he does you? You think I'm going to steal your precious chosen family from you?"

"You can't steal fuck from me," I say in an indifferent voice, "because sooner or later, everybody will see your true colors. And they're not pretty, sweetheart."

I move past her, moving to the bathroom and gathering all her beauty products from the shelves next to the tub. She follows me in there and

Play My Part

shuts the door behind her, right before she starts screaming.

"Then what is it about, Lucas? Oh, please take mercy on me and enlighten me by showing me the true reason for you behaving like a fucking asshole!"

"Because I can't stand you anymore!" I scream back, throwing all the shit I gathered on the floor. "I can't stand you offering me half of you, I can't stand sleeping next to you and waking up to you reminding me about your fucking rules about not being too close in public. I can't stand living in this constant state of questioning if flowers are too much or if giving you a wink is too little. And all this is happening while you have no problem with offering Manon hugs and your stories in the most public place we've been to since we got here."

"The difference is that Manon doesn't tell me on a constant basis that he can't wait to marry me and have a family with me."

"Oh, I'm sorry then," I say sitting down on the edge of the tub, "I didn't know that I should've treated you like a fucking whore and tell you that I only want to use you for my own entertainment. That worked out for Bart, right? My bad for not taking a lesson out of his book. Maybe that would've actually made you want to marry me."

She gasps and looks at me with unshed tears in her eyes. I raise my shoulders, signaling her that I won't fall for that shit again. I'm done with wiping her tears and promising her that we'll sort this out. We're never going to sort this out and as much as my heart is begging me for one more moment, for one more kiss, and for one more touch, my brain screams louder that we won't have either of those. That I need her out of my life for good so I can find somebody who would accept me, who would fucking love me, and who would not abandon me and let me rot in my own misery.

"You have no idea how much I want to be all yours, Lucas," she says in a defeated voice, wiping her cheeks. "I don't think there's something that I want more in this world than that."

"Great way of showing it." I sigh and bury my face in my palms, rubbing my face. "You did nothing but hurt me these past weeks, Melody! You did nothing but force me to walk on a suspended wire, thousands of feet above ground while carrying the weight of the world on my shoulders."

"I know," she says sitting on the floor with her back against the door, "and I'm sorry for that. I didn't mean to, I swear. I just thought I could do it. I thought I could do it without telling you…" she trails off, looking at the wall behind me.

"Tell me what?" I frown.

My deepest, darkest secret," she whispers.

I don't know what the fuck she's talking about, but yet again, I feel deceived and played. All those times she said she could trust me with anything were nothing but lies, apparently. Every single moment I thought I'm the only person in this world who knew absolutely everything about Melody Byers was nothing but a figment of my imagination. Because, apparently, she was never as open as I thought she was.

"You're just making it worse, Melody," I say, taking a seat on the floor across her, spreading out my legs on the cold bathroom floor. "You're just telling me that you were never the person I thought you were."

"Oh, I was," she says, still looking transfixed at a point on the wall, "I just lost a part of me that I'll never get back."

"To Bart?"

"To Heaven," she says in a choked voice. "Or, at least, I hope that's where my unborn baby is now."

I feel my heart stopping in my chest and a lump forming in my throat that I can't swallow down despite my best effort. I don't know what the fuck I'm supposed to do now other than crawl and beg her to forgive me for treating her like I did earlier. But I didn't know. I didn't know because she didn't fucking tell me and I don't understand why it was so easy for her to tell me about Bart and give me a detailed description about how he abused her, yet she felt the need to hide a miscarriage from me. Unless it wasn't a miscarriage.

"Whose baby was it, Melody?" I ask in a scared voice.

After a pause that feels like eons, she starts crying harder, until her sobs turn to wails.

"Who was the father of that baby, Melody?" I ask again. I know who it was, I just need to hear it from her own fucking mouth.

"You were." Her voice is barely audible, but I feel like she screamed those two words directly in my brain.

I move closer, crouching in front of her, and grab her chin in my hand, forcing her to look into my eyes.

"And what happened to that baby?"

"Please, Lucas..."

"What did you do to my child, Melody?" I scream in her face so loud that I expect somebody to come knocking on the door making sure that I didn't kill her. But at this moment in time I feel like I would. She and everybody who helped her get rid of my unborn child. I could've had a son or a daughter with the love of my life. I could've had a family already. A fucking blood family, a small human being who would adore me and would have my blond hair and their mother's hazel eyes. I could've been loved since over four years ago by a person who would love me the same as I would them. And she fucking took them away from me. She took my chance of being happy and complete.

"I had an abortion," she admits, begging me for something with her eyes that are already swollen by how hard she's crying. "I did it for you, Lucas. Let me explain."

I stand up and punch the door behind her more times than I can count, stopping only when my hand goes through it.

"For me?" I shout. "You killed my child for me? You fucking took the thing I wanted the most in this whole fucking world for me? You made someone abandon me without even meeting me, Melody."

"You were just starting your career. Things were finally going in the right direction for you and…"

"You don't get to decide my life for me," I cut her off, screaming louder than I thought I'm able to. "You don't get to take my fucking baby from me without even asking me how I feel about that."

I feel hot tears running down my cheeks, and my ears are ringing while my heart is thumping in my chest. I could've heard a heart beating like this on a monitor, holding Melody's hand if she hadn't decided to be so fucking selfish and keep me away from this decision.

"You should've come to me," I say through gritted teeth. "You should've told me and we should've made that decision together! I would've fucking held your hand if we *both* decided this was the right thing to do. I would've taken care of you and apologize for not using a condom despite you lying to me that you were on the pill. I would've done everything you needed if you decided you didn't want that baby, if you would've fucking told me that you were pregnant with my child!"

"I didn't lie!" she screams back. "I took some herbal shit at the same time I was taking my birth control pills and I didn't know it interfered with it."

"I couldn't fucking care less! I could've been a father and you just decided to take that away from me, too. Wasn't my heart enough to take when you fucking left me after that night? You had to take my baby away from me, too?"

"You have no idea how much I wanted that baby, Lucas," she says in an aggressive tone when she stands up. "You have no idea how much I wanted to raise it with you and have a perfect family."

"Then why did you kill it, Melody?" My voice is hoarse from how much I screamed, but I can't stop myself from doing it. I fall on my knees in front of her and then lie down on the floor because I can't support my own body's weight. Apparently, our baby wasn't the only soul that left this planet by Melody Byers's hand because mine does exactly the same tonight.

Play My Part

"Because you were eighteen, Lucas." She lies next to me and looks into my eyes, but this time it's my turn to look at a point on the wall. "You were in no way ready to be a father. You had so much waiting for you!"

"That wasn't your decision to make, was it, Melody?" My voice is finally at a lower level, but it sounds robotic. Long gone are all the emotions I put in every word I uttered to her. Now I feel nothing but emptiness and a hollow void of deceit in my chest. "I would've cried, Melody," I tell her in the same voice. "When you told me that you were pregnant, I would've cried and hugged you. I would've promised to love and protect you both. I would've kissed you first and then your stomach."

She comes closer to me, cautiously wrapping her hands around me and resting her face on my chest while she continues sobbing. I wish I could cry too. I wish I could have more tears to shed for the baby I never got to meet.

"I would've asked you to marry me the next day and we would've moved into my mansion, turning Sandra's room into the most beautiful nursery for that child, and our future ones. We would've been so happy, Melody."

"But we can do it now, Luc," she says in a voice that doesn't sound like hers. She sounds completely mental and unhinged. "Now that I told you my secret and everything is out in the open, we can be happy and have that life now."

She takes my silence as approval and starts fumbling with my zipper and my belt, taking my cock out and rubbing it frantically.

"Stop, Melody," I whisper. "It's too late."

"No, no," she strokes me even faster and the only reason I get hard is that my body doesn't feel the same pain my soul does. I have no desire left in me, not for her, not for any woman out there, not to draw my next breath. "It's not too late! We will do everything you just said." She lifts her dress and moves her panties to the side, sinking on my cock and making it hurt because her pussy is as dry as the air in the desert. This is as unpleasant for her as it is for me.

She starts rocking her hips faster with every second that passes and the look on her face might make me feel sad or scared if I was able to feel any fucking thing except this numbness that seems to choke me.

"I'll stop taking my pills tonight and you can fuck me as many times as you want until you make me pregnant again," she says with a fucked-up smile on her lips. "And even after that. You can fuck me anytime you want, I swear. You don't even need to ask, you can just throw me on the bed and thrust inside me and I'll love it. We will be so happy, Lucas. Can you imagine how happy we'll be?"

I keep staying silent, sacrificing another piece of myself to feed her madness and give her the illusion that I actually believe the insanities that come out of her mouth.

"I'll make you the father of so many beautiful babies, Lucas. It will be just us and them. We won't need anybody else. Just our happy family."

I fucking despise her right now. How easy it is for her to talk about the things I dreamed my whole life and living under the impression that from now on nothing can keep us apart. That because she finally has the same dream I had for so many years, I will thank her for the opportunity and do what she said. I fucking despise her for not caring if I need to heal from the wound she caused me by being fucking selfish and inconsiderate. I fucking despise her with every part of my being.

When I come, I don't utter a sound. She moans and that makes me hate her even more because she is now as fake as all the other women I fucked. I thought I found my safe haven, only to realize that I stepped inside the last level of Hell.

"Did you enjoy that, Melody?" I ask her, hoping that she'll be fucking honest with me at least now.

"I loved it," she chirps.

"Good. Now get the fuck out of my house."

Chapter 15
Melody

He left me. He left me here, lying on this cold floor with nothing more than a memory of how happy I was in the past month and a dream of a perfect life. He broke me into pieces that are scattered all over the world, never being able to find their way back together.

Every time I stop crying, a new memory comes to mind and the tears are back. I remember how he looked at me that morning in the airport. I remember how he kissed me when he saw me in the living room of this house, bags and suitcases around me. I remember every time he told me he was mine, and I remember all the times I couldn't say it back. I remember every fucking moment we shared since we met again and I don't know how to forget them.

The bad memories are there, too, reminding me of how I was never good enough for him. How only my poor choices led me to this dark place, where nobody is holding my hand. I remember crying when I saw the plus sign on that pregnancy test and how I made an appointment two minutes after. I remember how I said I was in no way interested to check on the small life that was starting inside me and how I was absolutely positive I wanted an abortion.

I remember being on that table. I remember all the sounds around me, every word the people in the room said, and I remember how much I regretted what I'd done the second the procedure ended. I remember getting dressed while doing my best not to cry and refraining from calling Lucas and telling him about the terrible mistake I had made.

Would've he forgiven me? Would've he told me *Ssshh, it's okay, Mel. Please don't cry.* And hug me to his chest? Would've kept me safe from making yet another mistake and accept going out with my gynecologist?

The memory of my first date with Bart comes to mind and I feel nauseous. I remember how he told me that I made the right choice. That he admired how I was strong enough to make a decision like this because I wanted to focus on my career and my growth. How fucking charming he was when he ordered an expensive bottle of wine that he drank alone in less than an hour. The signs were always there, but I was too blind to see them. I was building a fantasy because I wanted to fill the emptiness in my soul. I forced myself to believe that Bart, the charming man with expensive tastes, will take care of me, respect me, and cherish me. I believed the lies he fed me and I ate my own dessert. I was, am, and always will be a collection of poor choices that forgot how to smile genuinely a long time ago.

"Hey, uhm, do you want some ice cream?" a voice that sounds like it's wrapped in satin asks me. "They have the double chocolate Magnum here, and trust me when I say that your tongue will have an orgasm the second you taste it."

I don't want to eat ice cream with Tzipporah. I don't want anything else other than people to leave me alone, hoping that at some point I'll be able to get up and go home. Or, most precisely, go to the empty house that's waiting for me in Austin. Because my home is the person whose child I murdered.

"*By the* morning breeze *I was right by your side, but your arms released me, now I'm flying high,*" I whisper the song that keeps playing in my mind since Lucas left this room. I don't know why this happened. Most probably because my brain can't take this amount of pain, so it found a song that expresses what I feel. I wonder if Juke Ross was suffering when he wrote it, or if he did that while thinking of souls shattering like mine has.

Play My Part

"I think "All This Love" by JP Copper is more suitable for this situation to be honest," she says in a kind voice, "but I'll take that as a no for ice cream. Anyway, I think you should get up, Melody. You've been here for two hours."

I thought I had been here for five minutes, not that it matters anyway. I had a month of unadulterated happiness and now an eternity of emptiness awaits. I don't care where I spend it, I just need to find a way to carry this burden and a mechanism that will help me suffer the consequences of my own actions.

"Can you please leave me alone?" I realize that my throat is sore and talking feels like swallowing a handful of needles. "I'll be out of your hair soon. Just give me a couple of minutes and I'll be gone."

"For fuck's sake, Melody!" I can recognize Yonathan's thick voice even if he would be whispering in a loud crowd. "Aren't you done yet with this pity party?"

"Please, Yonathan," I swallow the little saliva I have in my mouth, "I'm begging you to go away and give me two more minutes."

I hear them whispering, but I have no interest in hearing what they are saying. I just want to torture myself for a bit longer with images of me and Lucas being old and having tens of grandchildren from all the sons and daughters we could have had. Of me changing diapers while he cooks dinner, or of me telling him how tired I am right after he turns off the lights and hugs me so tight I can barely breathe. I took the life he wanted from him and he ended mine in return. It's more than a fair trade.

"Stand up," Yonathan says, but I pay him no attention. Maybe if I ignore him he will go away and take Tzipporah with him.

"I just want to be alone. Please."

"You've been alone here for enough time." He lets out a frustrated sigh. "It's four a.m., Melody, and I'm fucking tired."

"So, go to sleep," I whisper. "I'll be silent. I swear you won't hear a sound," I plead.

"Yon, maybe we should leave her a bit more?" Tzipporah asks in that sweet voice of hers. "I'm sure she'll let us know if she needs something."

"She won't," he deadpans. "Always the fucking martyr, this one. She's just going to stay here and torment herself because she thinks she deserves it."

I have no idea how he knows about my plans, but maybe my face betrays me. Maybe the makeup that I'm sure is smeared all over my face is the perfect depiction of what my mind conjured in the last couple of hours.

"Do you want to tell us what happened?" she asks me in a sad voice. "Maybe letting it all out will help you a bit."

"She was pregnant with Lucas and she had an abortion," Yonathan says before I even open my mouth to say something. "The problem is that he didn't know and now that she told him, he wants to kill her and she just wants to die. A match made in heaven, after all."

I smile despite myself, feeling my lips cracking.

"I see that Lucas already updated you."

"He didn't."

"Then how do you know?" I frown.

"I know a lot of things, Melody," he says in a bored tone. "And the ones that I don't, I do my best to find out."

"I'm not sure what that means," I choke, "except the fact that you're a hacker and broke into my medical records. Did you do it for leverage?" I start laughing hysterically. "I was on borrowed time anyway, wasn't I, Yonathan? You were just expecting for us to be truly happy, so you could deliver the final blow and destroy us both."

I keep laughing, rolling onto my back, and putting my hand on my stomach, trying to soothe the pain there, and that gesture immediately makes me cry because I now imagine how it would feel to lie like this in bed, next to Lucas, being excited that the baby kicked and asking him to put his hand next to mine so he could feel it, too. I'm laughing and crying and then laughing again. I feel like my sanity is hanging from a loose thread and the only thing that keeps me from completely losing my mind is the fact that I need to punish myself more. To make myself suffer for the rest of my life for one of the most stupid things I ever did.

I feel a pair of arms grabbing me from the floor and all of a sudden, I'm in the tub with cold water spraying all over my tired body. I try to stand up, but Yonathan takes the showerhead and just directs it at me, soaking me from head to toe.

"Are you fucking insane, Yonathan?" I scream.

"Finally," he exhales, "I thought you lost even the last ounce of sass."

"Sass?" I ask, taking the showerhead from his hand and directing it to him. "I'll fucking show you sass!"

I shove the water jet in his face and then move it toward random parts of his body, not caring about the fact that I'm creating a small flood inside this bathroom. How fucking dare he do this to me? How can be so fucking soulless that he cared more about always having an ace up his sleeve even if that would destroy the happiness of the people he allegedly cares about? What if I didn't tell Lucas? What if I decided to bury that memory and be with him?

"Calm down, Aquaman." He laughs, but it's not fucking funny. "We already have to pay for the door Lucas broke. No need to pay for the whole bathroom!"

I turn off the water, get out of the tub, and go to pick up my suitcases. I can't be in this house anymore with these fucking insane people and with the man who treated me worse than trash since we met. Fuck them. Fuck Yonathan, and especially fuck Lucas for not trying to see my side of the story. To walk a fucking mile in my shoes and be scared shitless of being pregnant by her best friend's brother. Her best friend's brother who was three years away from being the legal age to drink, for fuck's sake. It's easy for him to say now that he would've kissed me and asked me to marry him if I told him about the pregnancy because now the whole world would fucking swoon if he'd become a daddy. But at eighteen? He would've been a child raising a child.

"And where exactly are you going, Melody?" Yonathan asks in his classic bored tone.

"To go find a hotel."

"You do know you're outside Bucharest, it's four a.m. in the morning and you have to be on the filming set in three hours, right?"

"I don't have to be anywhere!" I scream. "Fuck you and fuck the movie! I don't want to see any of you for the rest of my life. Actually, if I see you three lifetimes from now, it would be too soon."

"Melody," Rah gets closer to me, putting her hand on my shoulder, "I know you're hurt. But maybe you should wait until both of you calm down and talk this out."

"No!" I resume walking. "Lucas told me to get the fuck out of his house, and that's exactly what I'm going to do. He wants to throw me out? Then I'll leave before he has the chance to do so. I'm done accepting his shit. I'm done torturing myself, doing my best to please him, and I'm fucking done with tasting bile in my mouth every time I have to look at him because I'm afraid he will leave me. I told him the truth!" I scream. "I fucking came clean, begged him, and promising him that I would even let him half-rape me if that's what he would need to forgive me."

"Melody, Melody, Melody," Yonathan clicks his tongue, moving closer to me, "did you really think that's what baby Temple would need? To fuck you against your will and make you a baby machine?" he says in the most disgusted voice one could imagine. "He needs you to accept that you wronged him," he deadpans. "He needs you to go out there and say that you're sorry, and that you will fix this, somehow. Both of you."

"But what about what I need?" I ask no one in particular, pointing to my chest. "What about how I heal from the trauma of being pregnant while being all fucking alone? What about what I felt when I realized that I let a man manipulate me, gaslight me, convince me that I deserve to be raped, and punched, and slapped because I will never find somebody else?

Play My Part

That no matter what I would do, Lucas would never have me back? Well," I half laugh, "I guess Bart wasn't so wrong, after all, was he? Because Lucas, indeed, would never want me again after tonight."

"Lucas will always want you," Yonathan dramatically rolls his eyes, "even if he's yelling that he doesn't now."

"Tough." I dismiss him. "He should've thought about that before calling me a whore, and behaving like a maniac."

"What did I tell you the night I brought you here, Melody?" he asks through gritted teeth. "Did I ask you if you wanted him or did I not?"

"You did, but…"

"Did I tell you that if you step inside this house, that means you will fight for him no matter what, consequences be damned?"

"Yes, but you were referring to what the world would say about us," I say in a determined voice. "You weren't talking about this kind of shitshow."

"And how would you know what I was talking about, Melody?" he asks in a tone that makes my blood freeze and Tzipporah gasp. Yeah, sweetheart, he's not so hot now, is he?

"I knew about the abortion two hours after we landed, Melody." He takes a seat on the edge of the bed, taking Rah's hand and bringing her next to him. I notice that he doesn't let her hand go after she sits down, but I keep looking in his hypnotizing eyes. "I needed to know everything about you, considering Lucas was completely obsessed with you. I needed to know if I should've encouraged him or not."

"You had no right." I clench my jaw so hard, I feel my morals cracking.

"Rights are relative. The richer you are, the more rights you have." He shrugs. "By the time the help in the house finished unpacking, I knew all there was to know about Melody Byers, ex-Trello." He pauses, daring me to say something, but the only thing I do is cross my arms, dropping the bags to the floor. If he decided to come clean about the horrible way he invaded my privacy, I'm more than willing to listen. I have absolutely nothing left to lose, and his confession might give me the closure I need, so

I can realize how absolutely mental all three of them are. "And I realized that your past didn't include something that baby Temple couldn't forgive. Something that would piss him off? Yes. Confuse him about his feelings? Sure. But giving up on you? No, not in any way."

I look at Rah, expecting her to be as horrified as I am, but all I see in her green eyes is curiosity, admiration, and desire. And that convinces me that she's just another person I need to put on my list of people to avoid at all costs.

"That is wrong on so many levels, Yonathan." I shake my head. "Completely and utterly wrong."

"Perhaps," he shrugs, standing up from the bed. "But if you think that's wrong, then what I'm about to do will either end with you grabbing a knife and stabbing me with it, or realizing you need to fight to get what's yours. I would prefer the latter, of course, but do know that if you choose the former, I won't hold any grudges."

"What are you planning to do, Yonathan?" I'm crippled and I feel my body starting to shake.

He grabs my wrist so tight that I think it will bruise tomorrow and drags me to the living room, where I see Lucas and Non sitting in silence on the large leather sofa. I try to twist Yonathan's arm because this is the last place I want to be right now, but he doesn't seem to notice the pain my movement is causing him. Or, at least, the pain I'm hoping I cause him.

"Gentlemen," Yonathan booms, throwing me on the ottoman in front of them, "can we have a bit of privacy?"

I look at him with my eyes wide open, feeling like I'm having a heart attack. He leans over me, spreading my legs with his knee. When I'm about to punch his beautiful face, he puts his lips over my ear and whispers, "Play along, Melody. I know you don't trust me, but I swear to everything I hold dear that I won't hurt you."

He never sounded more honest than he does now. Yonathan is always bored, sarcastic, or in a different stage of annoyance. But now both his

Play My Part

voice and his face are nothing but sincere. So I give him a barely visible nod, remembering that I already lost Lucas and if Yonathan thinks that this might bring him back to me, then I'm willing to do whatever he wants me to.

"What the fuck are you doing, Yonathan?" Manon's voice is the perfect contradiction to Yonathan's. If anger sounded a certain way, this is how it would sound.

"Finally taking what's mine!" he laughs. "I've been waiting for this for a long, long time!" He trails his finger over my shoulder, my arm, and my palm. "Tell me, Lucas, did she say my name when you fucked her the last time?"

I can completely understand what he's doing now, and part of me wants me to do exactly what he suggested and stab him until I drain all the blood from his body. But the bigger part of me tells me that I should try and play this completely stupid game.

"Do you mean earlier, when she was desperate for my cock, hoping that fucking me would make me forgive her?" Lucas says in a distant voice. But I know him. I know this is his way of reacting when he's completely suffering and hurt. He tries to offend the people around him, shatter them like glass, only to make them feel the same pain he does. Unfortunately for him, I know this game. I know every step he will take and how long it takes for him to crack.

"Not necessarily," Yonathan smiles devilishly, moving his fingers all over my legs, "I'm referring to the last time you actually did something to make her feel good. Did you know she likes it when you flick her clit before burying your tongue deep inside her?"

Lucas looks at him with his eyebrows raised in shock, and then at me, hate pouring from his eyes. So, I decide to push him even more and fake a moan the best I can, hoping it sounds at least a bit believable. I'm in no way as good at acting as they are, but I can only hope that all the mixed feelings boiling inside Lucas will keep him from seeing that I'm bluffing.

Miriam Rosentvaig

"Why do you look so surprised, baby Temple?" the man who is now toying with some strands of my hair asks. "Oh, wait. Don't tell me that you actually thought that your small fantasy is one step away from coming true?"

Lucas looks at Yonathan like he's his worst enemy. There is no trace of the warm, kind man he was until tonight. Now it's clear how much of Yonathan lives inside him. And I admire him a bit more for not letting this side of him come to surface except during life-changing moments. Like the one happening right now, that is affecting both of our lives.

Yonathan draws his index finger between my breasts, moving slowly to my stomach. My body starts shivering from the cold air coming out from the air conditioner directly on my wet skin covered by my soaked dress. Lucas looks at me and I laugh internally. I can't fucking believe that he thinks this is happening because Yonathan is bringing me so much pleasure.

"Take her dress off, Yon," Rah says in a sultry voice. "I want to see her tits."

I quickly change the first person on my kill list, crossing Yonathan's name and writing hers instead. I see her in my peripheral vision, going to the sound system and connecting her phone to it. The speakers are blasting Charlotte Lawrence's "Joke's On You" and when she leaves her phone on the coffee table, she starts singing the lyrics in a low, hypnotic voice. Of course she can fucking sing, too! This woman is absolutely flawless.

"Impatient little bird," Yonathan says in a soothing voice, "first we need to get rid of the unwanted people in this room."

Tzipporah comes closer to us, toying with the hem of her dress, blowing a kiss to the two men sitting on the couch.

"Does that mean we can take Rah and tag team her?" Lucas asks, standing up.

"I'll stay here," her accent gets thicker, the *R* sounding like her tongue is curling around the sound, "I like to watch." She lets out a laugh that sounds completely innocent, despite the fucked-up situation we all are in.

Lucas exhales loudly and his eyes follow Yonathan's hands that are

Play My Part

moving all around my body, except to my breasts and my pussy. I'm sure he feels like he would rather drink acid than keep doing this, so I decide that if he is willing to walk so many extra miles, I owe him to walk them, too.

"Is this true, Melody?" Lucas asks me in a choked voice. "Did you play me this whole time? Used me like a fucking tool?" My heart breaks seeing him like this, but he needs to see that I'm hurt, too. That I need him, too. That we need to heal, but we need to do it together. "To what end, Melody?"

"You wouldn't believe me," I shrug, "so I finally found someone who would."

Yonathan chuckles, kissing the back of my hand, and then my wrist. When his tongue crawls all over my arm, Manon stands up and goes to the dry bar, pouring himself a drink. It's the first time I've seen him drinking. Even when we were at the club earlier, he drank his usual canned Dr. Pepper. I can only hope that my only friend out of this bunch will be able to forgive me.

"Believe what, Melody?" Lucas's voice distracts me from looking at Manon. "That you fucking played me like a fool? That I was just a pawn in your fucked-up game of chess?"

"See?" I shrug. "That's why I gave in. That's why I agreed to give myself fully to Yonathan and not you! Because we might have started on the wrong foot, but now he understands that I made a mistake and he forgave me."

"He's not the one who you should apologize to," he roars, taking Tzipporah's phone and throwing it to the wall.

"You'll have to buy me a new one, buddy," she muses, taking his place on the couch. "Now, move aside and let me enjoy the show."

"Stop, Yonathan!" he screams again.

"You're not the one who can make me stop, baby Temple," he rasps. "The only one who can seems to enjoy what I'm doing."

He raises the stake by slowly lifting up my dress, and I send a silent prayer to God to keep his already deteriorated sanity in place enough for him to stop when he should.

"Such delicate skin!" he whispers. "I can't wait to see how it tastes!"

"Haven't you hurt me enough, Melody?" Lucas asks and when I look at him, I see tears running down his cheeks. "Did you have to do this, too? Did you have to fucking ruin my life?"

"You made your bed, now sleep in it, Lucas," Yonathan says before I can fall to my knees and beg Lucas to forgive me and to take me back. "I tried to teach you that every action has a reaction, and that the consequences of your mistakes will hit you right in the face sooner or later. I guess now it happened sooner."

"So, this is my fault, too?" he asks in an incredulous voice.

"Of course it is." Yonathan laughs, grazing my thighs with the tips of his fingers and looking into his younger brother's eyes, "you told her to leave the house. I took advantage of the opportunity, and told her to stay. Finders keepers, losers weepers."

"You didn't find shit." Lucas pushes Yonathan off me, making him fall to the floor and going down with him. He wraps his hands around his throat and screams like somebody is skinning him alive, "She's mine! And I will fucking rip you apart if you ever touch her again. You don't get to put your fucking filthy hands on her."

I stand up, but I feel a soft hand taking mine. I give Rah a questioning look, and she squeezes my hand.

"Just wait," she says in a low voice. "Don't show your cards just yet."

I nod and promise myself to fight the urge to go and wrap my hands around Lucas and beg him to stop. Maybe Tzipporah is right. Maybe all of us need this to happen so we can finally clear the air and inhale deeply.

"And why should I do that, Lucas?" Yonathan wheezes. "Just because you came inside her once?"

"Shut up." His scream is a mix of anger, disappointment, and fear. "Shut the fuck up."

Play My Part

"Poor baby Temple," Yon mocks. "Having to accept that another human being he loved is dead. Cry me a fucking river."

He punches Yonathan so hard, the crack can be heard in every corner of their huge living room. But Yonathan doesn't seem fazed.

"Right. Because punching me will definitely bring them back." He coughs, his blues spitting fire into Lucas's greens. "They're dead, Lucas. Fucking six feet under and dancing with the angels you're so keen to believe in."

His tears are falling on Yonathan's wrinkled jacket, and I can see the grasp he has on Yon's neck loosen. He doesn't say anything in response, he just keeps staring at the man he has pinned to the floor.

"Keep in mind, Luc, that by focusing on the ones who aren't breathing anymore, you're slowly killing the ones who are still alive."

"She took my child from me, Yonathan," he says between sobs. "My baby boy or my baby girl."

"She took her child from her, too, Lucas." He wraps his hand around Lucas's wrist, pulling him into his arms and hugging him on the floor. "You're stronger than you think you are, baby Temple. Don't ever forget how much shit you swallowed from life, yet here you are. Shining in the spotlight, and being this generation's most talented actor."

"I thought that was you."

"Ask me again tomorrow and I'll tell you it's me." Yonathan laughs, gently pushing him away.

They both lie on their backs in the middle of the living room and I let out an exhale, trying to remember if I breathed in the past couple of minutes.

When Lucas looks at me with those green eyes that will never fail to make my heart stutter all I can do is nod. *We can do this.* He nods back. *I know we can.* Our thoughts seem to float around the room, disrupted by Manon clearing his throat and extending his hands to both of his friends.

"I honestly think I should be in the spotlight next time," he tells Yonathan, "I feel like the part of hugging her was too small for my unparalleled talent."

"Yeah, and if you ever make me play the role of a creepy voyeur again, I'll cut your dick off and feed it to the dogs," Rah says in a deadly serious voice.

"You orchestrated all this shit?" I scream at Yonathan who is arranging his tie, going back to the old, bored version of himself.

"If you're going to give me the *You had no right. How dare you, slap, slap, I hate you* speech, spare me." He rolls his eyes and comes to stand in front of me. "The good part is that now, you're starting to grow on me. Stick around, will you?" He gives me a wink and then turns to look at the gorgeous woman on my left. "And don't pretend you don't like to watch, little bird. I can read you like an open book."

He turns on his heel, waving his hand to Manon and Rah to follow him, leaving Lucas and I staring at each other.

I have never been more scared in my life.

Chapter 16

Lucas

The way she looks right now makes me go feral. The wet dress hugging those fucking hips. That little strap falling off her shoulder, allowing me a better view to her left tit, and that face that looks like she's got her throat fucked for countless hours. All that makes me take two long strides, grab the back of her head, and stick my tongue in her mouth, tasting the salt of the tears she shed.

She whimpers when I put my hand on her round ass, pushing her pelvis into mine to make her feel how hard I am. How hard she makes me even though my feelings are so fucking conflicted that I don't know where my love for her ends and where all the rage, hate, and disgust start.

"This doesn't change the fact that a part of me still fucking hates your guts." I tell her before shoving my tongue back down her throat and letting my hands roam all over her damp body.

"I know," she says, cupping my face. "But I want you to let that part of you come to play. Let it get to know me." She takes one hand from my face, wrapping it around my dick through my pants. "Let it fuck me the way it wants, so, maybe, that part could forgive me, too."

"If I do that, it won't be pretty, Melody." I groan. "You should never ask for the monster to devour you whole."

"What if I need it to devour me? What if I need to be punished in the most brutal way so I, too, can forgive myself for what I've done to you?"

she says in a pleading voice, and the fact that she wants me to be rough with her makes me even harder.

I wanted her to take what she wanted from me. I wanted her to use me for her own pleasure, and that brought me pleasure, as well. But now I feel entitled to her body. I feel like I deserve to use her, make her bend and break only to bring me pleasure. I feel like every action I would make while fucking her would be justified by what transpired earlier and I fucking well earned the right to claim her.

"Be careful what you wish for, Nightingale," I whisper in her ear, "because wishes aren't always made of stardust and honey. Mine, for example, are rooted in selfishness and sin."

"I'm not scared of you, Lucas." She smiles, trying to convince either me or herself that what she said is true. "I want to know every single part of you, even the ones that you keep from the public eye. Especially the ones you keep from the public eye."

She kisses me like I kissed her earlier, our tongues devouring each other's like two hungry lions fighting over the last piece of meat they found. The things I want to do to her, or better said, the things that I will do to her, since she just gave me the green light, might make her change her mind. She's used to nice, obedient Lucas. The one who always roots for her and holds her hand every step of the way, not questioning the orders he received. She had puppy Lucas and never met hungry Lucas. The one that will leave her body bruised and her pussy sore.

"Get on your knees, Melody," I tell her in a low voice.

She hesitates, and I arch an eyebrow, looking at her and getting angrier by the second because her reluctance only postpones what I have in mind for her. *We're going to have so much fun when we'll ruin her,* the monster living in my brain whispers, and I can only agree.

"Somebody might come back," she says, looking at the closed door to my right.

"And don't you want to let them know who fucking owns you,

Play My Part

Melody?" I push her shoulders until she has no choice but to kneel in front of me. "Don't you want to show them how much you like sucking my cock? Don't you want for them to know who you fucking bow to?"

She gives me a spiteful look which I can't help but return. "Either you open your mouth and let me fuck your throat like the lying slut you are deserves, or I'm going to find somebody else willing to do it. Don't waste my time, Melody," I say through gritted teeth.

She starts crying again, but angrily wipes the tears that fall the second they do. She looks at me for a couple of seconds before opening her mouth and sticking her tongue out, and it doesn't take me more than two seconds to unzip my pants, take my cock out, and do exactly what I told her I would do earlier.

When the tip of my dick reaches the back of her throat, she gags, and that only makes me take her head between my hands and start fucking her face, letting out all the rage, all the anger, and all the fucking disappointment. I take everything out on her and allow myself to let loose and punish her for every little thing she ever did to me. For abandoning me five years ago. For marrying Bart. For taking the chance of having a baby with her away from me. For lying to me. For fucking deceiving me. Every thrust is the representation of another mistake she made.

"Suck it harder," I pant. "Make that mouth worth my while."

She looks at me with her hazel eyes that are always expressing exactly what she feels, and this time I see rage and hate pooling in them. Apparently, we finally managed to feel the exact same things toward one another. Despite the way she looks at me she indulges me and starts licking the tip of my cock, lapping all the precum that's leaking from it.

I pull her hair back so fast that it takes her a second to realize what happened and to close her mouth. She starts coughing, and all the juices that are coming out of her mouth makes her look more of a mess than she already did. I chuckle when I think about how she will look when I'm done with her.

I kneel on the floor in front of her, and grab her face with my left hand, taking her dress off with my right one.

"Are you sure you don't want to run, Melody? There's still time," I tell her while I put two fingers inside her pussy. "You can still tell me *no* and go find another fool who will love you the same way I did."

She wraps her hand around my wrist, trying to stop my movements, and that makes me fuck her harder with my fingers. I know what I said hurt her, and that's exactly what I wanted. I want to see her in fucking pain. I want to see her crawling and begging God to make the hurt go away because she can't take it anymore. I want her to feel the same way as I do.

"Did?" she asks, her body shaking from what I'm doing to her. "The same way you did?"

"You don't expect me to keep loving you, do you?" I laugh. "I fucking hate you so much, Melody." I grab her face and kiss her again, my fingers bringing her closer to orgasm every time I move them in and out of her. "But unlike you, I'm not going to force myself on you. I'm not going to fuck you when you're in the ultimate state of pain. I'm getting you ready, Melody." I humorlessly laugh. "Because I'm a better person than you are and because I wouldn't hurt you. Not even now when you fucking hurt me so bad, I wouldn't harm you."

"I'm sorry," she whispers before her eyes roll to the back of her head and she comes all over my fingers. I put them in her mouth and she starts sucking them immediately, all this time whimpering and crying. I feel a heat warming up my chest when I see her like this, but I do my best to extinguish it. My monster didn't get enough. My monster still needs to feel her pain and he isn't done ruining her.

I lift her from the floor and throw her on the ottoman Yonathan dragged her to earlier.

"Did you like it when Yonathan touched you? Should I call him and let him fuck your ass while I'm coming inside that greedy pussy of yours?" I ask her in a borderline insane voice. Because I actually feel insane. Watching Yonathan touch her, even if it was just one of his fucking stupid games to make me realize that I need to leave the dead be dead and live amongst the ones who are alive, was the worst kind of torture I ever endured. Except finding out that my parents were dead. That was a different kind of torture, but painful nonetheless.

I look at her naked body when I pull down her panties, and it's then that it dawns on me that I can't breathe when she's next to me, but I'd be fucking dead without her. I was willing to do everything for her, and, on some level, I still am. I can't be without her because the second she leaves she will take my heart's ability to pump blood. I have been obsessed with this woman every breathing second for the last nine years and I will keep being obsessed until I draw my last breath.

"I didn't," she says, her chin trembling. She's fucking afraid of me. She promised she won't be, yet she is. I let her witness the ugliest part of me and I scared her. But it's too late for regrets. I will take this as far as possible because I need to let this out. Right now, I need this outlet more than I need her and if I make her leave, then, as Yonathan said, I will suffer the consequences of my actions. "I don't want anyone but you. Please, Lucas," she says, covering her face with her hands, "believe me when I say that I don't want anyone but you. That I don't want anything else other than your forgiveness and another chance."

I drag her body until her ass is on the edge of the small seat, and kneeling again, I stroke my cock two times before pushing its tip as hard as I can to her clit. She screams and arches her back, and I grab her left tit to keep her in place. Rolling her nipple between my index finger and thumb, I slap her pussy with my hard dick and the noises she makes sound like somebody is crucifying her.

"What about Manon?" I ask through gritted teeth, going inside her inch by inch. "Would you like me to share you with him? You seem very fond of him."

"No!" she screams, bucking her hips to get more friction. "I don't want you to share me with anybody and I don't want to share you with anybody either. I only want you, I swear!"

"Who owns you, Melody?" I ask in a calm, curious voice, giving her another inch.

"You do."

"Fully?" I ask in the same tone.

"Completely! I swear I'm only yours. Nobody else's!" She tries to scoot closer so I can go deeper, but she understands she needs to stop when I slap her tit.

"Are you keeping more secrets from me, Melody?"

"I'm not," she whines.

"And will you ever do it again?"

"Never!" her breaths get shallower when I give her half of my cock. "No more secrets, I promise."

"I don't know if I should trust another one of your promises." I click my tongue and pull out of her. Standing up, I tuck myself in and take a seat on the couch, bathing in the shock and disappointment written all over her face.

"I hate you!" she finally screams after a long pause. "I fucking hate you, you selfish, miserable, fucking piece of shit! I hate you so fucking much!"

I give her a simple nod, stretching my arms out across the back of the couch. I realized what I needed to realize. Now it's her turn. It's her turn to accept the fact that there's a part of her that hates my fucking face and she needs to let that part of her forgive me the same way mine did her.

I know there's a long way to go until I completely heal from all the disappointment, but I know now that I'm willing to walk that road. I know that she didn't have that abortion because she didn't care about me, but because she cared too much. I know that she gave up on a part of herself, she gave up on the chance of being a mother only because she thought that would make me happy. And I know she hates me because she thinks I'm

Play My Part

the reason for her not being able to fulfill her dream.

"As you should." I nod again. "Now what are you going to do about it?"

I take my own phone from my pocket and quickly connect it to the audio system in our living room and push Play on "Not Enough" by Elvis Drew and Avivian and give her a challenging look.

She stands up, shrieking from the top of her lungs. It takes her no more than three seconds to reach me, and she slaps me harder than she did earlier in the car. I say nothing, not only because I think I deserve it, but because she needs this. She needs an outlet, too. She needs to let it all out so we can finally start building the world we agreed we need.

Her long, dark mane is flowing around her shoulders with every slap she gives my face and with every punch she throws at my chest. I'm not sure she realizes that she's fully naked, letting those beautiful breasts bounce left and right. I take into consideration the fact that I might have lost my sanity since I am now rock hard. Because finally seeing the raw version of her, not the one who was always paying attention to every step she took, to every word she uttered, was just a ticking bomb. And now that it exploded, it's the most beautiful fireworks show I've ever seen.

I can't help but adjust myself, palming my cock through the material to relieve some of the pressure I'm feeling, and she notices exactly what I'm doing. She stops dead in her tracks and looks at my hand, biting that plump lower lip so hard she draws blood, and licking it right after.

"I'll ask you again, beautiful Melody," I say. "What are you going to do about it?"

"Oh, so now I'm back at being *beautiful Melody*?" she spits. "Fuck you, Lucas!"

"Please do," I say in an honest tone. "I would love nothing more."

She lets out a psychotic laugh, but I see the blush in her cheeks. She wants that even though she thinks it's wrong to do it. Even if she knows that the norm is that fucking the man who humiliated her earlier can only mean stooping a new low. But in our world, there are no norms. No general truth except the one we believe.

When she understands that I wasn't joking, she looks around, trying to keep the tears at bay. My fierce queen is confused and she has all the reasons to be. This night has been a fucking lot, and I'm not sure if people go through all that shit in a lifetime, let alone in a little more than six hours.

Neither of us say anything because she needs to make a decision and I need to give her the necessary space to make the right one. Wiping her face with the back of her hand, she goes back to looking at me, and this time I can't help but smile when I see that fucking sparkle back in her eyes. She's so radiant now that the sun is just a poor firefly in comparison to her.

"I wanted a girl," she says, crawling in my lap and taking my T-shirt off. She kisses my chest hungrily and desperately, flicking her tongue over my nipples at the same time she unbuckles my belt and rips the button off my pants. "She would've been called Leena Trinity, so she could've had your initials and because the first movie we ever watched together was *The Matrix*."

I let out a long exhale, trying to keep my temper in check and stop myself from crying hearing how she remembers this small, insignificant detail of our lives. She stands up and drags my zipper down and pulls my pants and my boxers off, and removes my shoes, leaving me as naked as she is. She looks at me, waiting for a reaction, and I have the feeling that our future is solely depending on what that reaction will be.

"I would've spoiled her rotten," I say in a choked voice, "and I would've made her mother jealous because she would've had to share me with that small lady."

She sniffs and crawls back in my lap, and this time she doesn't waste time with teasing or with any other kind of foreplay. She impales herself on my cock like she did earlier on that bathroom floor, only this time it's completely different. This time I want her so much that I want to rip her flesh apart so I could run through her blood the same way she does through mine.

She moans when I fill her up to the hilt and crosses her arms behind my neck.

"She would've been so beautiful, Lucas," she whispers and gives me a look filled with hope.

"Not as beautiful as her mother," I whisper back in her ear, "but a very, very close second."

"I want to do some really filthy things to and with you, Lucas," she says in a sultry voice. "I want to fuck the frustration out of you and I want you to fuck the longing out of me. I want you to fuck me like a dirty whore and I want to fuck you like you're my personal plaything, whose only purpose is to bring me pleasure."

I chuckle before kissing her shoulder. "I'm nothing if not your personal plaything, whose only purpose is to bring you pleasure."

She kisses my neck in return, biting so hard that I can't help but grunt when I feel her teeth piercing my skin, followed by her tongue that is licking my blood and soothes the pain.

"I want to mark you," she whispers in my ears. "I want the entire world to know who you belong to!"

"Do it!" I nod. "Let the world know that you own me the same way I own you."

"Will you mark me, too?" she asks, finally starting to move her hips. I love feeling her warm, wet pussy wrapping my cock, but going in and out of her while feeling that sting on my neck brings my pleasure to a whole new level.

"Only if that's what you want." I raise my pelvis to meet her thrust for thrust.

"Ask me nicely and I'll think about it." She brushes the hair from the right side of her neck, shoving that almost translucent skin in my face.

"Please," I say in a high-pitched voice. "Please let me bite your beautiful skin and let everybody know that you're mine."

Miriam Rosentvaig

She doesn't say anything, preferring to nod and focus on massaging my cock with the walls of her pussy that are now clenching. I dig my fingers in her hips and my teeth in her neck, sucking her skin the same way I made her suck my cock earlier. I fill my mouth with it, creating as much suction as possible and biting until I feel the copper taste flooding my mouth. And I don't stop. I won't stop until she tells me to. Because she's my queen and I'm her humble servant, and I can't do more than obey every one of her commands.

She pushes my head aside and it takes a lot of effort to let her skin go. I'm addicted to her taste and to her smell, to everything she represents, and letting a piece of her go is harder every time I need to do it.

"Who owns you, Lucas Temple?" she asks in a moan, fucking herself on my dick with a strength not even I'm capable of. I'm so fucking deep inside her that I feel her cervix hitting the tip of my dick. "Who's the only woman you'll give your perfect cock to for the rest of your life?"

"You are," I say, letting my forehead fall on her shoulder.

"Who's the only woman whose pussy you'll lick and whose juices you'll swallow?"

"You, only you! I swear, only you!" I feel my spine tingling from the orgasm slowly building and I moan as loud as I can when I feel her hand gently squeezing my balls.

"That's right, Lucas! I'm the only woman you'll ever fucking want." She pulls my hair so hard I'm sure she ripped some of it, but I don't care. She can rip me limb from limb and I'll still do whatever she wants. I'll still be hers. Always hers, only hers. "Did you forgive me, Luc? Did you forgive me for being a lying, conniving slut and keeping that secret from you?"

"Yes!" I exhale.

"Say it!"

"I forgive you!" I look into her eyes to let her see that I'm nothing but honest.

"For what?" she screams, lifting herself until only the tip of my cock is inside her, and slowly bouncing on it.

"I forgive you for being a lying, conniving slut that kept that secret from me!"

"Such a good boy," she teases, lowering herself and putting my cock back inside her. "Such a good boy for forgiving his dirty, nasty whore." She licks the column of my throat while laughing. "Do you want to come, Lucas?" She sounds like the best kind of seductress and that makes me scream.

"Yes! Please let me come for you! Please let me come in your tight pussy!"

"Do you want to come inside me?" She quickens her pace, and I need to clench my abdomen to keep myself from coming. "Do you want to fuck another baby into me, Lucas?"

I swear I feel like I'm dying hearing those words coming out of her mouth.

"I would love to fuck a baby into you, yes! Please let me breed you and make you a mother. Please, Melody. I'm fucking begging you!"

She moans loudly and takes my hand, moving my index finger to her clit. She doesn't need to tell me what she wants because I immediately start rubbing fast circles on it.

"That's it, Luc!" she screams. "Fuck! That's it! Make your dirty bitch come on your thick cock when you're coming inside me. Fucking. Make. Me. Come." She punctuates every word by going up and down all over the length on my cock and when I feel her pussy clenching around my shaft I let go, coming so hard I see fucking stars.

"Fuck, Lucas. That's a lot of cum." She doesn't slow down her movements. If anything, she moves even faster. "That's it. Fuck that cum deeper in my hungry pussy."

I slowly push her off me, feeling my cock already hurting from being overstimulated, but she doesn't budge. Frowning, I take a look at her and she gives me a coy smile in return.

"More." That's all she says before getting off me and getting on her hands and knees on the couch next to me. "And harder this time."

"I can't." I swallow and lick my lips, trying to make my dry mouth function, "I'm too sensitive, Mel."

She shrugs, looking at me over her shoulder and spreading her pussy, letting my cum fall from it onto the couch. My cock, of course, reacts immediately, getting even harder than before.

"I see someone disagrees with that statement." She laughs, nodding to my now fully erect dick. "He seems excited by my suggestion. Now fuck me, Lucas."

I roll to my side and sit up on my shaking knees, grabbing her ass cheeks in my palms and thrusting inside her in one go. She's so fucking wet from both my cum and hers that I slip right inside her without any effort.

"Fuck, Melody!" I bite my cheek, trying to cause a different kind of pain so I can focus on that instead of the one my overstimulated cock feels. "I love how your pussy feels so fucking much."

"Then fuck that pretty pussy. Show her how much you love it."

I give her long, deep strokes and wrap her hair around my fist, pulling her head back.

"I love it when you use my hair as a leash," she moans. "I love being your bitch in heat and being fucked properly with your thick cock."

"You're such a filthy girl, aren't you, Melody?" I say.

"So, so filthy," she whimpers. "I can't wait for you to lick me clean."

The thought of licking her pussy while she still has my cum inside her makes me fuck her like an animal. I've never tried this before, but apparently, she just unlocked a new kink for me. And I can't fucking wait to see how it feels. I know this is not payback for making her taste herself because she loved it. She was the one asking for it, actually. This is something that would make her pussy even wetter and fuck me if I wouldn't love to feel that on my tongue.

"I'm gonna feast on that pussy like my life depends on it," I tell her, pulling her hair even harder. "I'm gonna eat it until my jaw goes slack, Melody."

"Do you like eating my pussy, Lucas?"

Play My Part

"I love eating your pussy."

"I love sucking your cock."

"I love you!" I blurt out. And the best part? I don't fucking regret it.

"I love you," she replies instantly. And the best part? I come on the fucking spot.

She lets me set the pace while I'm groaning, moaning, and screaming that I love her all over again. When I finish emptying my balls inside her, I turn her around on her back and without further warning, I start sucking her clit while pushing every drop that leaked outside of her beautiful pussy back inside with my fingers. Only when I'm done, I lower my tongue to her slit, lapping up all that salty liquid and swallowing when my mouth becomes too full.

Her body is a quivering mess, but I raise the stake, putting her knees on my shoulders and lifting her lower body in the air. With my already wet fingers, I start taunting her puckered hole and when I get to the second knuckle she lets out the most beautiful scream I've ever heard.

"Do you like having my cum in your ass, too, Melody?" I ask between licks.

"I love it."

"I love you," I say again, and this time it's her who comes when she hears those words. "I love you so fucking much, my beautiful nightingale!" I continue licking her and playing with her ass through her orgasm.

When she shifts uncomfortably, I go lie next to her and hug her tighter than I did when I saw her in the airport in Austin. Because it feels like I found her again, only this time it's my Melody I found. The woman who stole my heart without knowing and with no intention of ever giving it back. My queen, my nightingale, the owner of my soul and the reason for wanting to wake up every day from now on.

She hugs me back and kisses me with caution, but I deepen the kiss, letting her know that she doesn't need to be scared. I've got her. And she's got me. And we'll forgive each other fully, more and more with every day that passes.

I break the kiss and smile at her, and she starts laughing.

"I'm happy," she whispers, nuzzling my chest. "For the first time in my life, I feel genuinely happy."

"I'm happy, too, Nightingale." I kiss the crown of her head and toy with a strand of her hair.

"I'm so happy you two are happy." Yonathan's sarcastic voice fills the room, making Melody scream and me cover her body with mine. "Now get the fuck cleaned up because we need to go to the set!"

He looks like he slept like a baby for more than ten hours, not like he went to sleep a couple of hours ago after being punched and arguing with me. Rah comes in two seconds later, putting her hand on her chest when she sees us.

"Oh!" she says. "That's a nice ass."

"All mine!" Melody screams from beneath me, and that makes me kiss her again. My possessive, beautiful queen didn't lie. She really wants the world to know I belong to her. And I would love nothing more than to let her do just that.

"It's average," Yonathan remarks, and if I didn't know him, I could've sworn I heard a hint of jealousy in his voice. "Wait, till you see mine!"

"Till she sees your wha-wooooow!" Non joins them and stops dead in his tracks on Rah's right. "Nice ass, baby Temple." He laughs and makes me groan and bury my face in Melody's neck.

"If all of you could stop staring at my ass and get the fuck out, that would be great," I say.

"Should I tell Joshua to change the scene we're supposed to film today to one where I'm masturbating thinking of you?" Tzipporah asks in a kind voice. "I don't want you to feel, you know, uncomfortable. Plus, you might want to get some rest, since you had a, uhm, busy night."

"No!" Melody says before I can tell her that's a good idea. "We'll be ready in half an hour. And Lucas knows exactly who he belongs to."

Play My Part

"And who's that?" Manon asks, a smile blossoming on his face.

"To the woman who he loves," she says, not taking her eyes off me. "And to the one who loves him back. Completely, madly, and desperately loves him back."

Chapter 17
Melody

"So, how was couple's therapy?" Manon asks us the second we step inside the living room. It's pouring rain outside today, and the trip from our therapist's office back home took us three hours. When it usually takes us one.

"Therapy was good," Lucas smiles and wraps his hand around my waist, "she said that we're making huge progress and that she's proud of us."

I lean my head on his shoulder and give Non a tired smile. I feel completely exhausted these days, and the thought that we came here only two months ago makes me even more tired. Not only because work is getting more and more packed with every day that passes. I still love what I'm doing and as much as the workload grows, my motivation does the same. I can't wait for next week's event, where we are officially presenting the crew to our sponsors. It's an exclusive event, and I need to work my ass off for it to be impeccable, but I love working on it nonetheless. Especially since Charlie, who for some reason went back to the States a month ago, put me in charge of it. I'm working with three of my colleagues, and booked an impressive collection of different services. Caterers, security, decorators, everything that an event like this needs, we already have it. And we already sent them the instructions, so starting tomorrow I'll stop attending filming to go to the venue and to make sure everything is going according to plan.

"Did you run into Edward on the way here?" Yonathan arches an eyebrow and looks at Lucas with curiosity in his eyes.

"Norton?"

"Cullen!"

"Who the fuck is Edward Cullen?" Lucas asks in a confused tone.

"Oh, I'm sorry! I didn't realize that you're too cool for *Twilight* now that you have a girlfriend." Yonathan rolls his eyes and takes a seat on the leather chair in the living room.

"I was always too cool for Twilight," Lucas laughs, "I'm more of a Lestat de Lioncourt type of guy."

I sit down on the couch and pat the seat next to me, encouraging my boyfriend to sit down. My boyfriend who finally managed last night to fall asleep without crying, and telling me how much he wished he could've been there for me when I found out that I was carrying his baby. And who told our therapist today that he finally feels that the last shadow of resentment that lived inside him vanished into thin air. That he realized he's not afraid of dying, but his greatest fear is seeing more of his loved ones dead and him not being able to do anything to prevent it. And my boyfriend, who decided today that besides us going together to therapy in order to heal as a couple, he needs to go to therapy on his own to make the wounds on his soul stop bleeding.

Because no matter how many times I promised him I would never keep something away from him again, and that I am here to stay, he still doesn't fully believe me. And now, he knows that he's to blame, too, for not believing that somebody he loves would decide to stay by his side.

"Either way, care to explain why both of you have those Band-Aids on your neck?"

I look at Lucas and he gives me an encouraging nod. I smile shyly, turning my gaze to Yonathan, and trying to decipher what's behind that exterior he blatantly shows to everybody. It's not that I want to make it my life's mission to find out if there's more to him than meets the eye, I'm just curious about him. I'm intrigued by his random acts of kindness that are always followed by another proof of how crude and ruthless he is. He is, indeed, a mystery, but not one that I'm keen on solving. I can only hope that someone will show up in his life, willing to decipher him, to crack the code to his soul, so he can radiate the same way Lucas does. Because if there's one thing I know, it's that like recognizes like and if Lucas was drawn to him, he was drawn to Lucas the same way. And if Lucas learned some things from him, it's obvious that he learned some things from Lucas.

"We got tattoos!" I say.

"Matching ones?"

"Yes. A heart speared by an arrow, wrapped in a ribbon that says *I wuv you, xoxo*." I roll my eyes and laugh.

"If you're serious, Melody, I'm not one to back away from pouring gasoline on your skin and set you both on fire."

"What's it to you?" I stand up and go to the dry bar to get myself a bottle of water. "It's not like you're the one wearing this on your skin for the rest of your life."

"Shame by association is still shame," he cockily answers. "And I refuse to be associated with people who would do such a monstrosity."

Lucas starts laughing and comes to hug me from behind. I revel in his touch, smiling peacefully when I remember that a couple of months ago, I would've jumped from my skin if I was put in the same position. But now, I don't. Now I have a boyfriend who would take a bullet for me, and a fantastic therapist who heals more and more with every session we have together. I am complete, I am put together, and I am exactly who I want to be.

"Take him out of his misery, beautiful Melody," he whispers in my ear. "He's close to having a coronary, and I'm not sure the ambulance will get here in time."

I turn around and kiss his lips, putting a hand on his chest, right where his heart is beating.

Play My Part

"I got a crown with Lucas's initials hidden inside the stones encrusted in it," I say before taking a sip of my water. Manon, who was silent, as per usual, looks at me and gives me a sad smile. I know he has a tattoo on his back for somebody who meant the world to him at some point. He told me one night that he doesn't regret it, but that he would've done things differently if he had the chance.

"How original," Yonathan mocks, but that half-smile on his face betrays the fact that he's actually happy with my choice. I've got to know this man more than I ever wanted to, and I don't know how I actually feel about that. On one hand, I'm happy that we are now finally having a cease-fire. We don't necessarily hate each other, and sometimes, we even have a few laughs together.

I know I'll never be able to be as close to him as I am to Manon, to whom I get closer to with every day that passes, but I will settle for what I have. Beggars can't be choosers, and being on Yonathan's neutral side is more than I could want.

"And Lucas's is a nightingale."

"With dark, hazel eyes and ebony feathers," he adds, giving me a wink.

"So now you have a crow tattooed on your neck, baby Temple?" Yonathan laughs. "We'll tell the world it's a raven. Makes it all mysterious and shit."

"I'll tell the world that I made this tattoo for my nightingale," Lucas says in a serious voice, turning on the TV and sitting back down. "And they can do whatever the fuck they want with that piece of information."

I look at Yonathan, and that smirk on his face says how proud he is of Lucas. I'm not sure if it's a good thing or a bad one to make this man proud, but considering the fact that this seems to bring even more peace in our home, I won't dig deeper. I want this house to be as silent as it was in the past month.

I want to keep having breakfast together, and I want to tell the cooks to take a day off from time to time, so I can cook for my boyfriend and his friends. I want to spend the days with these people, and the nights in Lucas's arms. I want to talk to Manon and to Tzipporah about books, and I want to talk to the love of my life about our future. Because now, the future doesn't scare me anymore. If anything, it makes me excited to see it happening.

"Where's Rah?" I ask Non.

"She went shopping."

"Her? Shopping?" I'm surprised to hear that because I know how much Rah hates trying on clothes and that if she could live her life in jeans, a pair of Chucks, and tank tops, she would do it without doubt.

"Not clothes shopping. She said she wanted to make some additions to the house, whatever that means."

"Shouldn't we validate these changes with the head of logistics? Or the owners?"

"The head of logistics!" Yonathan shouts, making all three of us jump. "That's someone I haven't fucked yet. Do we have her number somewhere?"

"She's engaged," Manon says through gritted teeth, and I put a hand on his back, trying to calm him down. You would've thought that he already knows by now that if Yonathan lacks something, it's decency and scruples.

"Still a maybe." He laughs and I hear Lucas snorting to my left, and that makes me elbow his ribs.

"How would you feel if somebody talked about me like that?" I ask him in a scolding tone.

"Are you saying you want to be my wife, Melody Byers?" He gives me that boyish grin that never fails to make the butterflies in my stomach go wild and my nipples harden.

"I'm saying that it's not okay to disrespect a woman's commitment."

"Because I'd put a ring on that finger right now," he continues, completely ignoring me. "I'll go and buy the biggest diamond I can find and I'll propose as soon as I come back."

I grab his face in my palms and kiss him, showing him that I would say

Play My Part

yes if he asked me. I want another marriage, one that I'm sure will work and that will never be broken, not even after death do us part. I'm sure Melody Byers and Lucas Temple will find each other in the afterlife, too.

"Is that a yes?" he asks me when I take my lips from his.

"I didn't hear a question, Lucas." I playfully slap his shoulders, and lean forward so I can see Manon's face, who is now focused on the things he's writing in a notebook.

He started journaling the second our therapist, Runa, told him to. I honestly believe that she'll be able to buy a house after she's done with us, but she deserves that and a whole neighborhood for putting up with all our shit. She not only makes us take our skeletons from the closets we locked them in, but she forces us to analyze them and watch them rot. She's absolutely fantastic and I can't be more grateful to Non for finding her through his contacts here. I have no idea who those contacts are, since he spends every waking hour with us, but I'm sure he'll tell me more when he's ready.

The thunderstorm outside intensifies, the rain and the hail hitting the large window wall through which we can see the beautiful garden. The thunder is so loud, that the cars' alarms are going off in the garage and I can hear the maids cursing for leaving some of the windows open. I don't speak Romanian fluently, but, as it always happens when you learn a foreign language, the first things that stick are curse words.

"It's fucking June," Yonathan says. "We were supposed to welcome summer, not turn on the heating system."

"Did the weather ruin some plans, Yon?" Lucas teases.

"All the entertainment I need lives under this roof," he retorts.

The fact that he hasn't given up on trying to convince Tzipporah to sleep with him is something that surprises both me and Lucas. For a man who keeps saying he doesn't like to have his time wasted, a whole month of wooing somebody is pretty unusual.

The sound of the doorbell makes all of us jump from our seats. I guess

I'm not the only one who hates this kind of weather. I hear a conversation between one of our maids and a feminine voice that sounds familiar, and when the person on the other side of the door walks in the living room, I know why. Sandra Temple, or, better said, Sandra Bancroft, comes inside, wearing a white, long dress, and dragging a huge suitcase.

I jump to my feet and run toward her to give her a hug, but the fact that she doesn't hug me back speaks volumes. I suspected that she's angry with me for not getting in touch with her for so many years, especially since she did me a favor by taking my parents with her, but I thought she would understand. Besides, she could've picked up the phone and called me the same way I could've done it.

"I'm sorry," I whisper in her ear, still not letting her go. "I'm so, so sorry."

"Don't be," she says, crossing her arms after pushing me back. "You were always an ungrateful bitch, so now that my brother decided to make you his whore for a little while, I might convince you to pay me back all the money I've spent on your parents!"

"Then how about you pay me every penny I spent on your brother, Sandra?" Yonathan stands up and stops next to me. "I think my accountant still has the receipts, if you won't take my word."

"Yonathan," she nods in greeting, "never took you as a spokesperson. You live and you learn, I guess." She looks at her manicured nails and shrugs.

Yonathan opens his mouth to say something, but I speak before he can.

"I might be your brother's whore," I drag my long fingernail over the handle of her suitcase, "but at least I stayed in touch with my family. Unlike another ungrateful bitch in this room, who calls her only relative once a year. Can't your sugar daddy afford to pay for international calls?"

She takes one step in my direction and I push my chest forward. I'm done being intimidated by bullies. Yonathan trained me well, and even though he's completely unhinged sometimes and the rudest person I've ever met, his intentions were good. He was trying to protect Lucas, and he

Play My Part

was more of a sibling to him than Sandra was since she left the country. I have nothing to prove to her and if she wants to send my parents back home just to punish me or to get her revenge, then so be it. I have enough money in my bank account to buy them the house of their dreams in whatever corner of the world they want to spend the rest of their lives in.

"Fuck off, Melody!" She moves past me and goes to Lucas, giving him a hug that he returns awkwardly.

"What are you doing here, Sandra?" he asks in a cold, detached voice.

"Isn't a girl allowed to come visit her baby brother from time to time?" She laughs, faking innocence. "I missed you, that's all!"

"You haven't visited me the last six years. Why now?"

"Jesus, Lucas!" She dramatically puts her hand over her chest. "Do you think this is how Mom and Dad would've wanted you to treat me?"

I give her a spiteful look that she can't see since she has her back to me. But Lucas sees it and that's all I needed, for him to know that I'm here for him and that I will defend him if he needs me to. I won't let Sandra take advantage of that sensitive topic, and I'll die before witnessing her delivering more low blows only to get what she wants, whatever the fuck that is.

Lucas stays silent, preferring to look at the ground. The pain that is clearly written on his face for everyone to see makes me want to strangle that fucking bitch who came here and destroyed all the peace we were still building. We all lived in a house made of straw and she came and blew it away.

"Who the fuck left this suitcase in the middle of the living room and stained the floor?" Rah's pissed voice says from behind me.

Everybody looks at her in awe because she looks like the sun, a perfect contradiction to the storm outside and the one brewing inside.

"That would be me!" Sandra says, walking toward her, slightly pushing Manon with her shoulder. I now notice that he didn't utter a word since he saw Sandra waltzing in like she fucking owns the house. He didn't step up to defend Lucas, which is completely unusual. Especially since he and Sandra know each other from back in the days when she insisted on meeting both him and Yonathan before letting Lucas go in a different state with them.

"I'm Sandra! Huge fan!" she says in an excited voice, extending her hand.

"I'm Tzipporah. Not a fan of Sandra," my friend retorts in a deadly voice. "Care to tell me what the fuck are you doing in my house?"

Sandra takes a look at everyone around her, but nobody jumps to her defense. Not Lucas, who keeps analyzing the floor, not Manon who turned his back to us, preferring to look outside the window, and definitely not me and Yonathan.

"I'm Lucas's sister!" The way she says it, like she contributed to who Lucas is today, makes me want to grab her hair and kick her out of the house.

"Cool. Put that on a pin and wait with the other groupies," Rah says in the same tone from earlier. I now understand better why Yonathan can't seem to get himself to let go of her. They're like two peas in a pod. "I still don't know why the fuck you're in my house."

Sandra frowns and starts toying with the spaghetti strap of her dress. She's uncomfortable and it's obvious. Good. "I came to visit Lucas." She watches Rah taking a sandwich from her bag and unwrapping it.

Rah waves her hand, signaling she needs more details while she chews the bite she just took, but Sandra stays silent. After a long pause, Tzipporah finally swallows.

"Book an appointment with his agent and get the fuck out of here."

"You just met me."

"I wish I never did."

Yonathan starts laughing, taking Rah's hand in his and kissing her knuckles. The only jaw that drops to the floor is Sandra's because the rest of us are already used to this teasing game they play and seem to enjoy.

Play My Part

"Judgmental much, little bird?" he says in a low voice, holding her gaze. "Why wouldn't you give poor Sandra a chance? Maybe you'll be friends."

"I don't need more friends and she makes everybody here uncomfortable. Sorry, Luc, but she needs to go," she says in an apologetic tone, looking at my boyfriend across the room.

I know it's selfish of me, but I would love nothing more than for him to agree with Rah. I want her gone and I want her gone now. I want to fucking have a longer period of pure, uninterrupted bliss.

"You offended my future wife," he finally says in a deadly voice, "then you used our parents' memory to try and manipulate me to pretend like we're still thick as thieves." Lucas starts walking toward us, stopping only when he towers over his sister. "And to answer your question, no, I don't think Mom and Dad would like me to treat you this way. But they would've definitely hated you for becoming a selfish piece of trash, remembering about me only when you hit rock bottom."

"What are you even talking about?" Her laugh is so fake, even I notice it. And I'm not one of the best actors in the world. "I am riding the highest wave, my dear brother. Rock bottom isn't something I lose any sleep thinking about."

"Where's your wedding ring, big sister?" Lucas asks, taking her hand and raising it for a better view.

"At the jeweler's. It needed to get repaired." Her voice is shaking like she's about to cry because this is exactly her modus operandi. Whenever she wants something and the people around her aren't willing to give it to her, she starts crying. I always consoled her and told her that what she's going through is completely unfair, but now? Now I feel stupid for doing that and I realize I only helped her become more selfish and more spoiled.

"You're lying," Manon says, turning around. "Whenever you lie, you scrunch your nose. You did the same when you promised me and Yon that you'd come back to see Lucas every three months. Then and…" he trails off, leaving the sentence unfinished.

"I'm not!" she screams, taking her hand from Lucas's. "I swear I'm not."

"More empty promises, Sandra?" Manon says in a pained voice. "Your vows mean nothing to all of us here."

I try to understand how Manon knows Lucas's sister so well. When did he witness her lying enough to know her tells? *I* don't fucking know her tells.

According to Lucas, they all met a couple of times before her departure, and most of the talking was done by Yonathan, not surprisingly at all. Yet, I have this gut feeling that Manon and Sandra have a long history that no one talks about. Or, on second thought, somebody does talk about it, only she never had a name in all those stories I heard.

A new wave of anger hits me, realizing that she was the woman who hurt Manon so badly in the past. I don't have a clear timeline of the events, but I am absolutely positive, based on what he said and his reactions since she stepped inside the house, that she's the fucking snake who took advantage of him and his beautiful heart.

"Take your shit and go, Sandra," I say in a threatening voice. "We don't need to hear more of your stories. Not now, not ever. Just fucking go."

"Lucas?" She looks at her brother, but the only thing he does is hug me from behind, as he always does. This is his way of telling me *I have your back* and he came up with it after our second therapy session, when I told him I needed to know that he's here for me. Even if he doesn't feel comfortable enough to say it sometimes, I need to know.

"You heard my fiancée!" He kisses the crown on my head and rests his chin there. "Get your fucking attitude out of our house."

"I have nowhere to go," she whispers, and I could've been sorry for her if she weren't here for all the wrong reasons.

"Then it's a good thing I bought a hotel," Yonathan says in a happy voice. "Go and live there, rent-free. The only condition is you'll never get close to us again. I bought it because I was bored, so I don't care about who lives in it, anyway." He lets out a humorless laugh. "But, if you

Play My Part

ever pull shit like this again, you can say hello to a new cardboard house. Bucharest has some lovely bridges to protect you from the rain."

She gives each of us a pleading look, but when she sees that none of us is willing to offer her the mercy she craves, she nods and leaves the living room, dragging that suitcase again.

"Ew, Lucas," Rah says, finally finishing her sandwich. "How the fuck do you share blood with that lowlife?"

He smiles bitterly and lets out a long exhale before answering.

"She wasn't always like this. Or, at least, I never saw her like this."

"You never saw her for who she is," Manon says in the same pained voice. "She was always like this. Even worse."

And now, more than never, I know that I need to share my thoughts with Lucas. Because I promised him I wouldn't keep any secrets from him, and this is a promise I would rather tear my flesh apart than break.

"And when the fuck did you propose to Melody?" Tzipporah interrupts my train of thought. "I was out for three hours, buying the electric instruments for our living room, and you chose to propose right then? Rude, Luc! Rude and hurtful!"

"I didn't propose," he says in an amused tone. "But it's like I did."

"There's no *like you did*. You either did, or you didn't."

I start laughing, and drag Lucas out of the living room to our bedroom to keep Rah from continuing her interrogation. When I close the door, I take off my dress, my bra, and my panties and lie on the bed.

"Your turn." I flick my chin in his direction. "And make it fast because I need you to make love to me."

He takes off his clothes faster than I've ever seen him do it, and I can't help but laugh when he runs toward the bed.

"Does my beautiful queen need to be fucked properly by her king?" he asks, licking my neck, careful to avoid the bandage there. We got our tattoos in the same spot where we bit each other's necks a month ago. I told him I wanted to mark him and he told me he wanted to do the same to me, so we both decided a week later, when the bruises started to fade, and our friends stopped calling us horny teenagers, to make them permanent. To wear each other on our skin as long as our blood runs through our veins.

"I said I want you to make love to me, Luc," I say looking into his eyes. "I want us to truly feel each other and come together. I want this so much, my king."

I grab his cock and position it at my entrance. Raising my hips, I slowly let him slide inside me, inch by inch by inch, feeling him getting harder with every second that passes.

"You're so wet already," he breathes.

"I'm always wet for you," I moan when he's fully inside me. "I'm always desperate to feel you inside me, Lucas. I'm addicted to you the same way you are addicted to me."

He buries his face in the crook of my neck, gently grazing my shoulder with his teeth and massaging my tits with his palms. His thrusts are painfully slow, but I enjoy it as much as when I'm screaming that I'm his dirty whore who owns her good boy. We are always in tandem, a dance that will never be forgotten.

I start bucking my hips faster, desperate to find my release. He groans deep in his throat and I can tell by the way his movements become more and more uncontrolled that he's as close as I am.

I put my hand on his balls, squeezing gently, and he starts rubbing circles on my clit at the same time.

When we come, we come together, screaming each other's names, followed by *I love you*s.

I lie there, in his arms, listening to the storm outside, and enjoying the sunshine we brought together in this room. I bathe now in the love and devotion of Lucas Temple, the boy who smiled when he first saw me, the teenager whose virginity I took, and the man who I desperately adore.

And, now, I am completely and utterly whole, sane, and willing to start a family.

Epilogue
Lucas

I never lied to Melody. Now that I think about it, I can't remember lying to anyone for as long as I've lived. I was always an open book, strongly believing that the only things that lies can bring are complications and disappointments.

I know she thought I was joking earlier, when I told her I would go and buy the biggest diamond ring I can find and propose to her the second I get back home. But I wasn't; I want to marry the woman of my dreams and I want to marry her now, if possible.

That's why, as soon as I'm sure she's fast asleep, I silently get out of bed, put my clothes back on, and leave our bedroom. Theo answers on the first ring and, despite the fact that he tells me it's dangerous to go out in this kind of weather, I tell him this needs to happen. I don't care about the weather. Nothing can keep me from making Melody wear my ring from now until forever.

"Where the fuck are you going, baby Temple?" Yonathan shouts when he sees me running down the hallway. "It's pouring rain!"

"We'll talk when I'm back." I laugh.

Getting in the SUV that waits for me on the huge porch, I tell the driver that I need to get to the closest jewelry store in record time. I know they all close soon, and this is one of the moments I'm grateful for Melody's exhaustion this past month. I already booked an appointment for her to visit the best doctor I could find in this city because I need to know if there's something wrong with her. I know she will never quit her job, and despite the fact that her determination and dedication make me love her even more, if the doctor says she needs to take some time off, then I'll make sure she'll take some time off. Nothing will take her away from me. Not *her*.

Despite the thunderstorm outside, my driver gets me to the store in fifteen minutes. I go inside, tell the jeweler what I want, and she shows me an impressive collection of engagement rings. My ego tells me that I should buy the most expensive one, but then I remember how delicate she is. The only jewelry she ever wears are the silver watch on her left wrist, some small earrings that go well with whatever she's wearing, and a small necklace that my mother gifted her for her twenty-first birthday. So, I settle for the platinum one, with a small diamond on top of the two knots that mend together. Two knots representing her and me and a stone that shines bright, representing the love we feel for each other. Always together, united by something more powerful than words can tell.

As soon as I get out of the car, I rush inside, taking a moment to laugh when I see Manon and Tzipporah connecting some small drums and a guitar to the TV. They turn around when they hear my laughter and they laugh back.

"Where've you been, Luc?" Rah asks me with a knowing smile on her lips.

"Around." I shrug.

"Glad to see you're not dead," Yonathan says, sitting in the same spot he was in when I left an hour earlier. "Don't do this kind of shit again, Luc! I think Melody would rather wait for you to propose when the storm calms down rather than cry over your casket."

"You do know how to ruin the good mood," I tell him. "Try being happy for the people around you once in a while, will you?"

He doesn't say anything, but the way he looks at me tells me that he

Play My Part

is happy for me. Or, at least, as happy as he can feel considering the type of person he is.

"Time to wake up, beautiful Melody," I whisper in her ear the same way I do each and every time I wake up before her. "I have a surprise for you."

She opens her beautiful eyes and gives me a confused look.

"Why are you dressed? And soaked nonetheless. Have you been outside? What happened?"

I kiss her plump lips, stopping the line of questioning. Whenever she's agitated, she feels like she's left in the dark and tries to find out everything there is to know. But she needs to understand that the dark is a place she will never see again. Not as long as I'm next to her.

"I'll answer your question if you answer one of mine." I smile when I take my lips from hers.

She opens her mouth to say something, but she quickly changes her mind and nods instead.

I feel like I can't fit in my own skin and that I'm more anxious than I was in my life. Waiting to find out if I got the award or the part I wanted doesn't even begin to compare to how this event makes me feel.

I clear my throat, kneeling in front of the bed. My smart nightingale knows exactly what I'm about to ask her since she gasps and tears flood her eyes. She wraps the sheet around her body, a habit that she still hasn't gotten rid of, but she will. I will do my best to teach her how to love her body the same way I do.

I unwrap her and grab her naked body, making her sit on the edge of the bed.

"I love you," I say in a choked voice.

"I love you more," she swiftly replies, and that makes me chuckle.

"If you keep this up, I'll never get to ask my question."

She stays silent and I wipe the tears falling on her cheeks with my thumbs and give her lips a chaste kiss.

"I love you," I say again. "I don't know how to express how much I love you, Melody. I already told you that I knew you were it for me since the second I realized there was an it for me. You were, are, and will be the only woman I have ever truly wanted. I want you so much, my beautiful queen."

I take the ring box out of my pocket and open it, and that makes her cry harder.

"I want you to be mine in every way that matters, the same way I want to be yours. I want us to be brave and turn our dreams into reality. I want us to live, Mel."

"I want that, too." She nods eagerly. "I want that so much, Luc."

I let out a laugh when I take the ring out of its box and look into Melody's eyes. The same eyes that haunted my existence for as long as I can remember are looking back at me with so much love in them. And that is the only reason I feel like I'm the luckiest man alive. Not the success I have, not the money in my bank account, not anything else. She is the sole purpose of my existence.

"Will you live with me, Mel-Mel?" I ask her in a raspy voice. "Will you let me give you a perfect life, be the king the most beautiful queen deserves?"

She doesn't say anything, but jumps in my arms, bringing both of us to the floor. She peppers kisses all over my face, crying and laughing at the same time. I kiss her back and hug her with all my strength, needing her more than I did any other day.

"I would love to have the perfect life with you," she says. "I want to give you my life if you'll give me yours in return. I want us to be one, Luc-Luc."

I put the ring on her finger and kiss her savagely right after. Melody Byers will soon become Melody Temple. And now I feel like my mission on earth is complete.

Play My Part

Melody

Looking at the ring Lucas put on my finger two weeks ago, I let that honest smile blossom on my face again. It still feels weird to wear it since I didn't for such a long time, but I love it. I love how quickly it turns into laughter, too. I am the happiest woman alive and I had no idea I could feel this way.

I take my cell phone out of my shirt pocket. Only two minutes have passed since I checked it last time, but I need Lucas to come home faster. I know he had to stay longer tonight on the set because some scenes didn't go the way he wanted. And my future husband is nothing but a perfectionist. And the kindest soul, since he told Rah to go home because her performance was impeccable and it's his monologue he wants to shoot again.

I lean on the kitchen counter, taking another sip of my tea and silently watching Manon painting in the garden. It's already dark outside, but since our garden has more artificial light in it than a stadium does, he can easily spend the whole night there if he wants to. He's changed in the past couple of weeks and I know it's because of Sandra. I decided to ask him about her and then tell Lucas, not because he would think I'm saying this out of spite, but because I want to have the whole picture. I never thought I'd end up resenting my best friend and marrying her brother, but life always has a way to surprise us. And this is one of the best surprises I could've ever imagined.

I hear a commotion behind me and I turn around to see Rah running down the hallway. I call her name, but she completely ignores me, heading toward the exit. When I say her name the second time, I see Yonathan coming behind her and forcing her to look at him, grabbing her elbow.

If her face is devastation, his is determination, and I can't say I'm surprised. Tzipporah never wanted to accept the fact that everything that Yonathan touches turns to dust. In the very few occasions we talked about him, she always tried to convince me that behind that rough block of ice was a fire that could melt the whole world. What she fails to understand is that, even if she's right, the fire would never show its flames.

I take a sip of my tea and decide to watch the shitshow. Not because I want to pry or because curiosity gets the best of me, but because I want to be there for her the same way she was there for me all this time. The fact that I accepted Yonathan as a part of our lives, doesn't mean that if shit hits the fan, I won't be on Rah's side. I would love for us to be the same way the three men we are currently living with are, but we still have a long road ahead of us in order to get there. One that I'm more than willing to walk.

"What do you want?" she screams. "Get your fucking hands off me!"

Yonathan rolls his eyes, but I notice how fast he lets her go. Nothing like Bart Trello, indeed.

"How old are you?" he asks, piercing her with his gaze.

"Twenty-seven, but I don't see how…"

"And is there any particular reason for you behaving like you're fifteen?"

"I didn't know that fifteen-year-olds are decent enough to leave the room where they catch their boyfriends cheating on them!" she spits.

I frown when I hear that word. Boyfriend?

"Boyfriend?" Yonathan half laughs. Apparently, he and I finally have something in common. Who would've thought? "Honey," he continues in a condescending tone, "what would possibly make you believe that I am your boyfriend?" He spits the last word like it's poisoning his guts.

"You-you said that," she stutters. "You said all those nice things to me. You took me out, you wanted to kiss me, but you said you'll wait for me as long as I need you to."

He nods and takes a step back. When he looks at her, there's nothing but malice in his blue eyes.

"And who says I'm not still waiting?"

"You were fucking that whore!" She bellows. "You were smiling at me while you were inside her, you fucking piece of shit!"

Play My Part

"No need to call her a whore." I keep myself from snorting. Such a fucking hypocrite. "She was only willing to give me what you refused to." He shrugs nonchalantly. "Either way, the fact that I told you I want to kiss and fuck you, that I'll wait for those things to happen until you grow out of your prude phase, most certainly doesn't make me your boyfriend!"

"I trusted you," she says through gritted teeth.

"That definitely sounds like a *you* problem, not a *me* problem. I never asked for your trust, Rah." He sighs. "The fact that you decided to give it to me is none of my concern."

"But you did tell me that you couldn't wait for me to suck your cock," she says in a cold voice. "I suppose that is one of your concerns."

He pulls his sweatpants a bit higher and I now realize it's the first time I've seen him wearing anything but a suit. He looks more human now than he ever did, but he's still the same ruthless man despite his appearance.

"Correct! Fucking and everything related to it is one of my greatest concerns, given the fact that I have a life with very few of them. And since you act like your pussy is a golden sanctuary that nobody is worthy enough to touch, I decided to bury my cock in a pussy that welcomes me. A warm, wet hole is and always will be a warm, wet hole. As long as it's attached to a decent body, I have no problem fucking it until it turns red."

Tzipporah slaps him and I completely understand why. I would've slapped him sooner, to be honest. His face turns left from how hard she hit him, but his only answer is a dark chuckle.

"And here is that fifteen-year-old showing her ugly face again. Hurting others just because your brain conjured a fantasy so different from reality. Lucas understood that this kind of behavior wouldn't take him anywhere. Maybe ask him for advice?" he suggests in a mocking voice.

"Just go to hell and burn there." She dismisses him, turning her back to him and walking toward the door again.

"I permanently reside there, but the flames don't seem to touch me!" he challenges. "Any other demands?"

"As a matter of fact, yes!" her voice sounds as ruthless as Yonathan's is. "Don't fucking wait for me any longer. I'm sure I'll find someone better, someone who's able to offer me everything I want, including a better fuck than the ones you can think of!"

"You won't!" he shouts, sounding like she's not the one who needs convincing on that matter.

"I beg to differ, Mr. Friedmann," she says with a twisted smile on her face. "Because while you say you permanently reside in Hell and brag about the flames not burning you, you seem to have forgotten to check who sits on the throne that controls them. And mark my words, Yonathan, I will let them burn you and fall asleep to the sounds of your screams and your pleas for mercy!"

She storms out before Yonathan has the chance to say anything else. He lets out a frustrated sigh, and shakes his head, and that's when I see my beautiful fiancé going to hug him.

They stay there for a couple of minutes, neither of them saying anything. I know that Yonathan will never thank him and I know Lucas will never need to hear him say that. They are way past the stage of thanking each other for these things.

When Lucas lets his chosen brother go, I clear my voice, stepping out of the shadows of the kitchen. I don't need words either. I just need to feel him close. I put my hand in his back pocket, dropping the small object there, hoping he will notice. And he does.

Frowning, he takes out the stick from his pocket and starts crying as soon as he realizes what my pregnancy test says.

"No," he chokes out

"No?" I ask, panic and dread filling me.

"Is this real? You're… you are…" He takes two steps back and I feel the worst I've ever felt. He fucking wanted a baby. He talked about it all the time. I thought that was what he wanted, so I didn't feel the need to tell him I stopped taking my pills. I fucking ruined everything again.

Play My Part

He falls to his knees and I move past him, desperate to get as far away as possible from him. I can't do this now and I will never be able to do it. Lucas grabs my hand, making me stop, and I try to escape his grasp.

"What are you doing, Mel-Mel?" he asks while more tears are running down his cheeks.

"I can't be here, I messed up, I'm sorry!"

He crawls on his knees, and hugs me, putting his lips on my stomach and leaving them there for what feels like years. He keeps crying and I now realize he's crying happy tears. The happiest tears.

"Daddy is here," he whispers. "He's here now and he'll always be here. And he loves you so, so much. I can't wait to meet you, princess!"

I fall to my knees, grab his face, and kiss him, thanking him for existing in my life. He said everything I needed to hear, and I send a silent prayer to God that our baby heard him, too. That he or she will grow in my womb knowing how much we love them.

"I love you so much, Melody," he says between sobs. "I love you both so, so much!"

"We love you, too, Lucas. But if we have a son, never call him *princess* unless he tells you to, okay?"

"I will call our baby whatever the fuck they want." He laughs. "I will do everything for them, do you hear me?"

"So will I," I say, kissing him again. "We're going to have a baby, Luc-Luc! Our baby."

He picks me up and carries me to the bedroom, gently laying me on the bed. He takes our clothes off and kisses my stomach again and again.

And then he reminds me why I love him the way I do. He reminds me that I own him and that this is just the beginning. That we created life and happiness together, only by facing life's challenges while holding each other's hand.

"I feel like our lives just became a movie with a happily ever after instead of a tragedy," I tell him as I lie in bed, toying with his hair several hours later.

He looks at me, his hand on my stomach like he's trying to protect our baby from everything, and whispers,

"I don't care about the genre, Mel. As long as you're next to me, I'll gladly play my part."

- THE END -

Curious about what will happen between Tzipporah and Yonathan? Here's a small sneak peek at their story, that will come out in November 2022.

Tzipporah

He looks at me from my toes to the top of my head, boredom being replaced by disgust, and I have to make an extra effort to keep myself from hugging my stomach and crouching on the ground, waiting for him to leave so I can finally breathe. But I won't let him see me like that. Not now, not ever. Yonathan doesn't deserve the raw, vulnerable version of me. Nobody fucking does.

"You look like an underpaid whore." he says in that thick voice that brought me to the verge of insanity until less than six hours ago. The voice that made me question my decisions, and consider throwing everything I wanted and decided away, and beg him to sleep with me, just to make sure I'm everything he wanted. "The type of whore that sleeps with truck drivers for biscuits, not the classy, elegant one."

"And you look like the type of person who steals used toilet paper from public restrooms." I retort, squinting my eyes, and trying to read his expression despite the dark that surrounds us. If it wasn't for the headlights, we would've been in the middle of a dark forest, and I don't know how that makes me feel. Conflicted, I fucking suppose.

"But I suppose you didn't come here only to tell me that, right?" I ask through gritted teeth. "What the fuck do you want, Yonathan?"

"Who did you fuck, Rah?"

"Your dad. He asked me to help him with having a child who isn't a fucking imbecile, so I was more than willing to let him breed me as long as he eats my pussy properly."

He grunts and cracks his fingers and his neck. Then his open palms turn into fists, and I can see them shaking. I found one of Yonathan's wrong buttons, apparently. And I want to push it until he can't take it anymore.

"I called him *daddy* too, especially when he buried his cock so, so deep inside me. He made me scream so loud, I thought they would throw us out of the restaurant." I say in a sultry voice, and letting my Israeli accent make itself noticed. "But do you know what my favorite part was, Yonathan? When he shoved that thick cock of his down my throat and made me gag on it. God, how I love an older man!"

I don't realize what's happening until I feel warmth on my cheek. My face is on the hood of Yonathan's car and he's keeping me there with a hand on my head and another one of my lower back. I'm almost positive that my ass is almost on full display, and I now curse myself for choosing this dress because Yonathan deserves nothing, not even seeing my body.

"You'd be surprised to find out what a young man can do to you, Rah," he whispers, leaning close to my ear. "I can eat your pussy for hours and tongue fuck you while I'm playing with your small clit. I can fuck you for days in more positions than you can imagine, stretching that tight pussy until you beg me to stop. And I can definitely face fuck you and make you cry so hard that your tears will be smeared all over your neck and tits. You're missing out, Tzipporah."

I let out a laugh and that only makes him groan. If he thinks his words affect me in any way, shape, or form he's fucking wrong. They might have if he wasn't such a piece of shit.

"You couldn't do shit to me, Yonathan. You couldn't make me come even if you would be able to lick and fuck my pussy at the same time."

"Care to find out?" he keeps me pinned, blowing hot air on my neck and making me shudder. I feel so fucking angry that I want to find a piece of paper to write a disclaimer that I won't be held responsible for my actions this night.

I let out a moan and push my ass back hard. I'm surprised to see that he isn't hard yet, but when I start grinding on his dick, I feel a bulge forming and I laugh internally.

"Yonathan," I breathlessly say, grinding harder on him and making him breathe faster, "I want to find out. I want that so, so much. But before that I need you to do something for me."

He doesn't say anything for a little while, so I move my hips faster, until he finally asks me,

"I'm known for keeping track of the favors I grant. So what is it that you need, little bird?"

I lift my left leg and kick him as hard as I can in his knee. I don't care if I broke something, as long as he feels pain. And that's just a small demonstration of how much pain I want to bring upon him. Physical pain, mental pain, and heartache.

"For you to fuck off and crawl in the fucking depth of Hell that you escaped from, you fucking imbecile. Don't you ever dare touch me again or I swear to God I'll bury you in lawsuits and I'll go to the press crying."

I lean down so I can look in his eyes while he's groaning and keeping his hands on his knee, and grab his chin the same way he did mine for so many times. His eyes are promising mayhem, but my soul is promising destruction. And if we burn, then we burn together.

"Don't fucking underestimate me, Yonathan Friedmann. I bark, I bite, I rip flesh, and I go for the kill. Get the fuck out of my life!"

I turn on my heels, lifting my left's hand middle finger, and walk on the alley in the front of the car, looking for Theo so he could take me home.

I know I'm playing with fire, but luckily, I'm the one who lit the match. And nobody will tame the fire that's burning inside me. Not now. Not ever.

ACKNOWLEDGEMENTS

There are a lot of people I would like to thank, so here it goes.

To my beta readers, Jamie and Stephanie, you are more than I could ever asked for. Your input was absolutely fantastic, and it made Play My Part reach its maximum potential. I could never thank you enough for all your effort and I can only hope this was just the beginning of our story, and that you will accept beta reading for me again.

To my editor, Rumi, there are no words to express my appreciation. Your feedback wasn't only extremely valuable, but you delivered it in such a perfect manner, that I have no other choice than to give you a standing ovation. You are absolutely amazing!

To all the fantastic people from *Cover2Cover Author Services,* thank you for putting up with me. Your professionalism and friendliness are something I would never stop appreciating, nor would I take lightly.

To Chinmoy Designs, I'm not sure if you will ever want to hear from me, considering all the changes I wanted to make to this book's cover, but please know that I appreciate you immensely. To my old and new ARC readers, you are amazing and I am completely overwhelmed about the love you've shown me. I can't wait to share more of my work with you.

To my mom and dad who always let me pursue this crazy passion and encouraged me to act upon it, even though they have no idea how I turned out to be a writer.

To all my friends who didn't see me in the past months because I spent most of my free time writing.

To all the people on social media who supported me and decided to be part of my community. You are what I needed in my life without knowing.

Let me tell you that this book wouldn't have happened without

Gabriela, who is rooting for me each and every day. I love you, my sister from another mister!

I want to thank my boyfriend for putting up with me even when he was sick and tired of hearing about Lucas and Melody, and when he accepted that I want to spend some weekends writing this story.

To my absolutely fantastic E-girls who make me smile, laugh, and my heart swell more and more with every day that passes. It's an absolute honor to have you in my life and I can only hope that you love me the same way I do you. And, of course, to E, who besides creating the best community this world has ever known, one that I'm honored to be part of, is a great win for humanity, an absolutely fantastic human being, and a crazy talented professional. I am in awe! If you don't know who I'm talking about, just search for *voeros* on TikTok and let the magic happen.

And last, but surely not least, to all the people who fell in love with Lucas and Melody, and decided to read their story. You are my everything!

AUTHOR'S BIOGRAPHY

One cold day, Miriam remembered that she loves stories with a happy ending and the English language, so she decided to put her thoughts on paper. She never stopped, and she doesn't intend to.

When she's not writing, she sits on the couch with her Kindle in her left hand and a mug of coffee or tea in her right one. She's born and raised in Bucharest, Romania, where she still currently resides together with her boyfriend who has a passion for DIY projects, astronomy and history.

She's addicted to dark romance and fantasy as a reader, and to contemporary romance as an author. She loves writing broken characters who fix themselves and each other because she strongly believes that everybody needs a voice.

Miriam is a huge fan of fighting for the right causes, and does her best to right the wrong in the world.

She also loves the world of Communication and Public Relations and her BA in that area of expertise can confirm it.

She's addicted to coffee, plot twists, social media and her Spotify playlists that never fail to inspire her when she's writing.

She'd love nothing more than connect with her readers, so make sure to follow her:

Facebook: https://www.facebook.com/authormiriamrosentvaig/
Instagram: @author.miriam.rosentvaig
TikTok: @miriam_reads_and_writes
or join her Facebook group where she promises to be more than active: https://www.facebook.com/groups/368196488011435

You can check out the two books she published, available for purchase on Amazon and in Kindle Unlimited.

We Were Just Born (Dysfunctionally Perfect #1)

We Were Just Leaving (Dysfunctionally Perfect #2)

Printed in Great Britain
by Amazon

86635297R00149